make you mine

Honey Mountain Series ~ Book 3

laura pavlov

Make You Mine
Honey Mountain Series, Book 3

Laura Pavlov
https://www.laurapavlov.com

Cover Design: Emily Wittig Designs

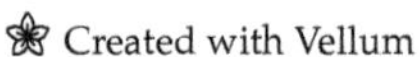

Mom,
Thank you for reading all my words and supporting me every day on this journey! Thank you for cheering me on every step of the way and being my biggest cheerleader! I am forever grateful!
Love you so much!
xoxo Buttons

one

. . .

Ashlan

I SAT across from Jace at his kitchen table as he pulled out a notebook and cleared his throat.

"I can't thank you enough for doing this. And I mean it when I say that when you find what you want to do with your life, I'll understand that it's not this. I know this is temporary. Just give me a couple weeks' notice when you want to bail, all right?"

"Of course. But I'm planning to stay for a while if you'll have me," I said over an embarrassing giggle. I mean, this man was something straight out of a sexy firefighter calendar. He was tall with broad shoulders, glistening tan skin, and every inch of him was chiseled and hard. Well, I couldn't technically speak for every inch of him. "Is it hot in here?"

Oh my gawd. Did I just say that out loud?

He chuckled this sexy, gruff sound that sent chills down my spine. "Let me check the thermostat. It is hot as hell outside today."

He moved to the wall beside the kitchen, and I quickly fanned my face frantically with my hand while his back was to me. He'd become a good family friend since he'd started working at the firehouse with my dad, and he'd been coming to our Sunday night dinners for the past few years. But lately, every time I was around him, I was a swoony fool. I didn't know what the hell was going on with me.

He was hot. Definitely hot.

And I was human.

"I've been setting up the guesthouse all day, so I'm probably overheated." I tried to make light of it, but the truth was —it could be snowing outside, and I'd be warm if I were sitting close to this man.

I wasn't proud of the thoughts I'd had lately, but I knew it would pass. I'd ended things with Henry, the guy I'd dated for a few months toward the end of school. It just wasn't going anywhere—he wanted to get serious, and I wasn't feeling it. So, I'd graduated from college and made my way back home to Honey Mountain.

I was going to write the book I'd had playing in my head for the past few years, and I'd taken a job to nanny for the two cutest girls on the planet, Paisley and Hadley King, while I pursued my dream.

Secretly crushing on my new boss was not a sin.

Was it?

Jace sat back down. His muscles strained against his white tee and my mouth went dry. He had blue eyes that were the lightest blue I'd ever seen. His brown hair always looked like he'd been tugging at it and managed to look sexy as hell with very little effort.

"Hawk and Niko helped me get a fresh coat of paint on the walls a few weeks ago. Looks like you and your sisters got everything moved and settled in there, yeah?"

Hawk and Niko were my sisters' husbands, and they were also good friends with Jace, so that didn't surprise me one bit that they'd helped out.

I nodded as I stared at his plump lips before clearing my

throat. "Yeah. Thanks for letting me stay there. It's such a cute place."

"Well, you're saving my ass. Since Karla left, the girls haven't had any consistency. We've had more nannies come and go than I can count. A firefighter's hours aren't always the easiest for people to accommodate. This will be really good for the girls. They were thrilled when I said you'd taken the job."

Karla was his ex-wife who'd skipped town with some random guy and left her girls and Jace behind. I admired the way he stepped up for his daughters. My dad was an amazing father and it hurt like hell that we'd lost our mama to cancer, but I couldn't imagine how much it would hurt if she'd chosen to leave. But Jace took it all in stride.

"You know I love your girls. And honestly, I'm happy to have my own place and not have to move back in with my dad. It just makes me feel like I'm somewhat of a grown-up, you know?" I'd seen them interact at Dad's Sunday dinners, and although Hadley seemed a little shy and limited on her vocabulary, Paisley was more of an old soul. I'm sure their mom leaving them had an impact on them both.

The corners of his lips turned up and my stomach fluttered. Jace was a serious guy, and after all he'd been through, I didn't see him smile all that often.

But when he did… I liked it.

Probably too much.

"Well, it's not much of a home with it being so small. But I'm glad you're happy with it. You know you can come over here any time if you want to cook in a larger kitchen." He slid over a set of keys. "These are to the main house. You'll stay here with the girls when I'm on duty at the firehouse, which is usually three nights a week. You know the drill, growing up with your dad. And then you'll have four nights to yourself. I may occasionally ask if you'd be willing to babysit a night here or there so I can go meet the guys for a beer or do a little work on one of the houses I'm renovating. But only if it works for you, and I'd pay you separately for that."

Did he date? My mind was spinning with questions that were too inappropriate to ask.

"Of course. You can ask me any time. And you're paying me plenty with the salary and the living accommodations." I knew Jace made money off of his house flipping side business that he did, which my brother-in-law, Niko, was now involved in as well. They were both talented when it came to renovating spaces, and apparently Jace King was doing quite well between flipping homes and being a firefighter, because this house was gorgeous.

"Well, I appreciate it. But I want to pay you for your time. My mom will watch the girls on the weekends for a few hours so I can work on whatever house we've got going at the time, but I don't like taking advantage of that. Hell, the girls are pretty good about chilling when I need them to in short doses. So, when you have to catch a shower or use the restroom, you just tell them to stay put until you come out. I usually put a show on in their playroom and they'll give you a quick fifteen minutes of peace. Just tell Paisley to keep Hadley with her."

I laughed. His girls were adorable. Well-behaved and sweet. "Okay. That sounds easy enough."

He handed me a piece of paper with a schedule on it. I have to say, I was impressed. It had everything laid out for me. What time they woke up, what time they napped, what they liked to eat. A lot of this stuff I'd already known because I'd spent a lot of time with them over the years, but I guessed this cheat sheet would come in handy when it came down to all the details. He had the pediatrician's information at the bottom, along with his parents' phone number in case of emergency.

"So, a few things you should know that you probably

aren't aware of from the time you've spent with them." His tone turned serious and when I met his light blue gaze, my chest squeezed at the concern I saw there.

"Okay," I said softly.

"Paisley is anxious about starting kindergarten for whatever reason. She's been in preschool and pre-K for the past two years, but she keeps talking about how scared she is for school to start in the fall. I don't know what's up with that, but let me know if she opens up to you about it."

"Got it. I think I was super nervous to start kindergarten too. It's all normal. You're doing a great job with your girls, Jace."

His smile was forced, and I saw it all in his gaze. The doubt. The worry. Maybe even some guilt about the fact that he was doing it on his own, trying to compensate for being a single parent.

"Thanks. I'm not sure how much damage her leaving will do to them, but I'm doing my best to give them a good life. As much as a grumpy firefighter can, at least." He shrugged and there was tease in his voice, but there was honesty too. "Anyway, Paisley will help out as much as you need her to. You know that. She's a go-with-the-flow type of kid. But she's got her quirks."

"Which are?" I hadn't noticed anything in all the time I'd spent with her. She was super polite and sweet and a ball of energy. Always helpful with little Hadley.

"She, uh, strips her clothes off when she goes to the bathroom." He barked out a laugh now. "Apparently, she takes them all off and folds them in a neat little pile by the door because she doesn't want her clothes to smell like poop."

My head fell back in laughter. I hadn't realized that's what she did, but it did make sense. "I did notice she takes quite a while in the bathroom, so now I understand why."

"Yeah. Her pre-K teacher was unimpressed about the little

habit because a line was forming outside the bathroom every time she took her turn."

"Well, no one should be rushed when it comes to doing their business," I said with a laugh.

"Touché. Couldn't agree more. What I wouldn't give to have a few minutes alone in the shitter now and then. I have to practically bribe them to give me ten minutes in the shower."

Jace King in the shower must be a sight. Visions of him washing his golden, naked body under a hot spray of water… there I go again.

I'd blame it on the fact that I'd been reading a lot of romance books lately as I geared up to start writing my own book.

And I'd possibly had a few sexy dreams about this man in the shower over the past few months. But I couldn't control what my subconscious did while I slept, right?

"Yeah. I'm sure. And where would you like me to sleep when I stay here at the main house?"

"So, when Mrs. Tusley was with the girls for those last few weeks of school, she stayed in the guest room. The problem is, both girls have occasional nightmares, and they like to climb into my bed. The guest room bed is small, and Mrs. Tusley was not a believer in letting the girls come into bed with her, and I don't know…" He scrubbed the back of his neck. "Maybe I'm fucking them up by letting them come in when they're scared."

"No. My sisters and I always went into our parents' room when we were young and had a nightmare. That's when you need to be comforted. I don't mind if they come to bed with me at all. Heck, for the longest time I used to take turns sleeping with all my sisters after my mom died. I welcome the company."

He raised a brow and I realized what I'd said.

"I mean, *the girls' company*. I hardly have any company in

my bed ever. I mean, not that I've never…" *Please, make it stop.* "The girls are welcome to come in if they get scared."

I reached for the glass of water that he'd given me and took a long sip, trying to regain my composure.

"I knew what you meant. And you're welcome to sleep in my room if you want. I'll make sure the sheets are clean for you. That way, if they come in, you'll still be able to get some sleep because the bed is plenty big."

"Okay. That sounds like a plan."

"I'm actually glad you brought it up. I, uh, I was hoping you'd understand if I asked that you not have any boyfriends stay over at the house when I'm on duty. Obviously, what you do in your free time in the guesthouse is your business, but I want the girls to feel safe when you're staying here with them. I've never allowed anyone to stay in my bed since Karla left, and I plan to keep it that way."

My face heated at his words, and I shook my head. "I would never do that."

"Fuck, I'm not trying to make you uncomfortable. Just needed to say it. You're young. I'm sure you have a million dudes chasing after you. But I just don't want to confuse the girls while you're with them. Obviously, you're welcome to have your sisters or a friend over any time. Just no strange guys." He chuckled.

My mind was still reeling that he'd just admitted he didn't bring women home. What did that mean? Did he just not have sex?

"I completely agree. That won't be an issue. I'm single." I held up my hands and fluttered them around like a crazy person. "I plan on writing when I'm not working."

"Yeah? I think that's great, Ash. What are you writing?"

I'm leaning toward writing about a sexy firefighter and his nanny.

Just kidding.

Not really.

"Um, it's a romance." I swallowed hard just as little Hadley came waddling over and walked right past her dad and over to me, holding her pudgy little arms up in the air for me to pick her up.

"Hey, sweetie pie. I'm excited that we're going to be spending lots of time together." I settled her on my lap, and she nuzzled her head beneath my neck. She smelled like sunshine and baby powder. Her light brown wild waves danced all around her face, and her hair didn't look like it had been brushed yet today. I knew Jace was doing the best that he could and the fact that he even attempted to do their hair was impressive to me.

"She still isn't speaking much, so maybe you can get her talking a little bit," Jace said, his voice low as he watched her with concern.

"Of course. I think we'll be just fine."

"Well, it's summer break, so they're going to be with you all day. You may be changing your tune here soon. A young girl like you probably wants to be hanging out at the lake with her friends, not hanging out with two little kids."

Young girl?

He'd pointed out my age twice now. I wasn't *that* young. I was twenty-two years old, turning twenty-three in a couple weeks. My mama always said I was an old soul. I never cared much for partying down by the lake or going out and getting crazy. Maybe it was because I'd lost my mother at a young age that I'd just become a homebody. I liked the comfort of being with my family. Always had.

"Don't worry about me, I'll be fine. I prefer staying home over going to Beer Mountain any day." I shrugged. It was the truth. And I was looking forward to getting lost in my words. "So, I'll stay in your room when I'm here, and we'll see how it goes."

"All right. I've been having some plumbing issues in my

master bathroom lately, but I have a guy coming over later today to get it fixed."

"Great. I'll just spend the rest of the day getting my place set up. I have a few pictures to hang, and Vivian made me some cute curtains."

He studied me. "Look at you. Making it all homey. I hope that's a sign you won't be quitting in a week."

"Not a chance."

Hadley squirmed to get down, and I pushed to my feet as the little angel wrapped her arms around my leg and kissed my knee which made me chuckle.

Paisley came walking into the kitchen wearing a princess dress with a tiara on top of her head. Her long brown hair ran down her back and she had her daddy's blue eyes. Both girls resembled Jace more than Karla, but Hadley had her daddy's coloring with big dark brown eyes and long lashes.

"Daddy, can Ashlan come over for pizza tonight?" Paisley asked as she stepped beside me and leaned her cheek against my side.

Be still my heart.

I'd always known I wanted to be a mother someday, and I couldn't wait for that to happen. I just hadn't found anyone I liked enough to date longer than six months.

"Not tonight, sweetheart. This is her night off."

Hadley moved toward her father and he plopped her on his lap and kissed the top of her head.

"Do you have another job?" Paisley asked me.

"I'm going to start writing a book," I said, and her eyes watered, her bottom lip quivering like I'd just broken her heart. "But I sure don't need to start that tonight. And pizza is my favorite."

Jace smirked, and his hand grazed over the beard that covered his jaw. "Don't let them be working you all the time, Ash. My girls may look sweet, but I swear they're little sharks."

"Well, seeing as tomorrow is our first day together, I think it would be fun to hang out a little tonight and they can show me some of their nighttime routine."

Jace smiled, and his face relaxed as he nodded. "If you're sure you don't mind."

"I'm sure," I said.

And just like that, my new life was getting started.

two

. . .

Jace

IT HAD BEEN three busy days at the firehouse. I was ready to take my ass home and see my little munchkins. I'd talked to Ashlan several times over the past few days, as I wanted to make sure she was comfortable there and the girls were adjusting. Apparently, both girls had nightmares on different nights, and they'd climbed into bed with her. Thoughts of Ashlan Thomas in my bed looking like a motherfucking vision had been difficult to ignore. The girl was too pretty for her own good.

Innocent.

Sweet.

Smart.

They didn't come any better than her. I knew I was lucky she'd been willing to take this gig that she was way overqualified for, but I sure as hell wasn't arguing. My girls were struggling, and I'd do whatever I could to help them.

The smiles on their faces when I'd told them that Ashlan was going to nanny for them. Hell, it's what I lived for. My ex-wife had bailed. It didn't hurt me in the slightest because we hadn't been happy since the day we got married.

If we were even happy on that day.

Sure, I'd tried hard to make it work. She'd given me the two best gifts of my life. But the woman was a train wreck. Always had been. We'd had a one-night stand and she'd shown up at my door nine months later, extremely pregnant with Paisley. I'd moved her in, and we'd given it a shot. We'd almost called it quits more times than I could count. She'd gone missing for two days a couple years back and then came home and begged for my forgiveness. Paisley was young, and I just didn't know if I could do it all on my own back then, so I'd taken her back long enough for her to get pregnant with Hadley. But we hadn't had sex since our youngest was born, so there wasn't much between us by the time she'd run off again.

This time around, I'd taken action. I wanted full custody of my girls, and she hadn't fought it. I'd sooner throw myself into a blazing fire than let her take them with her. They were worth all the suffering that I'd gone through with their mother. I'd filed for divorce, and she'd agreed to give me sole legal custody as long as she wasn't financially responsible for them.

She'd tried to step up after Paisley was born, but things had gone downhill quickly after we had Hadley. She said two kids were more than she could handle, and I'd had to hire help even though she stayed home with the girls. We had endless babysitters there on the nights I was at the firehouse, and then I took over on the days that I was home.

My girls needed more.

We all did.

"You out of here?" Jack Thomas, our captain, asked as he sat at the kitchen table finishing up lunch.

"Yep. I need to go see if your daughter is still in one piece after three days with the little munchkins."

"Cap, you think Ash can handle being with two little kids?" Rusty asked. "If so, maybe I should wife her up."

"Rusty, if you don't stop hitting on my daughters, I swear

to God, I will make you run drills out in the heat until your balls shrivel up into little raisins."

Rusty shivered in dramatic fashion, and I rolled my eyes. "I think some drills in the heat might do him some good."

"What? I'm sorry to tell you, Cap, but your girls are hot."

Niko chucked a biscuit across the table, and it hit Rusty square in the face. "Shut the fuck up about my wife and her sisters."

Laughter filled the room, and Rusty picked up the biscuit and took a bite. "So touchy."

"I'm sure she did fine," Cap said as he tipped his chin at me. "She loves kids and books. And I know she's happy that she didn't have to come back and live under her old man's roof. She's always been determined to show me how grown up she is."

I nodded. I agreed with him. Ashlan was not your typical twenty-two-year-old, out living her best life. I'd never heard of her getting into any trouble, and she'd always been great with my girls.

"I'll let you know." I clapped Niko on the shoulder.

"I'll meet you at the Elm Street house on Saturday morning," he said. Niko and I were wrapping up our most recent house flip, as our side business renovating homes was bringing in some good profits.

"Yep. I'll meet you there." I saluted all the guys.

"Take a shower. You smell like smoke and beef jerky," Tallboy shouted, and I flipped him the bird. He was right though. We'd had a late one last night, and we'd all been too tired to shower. I'd caught up on sleep because I'd need to be on my game with the girls today. I'd have to catch a shower later.

When I got home, it was unusually quiet. The house smelled like cookies and peaches, and as I glanced around the kitchen, it was spotless.

This wasn't a bad way to come home.

I couldn't remember the last time I came home to a clean house that smelled good.

"Hello?" I called out, and when I heard faint voices upstairs, I took the steps two at a time. When I got to the top, I found the three of them sitting together in the playroom.

Ashlan was sitting on the floor wearing a cute little sundress, her legs crossed beneath her with Hadley on her lap as she held a book in front of her while she read to the girls. Paisley was sitting beside her with her head resting on Ashlan's shoulder. I just took a minute to watch them.

My girls looked so content and relaxed. It was rare to see them sitting still like this. Their eyes were sleepy as they listened to Ashlan read. Hell, I felt like I could take a nap to the soothing sound of her voice. She closed the book and looked up to see me standing there.

"Oh, hey. I was just about to go put Hadley down for a little siesta."

I moved toward her, and lavender flooded my senses. Damn, Ashlan smelled good. I reached for Hadley and pulled her into my arms. "Hey, Sweet Pea. You want to take a little snooze?"

My baby girl burrowed her face into my neck, and I breathed in all that goodness. These two little angels were the reason that I'd keep working hard. They deserved better than the hand they'd been dealt, and I'd do whatever I fucking could to make things better for them.

I carried her to her room and set her gently on the bed. We'd recently moved her out of her crib, which made it a whole lot easier for her to come into my room at night. Her dark brown eyes blinked at me a few times and she tapped her cheek with her fingers, which was Hadley's way of asking for a kiss. I kissed her cheek and her little hand rubbed against my beard. She always giggled when it brushed her skin, but this time her eyes closed, and I placed her hand beside her and walked out of the room. The house looked fucking amazing. The playroom was organized, and I glanced in Paisley's room and noticed her bed was made.

"Did she go down okay?" Ashlan asked as she set the book on the bookshelf and followed me downstairs to the kitchen.

"Yeah. So, it went all right? The house looks amazing, and the girls are clean and happy. Hell, how'd you pull this off?"

"Daddy," Paisley snapped at me as she came down the stairs. "Billy Graber says that hell is a bad word. And you aren't allowed to say cuss words around kids. Isn't that right, Ashlan?"

Ashlan winced. "Well, it is right. I think people forget sometimes."

"Maybe he should have to go to timeout and think about his choices like we do at school?" Paisley asked, her hands on her hips as she raised a brow at me.

I rolled my eyes. I'd be damned if I was going to timeout every time I said a fucking swear word. Wasn't I already doing enough? I rarely went out, I had to have sex outside of my home, I'd allowed Paisley to paint my fingernails pink and been harassed by the guys at the firehouse, I'd gone to the store and bought the girls new panties last week—something I thought I'd never do, and I was cutting the crust off of sandwiches because it was their favorite even though I knew the crust was the best part.

But a man had his limits.

"I think timeout for an adult is…" I paused to think about my wording.

Fucked up.

Stupid.

Bullshit.

"Don't say it, Daddy. You're going to timeout every time you say a swear because we don't want Hadley to learn those words once she starts talking."

"Fine," I hissed. "But you're not much older than her, so why the hell do you know these words?"

She held up two fingers. "That's going to cost you two card changes. In my classroom, we get one warning and then you pull your green card. If you do something again, you get another card change. I'm sorry to tell you, you're on yellow already, Daddy, so you need to stand right over there and think about it. You're lucky you don't have recess, because you'd be missing it."

"Is that so?" I let out a long breath and moved to stand beside the counter. "When did you become such a bossy little thing?"

"Birth." She giggled. "I'm going upstairs to get some color cards made for you. It'll help you behave after you start pulling them. Billy Graber pulls lots of cards." She ran up the stairs and I shook my head in disbelief that I'd been home for just a few minutes, and I was already in timeout.

Ashlan's head fell back in laughter after Paisley left to make some sort of fucking color code system to call me out on my shit.

"Oh, you think this is funny?" I raised a brow at her.

"Sorry about that. But this is not a bad idea."

"Well, guess what?" I teased.

"What?"

"Timeout is not such a bad thing. Hell, I could use a few minutes to myself once in a while."

"I heard that bad word, Daddy. You're now on red," Paisley shouted from upstairs.

Ashlan's tongue swiped out to wet her bottom lip and she tried hard not to laugh. "Not a lot of wiggle room once you're on red, buddy."

"Sure," I said, leaning against the counter and crossing my feet at the ankles as I took her in.

She tucked her light brown hair behind her ear and smiled. So damn pretty. She wore a yellow dress with little straps over her tan shoulders. My mouth watered at the sight of her, and I silently cursed myself for wanting to reach out and touch her.

"Hadley talked a little bit today," she said as she moved to the sink and filled the Brita before putting it back in the refrigerator.

"What? What did she say?"

Hadley had only babbled and cried and grunted as her form of communication thus far. She was almost three and a half years old, and I knew she should be talking more than she was. The pediatrician thought it had a lot to do with the fact that Karla had run off without saying goodbye and their lives had been turned upside down the past few months.

But it's not like things were good when their mama was around. She was selfish and drunk more often than she wasn't. So unfortunately, I think it had affected my baby girl more than I wanted to admit.

"She said, 'Wuv you,' when she woke up beside me this morning." Ashlan shook her head and smiled like it was the cutest thing she'd ever heard. "And when I got her dressed and said that you were coming home today, she said, 'Daddy.'"

"No shit. Really?" I couldn't stop the smile from spreading across my face.

"Daddy!" Paisley shouted from upstairs. "Do better."

"Do better?" I whispered to Ashlan and shook my head. "It's going to be a long couple of days."

Paisley came bounding down the stairs with different colored rectangles.

"Did Ashlan tell you that Hadley talked a little?" Paisley asked, and I noted the fancy braid that ran around her head like a crown.

"She did. That had to make you happy," I said, knowing how much Paisley wanted her little sister to talk.

"Yep. You want to play magnets with me?" my little girl asked me, and I swear I'd give her the sun if she asked for it.

"Sure. I guess the shower will have to wait." I reached for her hand.

"All right. Well, I have a date with my laptop," Ashlyn announced.

"You're going to bring us cupcakes later, right?" Paisley asked, and I shot her a look.

"Hey, she's done enough," I said.

"Oh, she's not asking. I already told them I'd be going by Honey Bee's later and I'd drop off a treat for them."

"Thank you for everything. You did a great job. I really appreciate it."

Fuck, she was cute the way she beamed up at me, like it meant something to her that I was impressed.

She was Cap's daughter, and she was a decade younger than me.

Pull your shit together, asshole.

"Of course. We had a lot of fun. I'll see you guys later." She waved as she made her way to the door. "The sheets are clean on your bed."

That should have made me happy, but instead, I wouldn't mind the smell of lavender on my sheets.

"Thank you," I called out just before the door closed.

"I love Ashlan, Daddy," Paisley said as she led me up to her playroom.

"Yeah? More than Mrs. Tusley?" I chuckled, because my daughter had not been a fan.

"Yes. For sure. Mrs. Tusley smelled like mustard and pickles. And Ashlan smells like pretty flowers, doesn't she?" Paisley walked to the shelf and pulled down the tub of magnets before dropping to sit in front of me.

"She does. But mustard and pickles aren't bad," I teased.

"I know. But Ashlan's like a real mommy, and Mrs.

Tusley's like a mean grandma." Paisley dumped all the magnets out between us.

My chest squeezed at her words, but I wanted her to be able to talk to me about this shit. "Yeah? I'm sure it's hard not having your mama around sometimes, huh?" I reached for a few pieces and built a box.

"I don't miss my real mama too much because she wasn't fun."

"She wasn't?" I asked as I watched her build a second story on her box.

"She always wanted to take a nap, and she yelled at us a lot when you weren't home."

"How come you never told me?" Anger coursed through my veins. I knew Karla was no saint, but I didn't know she was cruel to our babies.

"Because she told me not to and said she wouldn't make me lunch anymore if I told you."

"Motherfuck—"

"Daddy," she said, raising a brow with the cutest little smile.

"Sorry, baby. I'll just put myself in timeout right here. I'm sorry that I didn't know how bad it was." Hell, I probably just didn't want to see it. I was trying to stay afloat with two babies and a disaster of a wife.

"It's okay. We've got a good daddy, and that's all we need."

My fucking chest tightened at her words. "I've got you, Buttercup."

We spent the next hour and a half playing until Hadley woke up. I took them both outside and turned on the sprinkler and then brought them in to get them bathed.

Once they were clean, I told them I needed to take a quick shower before we thought about what to do for dinner.

"All right. You two stay in here and play," I said as I turned on the Disney Plus channel. I wasn't a huge fan of them watching TV as I preferred for them to play outside, but there was a time and place for everything. And this would buy me enough time to get cleaned up. "Daddy's going to take a shower."

"Good. You smell like stinky fire," Paisley said, and Hadley clapped her hands together and laughed. I didn't know if she understood what people were saying half the time, but I hoped she was taking it all in.

"Oh, you think that's funny?" I teased, leaning down to each of them and rubbing my scruffy beard against their necks before kissing their cheeks.

The sound of their giggles filled the air around me as I made my way to the master bathroom. I turned on my shower and the damn showerhead drizzled. I'd just had the thing fixed a few days ago, and it wasn't working again. I turned off the water and made my way back to the playroom.

"Daddy's shower isn't working again. Did Ashlan mention it?" I asked.

"She takes baths like us, Daddy. She doesn't like the shower."

Damn. The thought of Ashlan Thomas sprawled out naked in my soaking tub had me clearing my throat.

"All right. I'll be in your bathroom. Use mine if you need to go potty."

"Okay," Paisley sang out while her baby sister giggled.

I was thankful for one working shower, and I let the hot water beat down on my back as I squeezed some shampoo into my hand and scrubbed my hair. These moments of peace didn't come often, and I was grateful for the few minutes of quiet.

Even if it wouldn't last long.

three

. . .

Ashlan

I KNOCKED on the door and when no one answered, I used my key to step inside. I'd gotten caught up writing several chapters and then made my way to my sister's bakery, Honey Bee's, just before it closed. I'd hurried to get over there because I wanted to drop these cupcakes off so the girls could have them after dinner.

"Hello?" I called out. Jace's truck was in the driveway, but maybe they'd gone to the park.

"Ashlan?" Paisley shouted, and she sounded upset as she came running down the stairs and lunged her little body into my arms. "You need to help Hadley. She's crying."

"What?" I tossed the box on the counter and started for the stairs. "Where is she?"

"In the bathroom. Her poopy's stuck in her bootie, and I was trying to help her." Paisley was crying now too, and I sprinted up the stairs and whipped open the bathroom door.

Jace King had just reached for a towel and stood there facing me—

Buck. Freaking. Naked.

I swear on all things holy—I'd never seen anything quite like Jace's sculpted body. Water droplets covered his tanned skin, and I couldn't look away. Every inch of him was firm and large. His hands. His shoulders. His…

I digress.

He took his time drying his hair before wrapping the towel around his waist. Maybe he was processing the fact that my mouth was gaping open and I couldn't move.

"Shouldn't you shut the door?" he asked, his voice gruff with a hint of humor.

My legs were frozen, but I forced my hand to reach for the handle and I yanked the door closed as hard as I could, but my feet were glued to the floor.

The door came hard and fast—no pun intended. It hit me square in the face and dropped me to the floor.

Paisley screamed as she came jogging up the stairs with a cupcake in her hand and saw me sprawled out on the floor as Jace hurried over to me with a washcloth.

"She's bleeding, Daddy," Paisley cried out and Jace bent down and covered my nose with a washcloth.

Oh my gosh. This is not happening.

He helped me sit up against the door and applied pressure to my bloody nose. Paisley was crying as she patted my head and smiled with chocolate cake in her teeth, and little Hadley came running around the corner with no panties on, wearing a tank top and pumping her little arms to get to me.

"I'm okay. I, um, I thought Hadley was in here crying because Paisley said her poop was giving her trouble." I tried desperately to explain why I'd just walked in on the man in the shower.

Hadley turned around and shook her bare butt at us, and sure enough, a little turd was dangling from her tiny hiney.

"Holy shit," Jace whispered as he pushed to stand, and his towel gaped open. His oversized penis was staring me and my bloody nose right in the face.

"Daddy," Paisley shrieked and pointed. "Your privates are showing."

Hadley turned around quickly to see what all the fuss was about, and she let out a bloodcurdling scream. Her pitch was high enough to shatter all glass within a ten-mile radius as she screamed at the top of her lungs and pointed at her father's... *privates.*

Jace adjusted his towel and picked up his youngest daughter and dropped her on the toilet. "Stay put."

He stepped over me as my body was blocking the doorway and he ran down the hall. He passed me again wearing a pair of sweatpants and headed for the kitchen. "Let me grab you an ice pack."

I scrambled to my feet and looked in the mirror before wetting the washcloth to clean up my nose.

"Are you okay?" Paisley asked as she watched me.

"I'm fine. I was just startled." I made my way over to the potty and leaned Hadley forward and chuckled when I looked down to see there was still some activity taking place.

"Is her bootie okay?"

"Yes, she'll be fine, sweetie." I reached for some toilet paper to wipe her up, and Jace walked into the room with a bag of ice. He took the toilet paper from me and handed me the ice pack.

"Hold this on there, and you'll be okay in a few minutes." He turned to Hadley. "Are you done?"

She shook her head and grunted and we all three laughed.

"Daddy, was that your penis? Billy Graber said he has a penis." Paisley giggled before stopping at the sink to clean up her frosting-covered hands.

"That kid's a wealth of knowledge, isn't he?" Jace grumped.

"Where's my penis?" Hadley's little voice whispered, startling all of us as she looked down between her legs.

Jace raised a brow, Paisley squealed, and I laughed.

"Daddy. Hadley's first sentence is, '*Where's my penis.*'" She fell on the floor in a fit of laughter and Hadley laughed too as she pointed behind her for Jace to wipe her bottom.

"We're not going to write that one down in her baby book. You don't have a penis, Sweet Pea." Jace lifted her off the toilet and set her on her feet. "Playroom. Now. I'll be in to get you dressed in a minute. Let me talk to Ashlan."

"You got any other words?" Paisley asked as she led her sister out of the bathroom and across the hall to the playroom.

Jace leaned forward and lifted the ice pack from my face to inspect my nose. "You all right?"

He was standing so close, his bare chest inches from my face. I could barely breathe.

"Yes. I'm so sorry about that. I thought Hadley was in here," I said, shaking my head as I rambled again.

He pressed the ice pack to my nose and stepped back. "Yeah, you mentioned that. Those reflexes weren't very fast though, huh?" He smirked.

"What? No. I just…" I set the ice on the counter beside the sink and checked out my nose in the mirror, desperate to do anything to avoid his curious gaze. "I was startled. That's all."

"Ah, I see. That door sure hit you hard."

"Yeah. I didn't see that coming." I shrugged and suddenly needed to get out of this small space. My breathing was labored, and I'd already made a fool of myself once today. "Okay, well. Thanks for—" Oh my gosh. Why must I continue to speak? "The, um, ice."

Thanks for the show is what I wanted to say.

"You got it. Sorry for all of that," he said with a chuckle. "Nothing like seeing a three-year-old naked with a poopy in her butt."

I covered my face and laughed. I was thankful that he was focusing on that instead of the fact that his nanny had been gaping at his *Johnson* before slamming the door on her own face.

"No problem. Cupcakes are on the counter, but I think Paisley already ate one. Have a good night."

I hurried across the hall and hugged both girls goodbye, and they were still giggling. Paisley kept saying the word *penis.*

"All right. That's enough penis talk for one night," Jace said as I made my way to the guesthouse and pulled out my phone. I needed to talk to my sisters *pronto,* before I overthought this to death.

I typed into the group chat text that I had with my sisters. We had an ongoing conversation going at all times.

Me ~ This is a 911 situation. Who's available?

Dylan ~ I live for these moments. Beer Mountain. Ten minutes.

Charlotte ~ I'm on my way.

Vivian ~ Niko just fell asleep on the couch with little Bee. I can sneak away for an hour.

Everly ~ Perfect. Hawk is working out and Mama's starving. Order me chicken fingers and fries if you beat me there.

Dylan ~ So bossy.

Everly ~ Try growing a human in your stomach and then talk to me.

Vivian ~ Ain't that the truth. I'll take a burger for whoever gets there first. I'm nursing. I need food all the time.

I chuckled as I hurried back outside and started the three-block walk to Beer Mountain. Nothing made me feel better than a Thomas girl happy hour.

When I pulled the door open, Dylan was sitting in our favorite booth flirting with Tanner, the bartender. The girl had no shame.

"I'll get this order in right away, beautiful." Tanner winked.

"You're too good to us," Dylan purred.

"Nothing I wouldn't do for the Thomas girls." He clapped me on the shoulder as he walked by.

"Thanks, Tanner," I called out, just as Charlotte, Everly, and Vivian walked in together.

We wasted no time, as we quickly hugged and joined Dilly in the circular corner booth.

"Drinks and food are ordered. For those of us who aren't with child or breastfeeding, we'll be eating nachos and tater tots. You're welcome." Dylan used her hand to motion to me. "The floor is yours."

I rolled my eyes at her dramatics and smiled when our server, Lily, set our drinks in front of us. I took a long pull from my beer and waited for her to walk away.

"Something happened," I whispered before setting my mug down and covering my eyes with my hand because the thought of what had just happened was still mortifying.

"Your nose looks a little swollen," Everly said as she studied me. "Did you get hurt?"

"Um, well, kind of." I shook my head before letting out a long breath. "I dropped the cupcakes off to the girls, and Paisley said that Hadley was crying because she had a poopy stuck in her bootie."

Dylan made a gagging noise and covered her mouth. "This is not what I signed up for. This is not happy hour talk."

We all laughed, and I filled them in on all the embarrassing details that followed. They all stared at me with wide eyes as their mouths gaped open. I told them that I tried to close the door but had managed to slam it on my face because my legs wouldn't move. And then I leaned back in the booth and waited for their response.

"Wait. It was *that big* that you were dumbfounded?" Dylan asked as Lily approached our table again and set down an obscene amount of food, and we were all trying not to laugh at Dylan's comment.

We thanked Lily and she moved back toward the bar. I

reached for a tater tot and popped it into my mouth. "Yes. It was a sight."

"I knew it. I mean, the man is ridiculously hot. Of course, he has a huge—"

"Package," I interrupted. "But that's not what I came to talk about. I just, oh my gosh, I walked in on him naked. I work for him. Now what?"

"Well, it was an accident. It doesn't sound like he's upset about it," Charlotte said as she waggled her brows. "But it does sound like you guys had a little moment there before he told you to close the door."

"Do you like him?" Everly asked as she studied me with one brow raised in that big sister way that she had about her. "I mean, obviously you're attracted to him. But, if it's just that, I think you can just act like it never happened and go back to normal."

"No. Of course not. I mean, yes, I like Jace. He's an amazing father and a really good guy. But he's a family friend, and he's got two kids, so no. Well, sure, maybe I've had a crush on him, but it's harmless, right? He's older than me. He'd never look at me like that. I just, yeah. No. Of course not. I don't like him in an inappropriate way." I crossed my arms over my chest and leaned back because I knew the more that I talked, the worse it sounded.

Yes, I had a massive crush on Jace King.

Who wouldn't?

He was beautiful and honest and sexy.

The table erupted in laughter before Vivian reached for my hand. "It's okay to have a crush on him, Ash. He's a gorgeous man."

"Well, we knew that before she saw his giant schlong," Dylan said.

"You better not tell anyone," I hissed.

"Hey, the size of his amazing penis is safe with me."

Dylan pretended to seal her lips, lock them up, and then throw the key over her head.

"Ignore her. No one is going to say a word. But Ash, he's a lot older than you and he has his hands full. He's a single dad with two girls, and trust me when I tell you… there is no one that doesn't look at you that way. But this is—complicated. And the only reason he isn't showing interest is because he knows that it would be—*messy*. And I don't know how Dad would feel about it." Everly reached for a French fry and took a bite.

I nodded. "No. It's just a crush. I would never act on it. And he's not interested in me, trust me."

"How did things end? I mean, outside of his towel gaping open in your face?" Charlotte covered her mouth to mask her laughter.

"Well, she got a bloody nose. Hadley had a poopy hanging from her tush, Paisley was horrified by her father's… *privates*—so I'm guessing Jace isn't sitting around happy hour talking about it." Dylan reached for her beer.

Vivian nodded. "Yeah, he's probably horrified by the whole thing."

He probably was. His nanny walked in on him naked. He was probably highly annoyed with me for even stopping by.

"Oh my gosh. I'm just going to pretend it never happened. I'm sure that's what he'll do too."

"It'll be fine. It's Jace. He's family. He's a single parent and trying to survive. I'm sure he won't say another word about it. Just act normal." Everly leaned back in the booth and rubbed her barely-there baby bump.

"How do you act normal when you see the guy you're crushing on naked, and he's hung like a racehorse?" Dylan said over a mouthful of tots.

"You're so crude," Charlotte barked at her twin. "It's an innocent crush. We've all had them. She'll get over it. I'd say

Jace King is probably the least attainable man in Honey Mountain."

Everly nodded and cocked her head to the side. "Have you talked to Henry again?"

Of course she was asking about my ex-boyfriend because he was all but perfect on paper. For starters, he was my age, and he'd been a doting boyfriend for the few months we'd been together. There was just no spark. He was a good friend and that's where I'd like to keep him.

"We aren't getting back together, if that's what you're asking. But I promise I'm putting this little crush to rest right now. I know it can't go anywhere with Jace. I've already forgotten about it," I said confidently.

"Why don't you try a dating app?" Dylan asked.

"That's a good idea," Vivian said. "Just be sure you meet at a public place."

"It's just not my thing. I just broke up with Henry, I'm not in any rush to date." I shrugged.

"Exactly. I tried it, and it wasn't for me either," Charlotte said as she reached for her glass of Chardonnay. "I prefer being set up by friends."

"Yeah, I'll bet you do. I'm sure you wouldn't mind if Jilly set you up with Ledger." Dylan raised a brow, and we all tried to hide our smiles.

From one girl with a crush to another—Charlotte had crushed hard on her best friend's brother for years.

"Shut up, Dilly. That is not true." Charlotte balled up her napkin and threw it at her.

"I don't know why you're all so afraid to admit when you want something. I have zero problem going after what I want. Unfortunately, there is no one that even piques my interest these days. The men here are so—predictable."

My head fell back in laughter. "I can't wait for the day that someone knocks you on your ass."

"Well, maybe if I walked in on a dude I was crushing on

and got a sneak peek of his goods—I'd be right there next to you. Sitting on my ass with an ice pack on my nose. *Hashtag, goals.*"

"She's already over it," Everly insisted.

My oldest sister had always been super protective of all of us, but especially me. I remember the first time I went out with a guy in college, she made me text her the minute I got home.

"Hey, Hawk has a few of his teammates coming to visit us for the Fourth of July in a couple weeks, and they'll be at the party. They're all really cute, and a few of them are single."

"That sounds great. I'm not dying to get into anything serious anyway. I want to focus on giving Paisley and Hadley some stability and outside of that, my focus is my writing."

"Ohhh, a fling with a hot hockey player. Yes, please." Dylan held up her glass, and Charlotte and I both lifted ours to meet hers. Vivian and Everly just laughed and shook their heads.

This was exactly what I needed. A little time with my sisters.

I already felt much better.

I was going to just act completely normal when I saw Jace next.

And all thoughts of a naked Jace King would be reserved for my fantasies.

Or the pages of my book.

This crush ended now.

four

. . .

Jace

THOSE BIG GOLDEN-BROWN *eyes stared at me, and my dick was painfully hard. Her lips were parted, eyes filled with desire, and neither of us moved. I reached down and stroked myself a few times, because this time I wasn't reaching for a towel or telling her to close the door.*

I wanted her.

Her nipples were impossible to miss through her thin sundress as her body reacted the same way mine was.

Want.

Need.

Hell, it had been so long since I'd actually wanted a woman, I didn't know what to do with these feelings.

I stepped out of the shower and moved toward her. My hand settled around her waist, and I tugged her against my body as her head fell back and her tongue dipped out to wet her bottom lip.

"Jace. I want you," she whispered.

"I want you too, Sunshine." My mouth crashed into hers.

"Daddy," Hadley called out from her bedroom, and I startled. I shot to a sitting position in my bed, realizing I was in the midst of a dirty dream with Cap's daughter.

Sunshine?

I'd never called her that, however, it was very fitting.

That's exactly what she was.

I adjusted myself and walked to the bathroom to wash my hands and splashed some water on my face before making my way across the hall to my baby girl's room. She'd been speaking a little ever since she'd found her voice. Her vocabulary was limited and unfortunately, the only words she'd spoken thus far were, *daddy, where's my penis,* and *wuv you*. But I'd take it.

Hey, I wasn't winning any father of the year award, so I'd count this as a win.

"What's up, Sweet Pea?" I said as I moved toward her bed and brushed the hair back from her face. Her little cherub cheeks were always rosy when she first woke up, and she blinked her dark brown eyes at me a few times.

"Wuv you," she whispered.

My fucking chest exploded. I'd never been a real sentimental guy before these two angels came into my life, but they'd gripped me by the heart since the day they took their first breaths.

"I love you too."

I scooped her into my arms and carried her to the bathroom. "Let's go potty and brush our teeth. Someone's got some major dragon breath."

She giggled before sitting on her little potty and concentrating real hard to pee.

"Good morning." Paisley appeared in the doorway, and I set her toothbrush beside Hadley's.

"Morning. How'd you sleep, Buttercup?"

"I slept great, Daddy." She moved to the sink and reached for her toothbrush before pausing to look at me in the mirror. "Can we go visit Ashlan today? I miss her."

It had been three days since we'd seen her. The girls and I had kept busy playing outside in the sprinklers, and I'd spent a few hours yesterday working on the Elm Street house with

Niko. My mom watched Paisley and Hadley for me, and Niko and I got the floors laid in the family room and kitchen.

Ashlan had definitely gone MIA, which was more than fair seeing as they'd been her days off. But with the last time I'd seen her being the day she'd walked in on me buck-ass naked, I hoped it wouldn't be weird when I saw her next.

Maybe she'd been traumatized by the whole thing. She'd gaped at me like she'd never seen a penis before, so maybe I'd scarred her for life.

Would she quit over this?

Hell, I should have covered up quicker. I'd been so mesmerized by the way she'd looked at me, lips parted and eyes half-mast—I'd taken my sweet-ass time wrapping that towel around my waist.

"It's her day off. Daddy goes back to work tomorrow, and you'll see her then." I gave Paisley the look to get a move on, and she reached for her toothbrush. "We're going to spend some time with your grandparents today, and then I'll take you two to the fair. How does that sound?"

Hadley stood up and clapped her hands together, and Paisley fist-pumped the sky as she continued brushing her teeth. I plopped my youngest daughter on the sink and told her to open up as I brushed her teeth, and she giggled the entire time.

"Ashlan does it better," Paisley said after she spit in the sink and rinsed her mouth. "She counts and tells Hadley no laughing until she gets to one hundred."

I rolled my eyes. My daughter sure did love putting me in my place every chance she got. "Is that so?"

"Yep." Paisley reached for a brush and ran it through her long waves before handing it to me. I brushed Hadley's hair and the static made it stand straight up, which caused all three of us to laugh. She did a silly little dance, and I walked to her bedroom and opened the closet. Karla used to fight the girls over what they wore, but I liked to give them the choice.

Man, kids had so few choices these days. The least I could do was let them pick out their own outfits.

Hadley pointed to her bumblebee costume from last Halloween.

"That's a Halloween costume, baby girl. And it's probably too small now." I pulled it down for her to see.

She clasped it in her hands and spun around.

Looks like we were wearing a bumblebee costume.

I helped her into her ridiculously small bumblebee outfit, and her little belly bulged in between the two pieces as I attached the wings. Paisley came around the corner wearing a pair of jean shorts and a tank top with some flip-flops. She was definitely the less flashy dresser of my two girls.

"What is she wearing?" She broke out in a fit of laughter.

"Bzzzzzz," Hadley said as she danced around the room. I'd count that as another word and add it to the list.

"It's a little small on her," Paisley said as she shook her head and smiled at her baby sister. I loved that these two loved one another so much.

"Hey. Choose your battles, Buttercup. Let her have this one. Sometimes people need a win." I scooped up Hadley and carried her downstairs to the kitchen, setting her in her chair. Paisley sat in the seat beside her while I poured them each a bowl of cereal.

"What's battles mean, Daddy?"

"It just means that you've got to choose your fights, right? Some things you feel strongly about and you don't back down. But the things that aren't that important, you let go. And sometimes, you've got to give someone a win."

"Is that what happened with our mama? You were tired of fighting?" Paisley asked as she shoveled a spoonful of Cheerios into her mouth.

I took my time to think about it as I set a small plate with sliced banana beside each of them before sitting down with a cup of coffee.

"Maybe. But you can't fight for something that you don't believe in. And your mama was sick, and she wasn't taking good care of herself, so this was for the better."

We'd talked about this many times, but I knew that we'd probably be talking about it over and over for a long time to come.

"Is that why she never calls to check on us or tell us where she is?"

"Yeah, probably. But one thing I want you to remember is that you're loved. Your mama may be sick, but she does love you. And I love you. Grammy, Pop, Uncle Hayden, and Uncle Travis love you." My parents and my brothers doted over my little girls, as I was the only one with kids.

"And Ashlan loves us so much," Paisley said with a wide smile.

"Wuv," Hadley said as milk dribbled down her chin, and I laughed.

Damn, these two owned me.

"Yep. There are a lot of people who love you two. You know that, right?"

Paisley moved to her feet and wrapped her arms around my neck. "We know, *Dad*."

"Hey, what happened to Daddy?" I teased as I pulled her on my lap.

"Billy Graber says that babies call their dads Daddy."

That little dick was starting to work my nerves. He had me standing in the corner every fucking time I swore out loud, he talked about his penis, and now he was telling my little girl not to call me Daddy?

That pissed me the fuck off.

"Billy Graber is a little shi—stinker. You best keep calling me Daddy, Buttercup, or I'm going to go have a little talk with Billy."

She laughed as she carried her bowl to the sink. "I think my pre-K teacher, Mrs. Hardy, thought he was a stinker too."

Hadley pinched her nose and scrunched her face because we were saying stinker. Even if she wasn't saying much, I was convinced that she was taking it all in.

"Come on, my little stinkers, let's go by Grammy and Pop's for a few hours, and then I'll take you to the fair later."

My parents gushed all over my two girls. They colored, they played hide-and-seek, and then my dad took them out back to kick a ball around.

"How's Ashlan working out? I'm so happy she agreed to nanny for you." My mom sliced up a tray of vegetables and set it on the table for the girls.

"She did a great job. I'm just hoping she sticks around for a little bit. At least until Paisley starts school and gets adjusted. I can get Hadley into preschool in January too, so they'll be covered during the day."

She nodded. "You know they can stay with us on the three nights that you're at the firehouse. We love having them here."

"Yeah, thanks, Mama." I kissed the top of her head. "If I need to, I'll take you up on that. But I'd like to keep them in their beds and on their routine if I can. Especially with school starting."

"That makes sense." She chomped down on a carrot before my dad and the girls came flying into the house.

We hung out for a few hours and had lunch with my parents. When we were getting ready to leave, my father farted, which sent both girls into a fit of giggles.

"You think that's funny when Pops has to toot?" my father asked as he tickled them both.

"I don't think it's funny," I said, as the foul scent wafted around the room. "Let's go, munchkins."

They kissed them both goodbye and I loaded them up to head to the fair.

"You think Uncle Hayden or Uncle Travis will be at the

fair?" Paisley asked as we drove toward downtown a few blocks away.

"Nah. Uncle Hayden is out of town visiting some friends from college, and Uncle Trav took his boat out today on the lake." Travis owned Honey Mountain Rentals, which had turned into a year-round business for tourists who wanted sporting equipment. It also meant that we had access to every type of sporting provision known to man.

"I want to go on the boat again," Paisley said as I put the car in park and climbed out of my seat. I unbuckled Hadley and set her on the ground.

"You hated the boat last time we went out, and Hadley puked all over me." I shook my head as I remembered the dreadful day about a year and a half ago when my brother had just gotten the boat and convinced us to bundle up and go out on the lake for a quick spin even though it was cold as hell. My ex-wife had gotten plastered per usual, my girls were both miserable, and Karla had called a friend to pick her up and never came home that night. I'd been taking care of the girls, and that's when I told her I was done. There was no coming back from the shit she'd pulled.

"I don't remember any of that." Paisley was out of the car and reaching for my hand as we made our way toward the entrance of hell.

Also known as… the Honey Mountain fair.

I'd been coming here since I was a kid. There were rides and treats and face painting.

Enough sweets to put a kid in a sugar-induced coma.

"Daddy, I want to go on that ride," Paisley shouted. I scooped Hadley up in my arms and followed close behind my older daughter.

"Hey, now, Buttercup. If it's a ride your sister can't go on, you're going to have to either ride alone or skip it. I can't leave her alone if I go on with you."

"I know. I'm fine going on by myself." She led me straight

for the ride that would make a grown man chuck his cookies. It was the spinning tops and my least favorite.

"It's called the Devil Whip," Paisley said with a big smile on her face.

"I don't think you want to go on this one. It'll make you sick." And where the fuck did these names come from? It's a family fair.

"Billy Graber said the Devil Whip ride is for the cool kids," she said as she chewed on her thumbnail and stared at the ride.

That little fucker needed to find a hobby and stop filling my little girl's head with bullshit. They'd been out of school for two weeks, and she was still quoting the little bastard.

I bent down and set Hadley back on the ground and looked Paisley in the eyes. "Do you want to ride this? I don't think I can take Hadley on this one, Buttercup. Maybe we should start with something easier."

"Ashlan," she shouted directly in my ear as she pointed over my shoulder, and I pushed back up to stand. "Ashlan's here, Daddy."

"Yeah, I heard you," I grumped because everyone within a ten-mile radius heard her shriek.

"Hey. Did you guys just get here?" Ashlan asked. She wore a pair of white shorts and a black tank top, and her hair was pulled back in an elastic band. She looked gorgeous.

And sexy.

Jack's daughter, asshole. His youngest daughter.

"Yep. We just got here." Paisley reached for her hand. "Will you ride this one with me?"

"Of course, I will." Ashlan gave me a forced smile as she followed Paisley up to the front of the line.

Maybe I'd traumatized her the other day.

She was young.

It was just another reminder that Ashlan Thomas was the most off-limits woman in Honey Mountain.

five

. . .

Ashlan

"AND WHAT DOES A DOG SAY?" I asked Hadley, and she giggled and barked.

"Ruff, ruff." She then stuck her tongue out and panted.

The little angel's vocabulary was growing at a rapid rate. She was a gentle soul, and I think she just needed that one-on-one time talking with her to find her sweet voice.

"Yes. And what does a piggy say?" I asked.

"Oink, oink." She scrunched her little nose, and I laughed.

"Where's Pay-Pay?" she asked. She hadn't said Paisley yet, but Pay-Pay worked just fine.

I handed Hadley the book and pushed to my feet. "She's in the restroom. But let me check on her."

I walked across the hall and knocked on the bathroom door. "Everything okay in there?"

"Yep. Just getting dressed." Paisley still took off all her clothes to use the restroom. And so what? It was her thing. My sisters and I all had our things. I saw no problem with it.

"Take your time, sweetie." I'd been working here for almost four weeks now, and I'd really found my rhythm.

It was funny because those last few months before I graduated from college, I was in a complete panic about what I wanted to do with my life. And somehow I'd fallen into the dream job. I loved taking care of the girls. Reading with them and baking with them, and we were putting in a little garden in the backyard. It's like this is where I was meant to be. And on my days off, I wrote like a madwoman. I'd gotten completely lost in my words over the past few weeks. I was already more than halfway done with my first draft, and everything just somehow felt… right.

The doorbell rang, and I remembered that Jace had told me the plumber was coming back. Jace would be home any minute now from the firehouse. We'd sort of avoided each other at all costs since penis-gate had happened, outside of talking about the girls and our brief time hanging out at the fair. He kept the conversations very minimal, he avoided eye contact, and I didn't fight it. I had a hard time looking at him without picturing him in all his naked glory.

We texted all day about the girls when he was working.

It was all very… professional.

"I'll be right back, Paisley," I shouted through the door and scooped Hadley up in my arms. "The plumber's here."

"Okay," she called out.

I ran down the stairs and opened the door to see Grady Wheat standing there. He was a few years older than me, and I didn't know him well, but we'd both grown up here in Honey Mountain.

"Ashlan Thomas, this is about as pleasant a surprise as one could ask for. I was expecting a grumpy firefighter." He smirked.

I laughed, and Hadley's little hand caressed my cheek. "Yeah, I'm nannying for the girls. Jace will be home soon. He said if you beat him here just to send you upstairs and you'd know what to do?"

"Yeah. Danner had another guy out here a while back that clearly didn't know what he was doing. So, you're getting his best guy." He chuckled before his eyes slowly scanned my body from head to toe. "I guess Jace scored on his nanny, huh?" He walked right by me and stepped into the kitchen.

What? His creep factor was quickly rising.

"Okay, you can head on up to the master bathroom. It's the last door on the right."

My instinct told me not to walk in front of him, for fear he'd be perving and checking out my ass. That's the vibe he was putting out there. So I motioned for him to go first. Paisley stepped out of her bathroom and stared at him.

"Who are you?" Her tone was all sass.

"I see this one has the personality of her father." He barked out a laugh. "I'm the plumber, little lady."

Paisley moved beside me, and I wrapped an arm around her instinctively. "You can head into the master bathroom at the end of the hallway. I'll make sure Jace is on his way home."

"No hurry. But I may need you to come assist me because I'll have to turn on the water, and I'll need someone to check the pressure."

"Okay, just let me know," I said, my tone curt. I didn't want to be stuck in a small space with this guy. I didn't know why. He hadn't done anything out of line, per se, but my father had always preached about being aware of my surroundings and to trust my instincts. It wasn't like I thought the man was going to hurt us, but he just gave me a weird vibe.

I led the girls into the playroom and put on their favorite movie and pulled out my phone to text Jace. I chewed on my thumbnail as I thought of what to say. I didn't want to overreact, but I sure wouldn't mind if he came home right about now.

Me ~ Hey. Grady Wheat is here, so hopefully you're on your way.

"Ashlan," Grady called from down the hall. "I do need your help with this."

Paisley's eyes grew wide, and I patted her head. "I'll just be a minute. Can you two stay in here until I get back?"

"Yes," Paisley said as she dumped the tub of magnets on the floor between her and Hadley.

"Wuv," Hadley said, kissing the palm of her hand and blowing it at me.

"Love you, too." I laughed as I left the room because I was literally going a few feet down the hall.

Grady stood in the shower and had a screwdriver in his hand as he dismantled the showerhead.

"Hey, I'm here to help."

"Great. Come on in here and hold this showerhead in place for me if you don't mind."

"Oh, sure." I stepped into the walk-in shower and my chest was nearly touching his. I tried to back up as much as I could and still hold on to the piece that was hanging from the ceiling. I pushed up on my tiptoes, and he moved even closer to me as he reached his hands above my head.

"I don't want it to fall, but I'm having a hard time holding this on my tiptoes. Do we have a ladder we could use?" I asked as my balance wobbled a bit.

"Nah, I've got you." He kept working with one hand and his other hand moved to my waist. I sucked in a breath because red flags were going off. If he had a free hand, why the hell did he need me? He could hold the showerhead with his free hand.

"Are you sure you need me in here? I really should go check on the girls," I said as I squirmed in discomfort.

"I most definitely need you." His hand tightened on my hip, and I swallowed hard to keep the nerves away. "How about you meet me at Beer Mountain tonight and let me buy you a drink?"

His other hand came down on my waist and he tugged me closer to him.

"What are you doing? Take your hands off of me," I said, not hiding my fear any longer.

"Are all the Thomas girls this feisty?" he said, his tone gruff as he tugged me against him harder this time. My hands fell from the showerhead because I'd rather be knocked out by a big piece of metal than be ground up against by this animal. I shoved him hard against his chest and he just laughed and squeezed my waist with more force.

The showerhead did not fall, and I realized he'd used that as a ploy to get me in here. My heart started racing and sweat gathered at my hairline.

"Let me go right now," I hissed.

"Or what?" He chuckled and his tongue swiped out to wet his lips as bile grew in my throat. He wasn't going to do anything, was he? His parents owned the dry cleaners that I went to. This had to be a misunderstanding.

Stay calm.

I remembered the defense moves my father had taught all of us and just as I shifted to lift my knee in an attempt to nail him in the balls, there were hands on my shoulders pulling me back.

"Get the fuck out of my house right now, before I beat your ass to a pulp." Jace's arm came around me as he moved us out of the walk-in shower, my back against his hard chest. His arm covered the front of my chest protectively, and I could feel the anger radiating from his body.

"Dude. I didn't know you guys were together. I was just having some fun." Grady chuckled, but I didn't miss the fear in his gaze.

"You didn't need her in there. That showerhead is secured, you piece of shit. Leave. If Ashlan and my girls weren't here right now, I'd be teaching you a lesson you'd never forget. No promise that won't happen at a later date. I'll be calling Danner right away to let him know how fucked up this was. Get your crap and get out of my house now." Jace's hand dropped from my body as soon as Grady hustled past us. Jace followed him out of the bathroom and I heard him shout at Grady again just before the door slammed shut.

I was stunned. I fell against the bathroom wall and tried to process the last few minutes.

What the hell just happened?

I heard Paisley asking her dad what was wrong, and Jace said everything was fine and to stay in the playroom for another minute before he came barreling into the bathroom.

"You okay?" He assessed me like he was looking for signs that I'd been hurt.

"Yeah. Of course. He didn't do anything. I mean, outside of being super creepy."

"He had his hands on you," he said, reaching for my wrist and inspecting my arms one at a time, for I don't know what.

"He didn't touch my arms. He was focused on my hips and my waist. I want you to know that I was just about to knee him in the balls when you came in."

His hands were on my upper arms, rubbing them up and down in a comforting way. "I'm so fucking sorry I let him come in here with you. I've known him for a long time, and I've never liked the dude. I had no idea he was working for Danner. I thought Ray was coming back."

Ray was a nice elderly man who'd lived in Honey Mountain for a long time.

"I'm not hurt, Jace. It was just a little nerve-racking."

His hand came to my cheek, and I nearly lost my breath as I looked up into his light blue gaze. He just studied me, and I couldn't move. His face dipped closer and the desire I felt was unexplainable.

A force so strong I couldn't stop it if I wanted to.

And I did not want to stop this.

His mouth just a breath from mine.

Everything stopped all at once.

My lips parted with invitation and my hand came over his on my face. Needing to feel that warmth.

"Daddy," Paisley called from the playroom, and Jace abruptly pulled back and dropped his hand.

"I'm really sorry about Grady. I'll call Danner right away," he said, clearing his throat and motioning for me to lead the way out of the bathroom.

Had he just been about to kiss me, or had I imagined the whole thing?

"Okay." I nodded as I walked out ahead of him. Now this was a man I wished was checking out my ass when I walked in front of him.

I stopped in the playroom to see the girls.

"Did the plumber man fix the shower?" Paisley asked.

"No. We'll get someone else out here right away." Jace shoved his hands in the pockets of his jeans.

"Can Ashlan stay for lunch?" Paisley asked.

"No," Jace answered before I could even answer the question. "She's leaving. She's off the clock."

Ouch. This man was going to give me whiplash. Maybe I'd imagined the whole thing. I leaned down to hug each of the girls goodbye and Hadley held on tight and wouldn't let go.

"Love you. I'll see you in a few days." I set Hadley back on the floor, and she blew me a kiss before walking over to her stuffed animals to continue the game she'd been playing. Paisley was back at the magnets, and Jace followed me down the stairs to the door.

"You sure you're all right?" he asked, but his voice was curt this time. The tenderness was long gone. When I turned around to face him, he stood at least four feet away from me.

"Yeah. I'm fine." I rolled my eyes, which was definitely not professional, but I didn't like how quickly he'd gone from hot to cold with me.

"Great. See you in a few days."

I don't know why I was so offended. Hell, I was more angry about the way he was being so cold than I had been about Grady the perv.

"See ya." I turned on my heels and stormed out the door.

I marched into my cute guesthouse with the vintage wood floors and the adorable décor and dropped on the couch before reaching for my laptop. Thankfully, the hero in my story was not giving the heroine whiplash.

He was romantic and swoony and sexy as hell.

A lot like Jace King, minus the romantic and swoony part.

But yes, definitely sexy as hell. Although Jace was swoony when it came to his girls. And he'd been super swoony when he'd stormed into the bathroom and kicked Grady out of the house. But he wanted to keep me at arm's length, and I needed to respect that.

He was my boss after all.

I wrote for the next several hours, and Dylan and Charlotte brought over tacos from our favorite place, as we made plans for my birthday which was the next day.

"So, any more sexy time with Big Daddy?" Dylan asked over a mouthful of taco.

"No. That crush is long over. We're acting completely professional, and I swear he avoids me most of the time."

"Well, he did come rescue you from that jerk, Grady." Charlotte dabbed at her mouth with a napkin. I'd left out the part about him almost kissing me, because if I'm being honest, I wasn't even sure anymore if it had really happened.

"Okay, so Beer Mountain tomorrow night, and then we're going to the barbecue at Ev and Hawk's on the Fourth. There will be some hot hockey players there for sure." Dylan wiggled her brows.

"That sounds like a perfect weekend. Bring on the hot hockey players," I said, holding up my paper cup filled with the boxed wine Dylan had brought.

"Hawk said only two of the guys that are coming are

single, so one of us is going to be missing out." Dylan clinked her cup against mine.

"Actually, I met this guy at the coffee shop yesterday. He's somewhat new to town, and he asked me out. I invited him to meet me at the party because I thought it would be a safe place to see if I liked him," Charlotte said, smiling at us as she shrugged.

"Interesting that we're just hearing about this now," Dylan said, narrowing her gaze at Charlotte. "Why didn't you invite him to Beer Mountain tomorrow?"

"That's too intimate. The party will be big and fun. It'll be less pressure."

"Well, it looks like it's you and me, Ash." Dylan took a sip of her wine.

"I'm not really in the dating mood lately. I'd rather swoon over my leading man that I'm writing right now."

"Ohhhh. Tell us about him." Charlotte took a sip of wine and leaned back on the white slipcovered couch I had in the small living area.

"He's a fireman, you know that."

"Obviously you have a thing for firefighters." Dylan smirked.

"Hey. I respect firefighters. We've grown up surrounded by them since birth."

"I do too. Ignore her." Charlotte pointed at Dylan and raised a brow, causing her to stop talking. "What does he look like?"

"He's tall with broad shoulders, brown messy hair, and the bluest eyes I've ever seen."

"Let me guess. Big muscles. Well-hung. A little broody. Sexy as hell?" Dylan teased, and a grin spread clear across her face.

"You just described every hot guy we know." I laughed as the wine was starting to hit me. I wasn't much of a drinker, and it didn't take much to get me tipsy.

"Or one man in particular. Does said hero have any children?"

"Nope. He's single and ready to mingle," I said, raising a brow in challenge. "I don't know anyone like him."

Hey, it was the author's job to protect her hero.

I could only write what I felt.

If he happened to look similar to my current boss, that was not my fault. Jace King might be off-limits in real life—but this was fiction.

six

. . .

Jace

"DO you think Ashlan got the gift we left for her on her doorstep with all the cards?" Paisley asked as I tucked her into bed.

"She'll get it when she gets home, Buttercup." I kissed her forehead and moved to the door before turning the lights off.

It was Ashlan's birthday, and everyone was at Beer Mountain celebrating. Niko and Hawk had tried to convince me to have my mom watch the girls so we could all go out tonight, but after what happened yesterday, I needed to keep my distance. Hell, I'd nearly kissed the girl after she'd been violated by that prick Grady fucking Wheat. Danner had let him go the minute he'd heard what happened. Serves that fucker right.

But what the fuck was wrong with me?

Hell, I'd wanted to taste those soft lips of hers. My dick had been having a fucking meltdown ever since. It had been so long since I'd wanted a woman like this. Sure, I'd messed around occasionally, a man had needs. I'd gone years without having sex with my wife. I'd gotten used to relying on my hand when I needed the release. But I'd never wanted anyone the way I wanted Ashlan Thomas. And the girl could not be more off-limits.

She was Cap's daughter.

The youngest of the Thomas girls.

Too young for me.

Cap would lose his shit. And why the fuck would a twenty-three-year-old girl who was smart and talented and beautiful—want to mess around with a single dad who was nearly a decade older than her? Technically, she was nine years younger than me as of today, but still. She wasn't someone I could just have sex with. It would have to be an all-or-nothing thing with a girl like Ashlan, and I didn't have much to offer. My time was spent between my girls, putting out fires, and renovating homes. A girl like Ashlan deserved the fairy tale.

And that was something I didn't even believe in anymore, if I ever did.

I needed to get her out of my system.

So I'd shut that shit down yesterday just before I'd almost crossed the line.

I was a selfish prick. She was Cap's daughter and my girls adored her. Kissing her and acting on these feelings would only make things awkward. Hell, we'd barely looked at one another for weeks after she'd walked into the bathroom and got a sneak peek of my goods.

And let me tell you—the way her mouth gaped open was something I couldn't get out of my head.

She was fucking beautiful.

And sweet.

And good.

Too good.

Too good for me, no question about it.

Sometimes you needed to be the grown-up, and that's exactly what I was doing.

I paused to make sure Hadley was asleep and closed her

door a little bit so the TV wouldn't disturb her. I made my way downstairs and cracked open a beer before dropping on the couch and watching some UFC. That would get my nanny out of my mind. Watching two dudes fight to the death.

I spent the next hour doing just that when a knock on the back door startled me.

I moved to the kitchen door and pulled it open to see Ashlan standing there in a white tank top, a short jean skirt, and a pair of white tennis shoes. Her light brown hair fell just past her shoulders, and her dark brown eyes locked with mine. Her plump lips were painted pink, and she smiled as she took me in.

"Hey, birthday girl. You just getting back from Beer Mountain?"

She bit down on her juicy bottom lip, and I shoved my hands in my pockets to keep from reaching for her. "Yep. The party's still going, but I ducked out early."

"Of your own party? You had enough?"

"I have a three-beer limit," she said over a hiccup and covered her mouth with her hand before her head fell back in a fit of laughter. "Clearly, I hit my limit."

"You want to come in?" I asked when I realized I'd left her standing out on the front porch.

"No. No, I didn't come over here to bother you. I just wanted to thank you for the sweet birthday gift. I found the package on my front doorstep when I got home. That was very kind of you." She leaned against the doorframe, and her smile stole the air from my lungs.

"That was all the girls." I cleared my throat.

"Really? The girls are so thoughtful to get me a leather-bound journal with my name personalized on it. They must have planned ahead, huh?"

I chuckled. "All right. They were the ones who insisted on the little cake and the cards. I just wanted to thank you for all that you are doing for them, for me—" I paused because I needed to be careful with her. The temptation was stronger than anything I'd ever felt with anyone, but I wanted her to know how much she meant to us, without letting her know how badly I wanted her. "I thought maybe you could use it to organize your thoughts for your book."

She cocked her head to the side and hiccupped once more. She was so fucking cute. There was such a genuineness about this girl. A goodness that I craved deep down in my soul. A goodness that I knew I didn't deserve. Not anymore. I'd made my choices, and I wouldn't change a thing because it brought me the two best things in my life. But my future was not my own, and I needed to remember that. I had two little girls that would always come first.

"Definitely," she said. "It was the perfect gift. But you almost gave me the perfect gift yesterday too. I wasn't sure if I imagined it at this point because it sure felt like something was happening there. And the curiosity is killing me."

Oh, fuck.

"When I kicked Grady to the curb? You didn't imagine it. His ass got fired too. Apparently, they've had other complaints about him, so I won't be using Danner's company any longer, because he knowingly sent that asshole to my house. I've got someone else coming next week, and I made sure to schedule it when I was home."

Her cheeks pinked because she thought I didn't understand what she was asking me. She wanted to know if I'd almost lost control yesterday. I'd almost kissed her. She knew it. And I knew it. Hell, we were both fighting this pull between us. I'd come to learn that sometimes doing the right thing was hard as hell. Raising my two girls alone—it was fucking hard. I wanted to give them everything and I didn't know if I was capable. If I was patient enough. Smart enough to pull it off when they were teenagers. But I would damn well try. And walking away from this attraction was the right thing to do. Not for me.

For her.

"Oh, yeah. Thank you again for that. I heard you paid Grady a visit last night at Beer Mountain with my brothers-in-law."

"Those two can't keep their fucking mouths closed. I may have gone over there to have a little talk with him, because what he did was so out of line. He won't be bothering you again." I'd seen red after what happened yesterday. I'd had my mom come watch the girls, and Hawk and Niko had met me at the bar where we knew that piece of shit was hanging out.

He wouldn't so much as look at Ashlan Thomas again. I'd seen the fear in her eyes when I'd shown up in that bathroom yesterday. She tried to play it off, but I knew she was scared. And that shit didn't sit right with me.

"Well, thank you. You didn't have to do that. But I wasn't actually talking about what you did with Grady. It was the thing that almost happened right after. Sometimes I think writing romance is making me imagine things," she said as she shook her head and walked toward the guesthouse. "Good night, Jace."

I should let her go.

Should let it drop right here.

But the sadness in her pretty dark brown eyes was too much for me. "Sunshine."

She turned around and her eyes widened. "That's new."

"It's also very fitting." I walked a few steps toward her but kept a healthy distance at the same time. "You didn't imagine anything yesterday."

"I didn't?" she whispered. "Did I imagine you avoiding me the past few weeks? Were you mad that I walked in on you in the shower?"

"Definitely not mad." I chuckled. "You didn't imagine yesterday, nor did you imagine the fact that I've been avoiding you a bit as well. There is something here, but it doesn't make it right."

"Why?" She looked so wounded and took a few steps toward me. Her chest bumping into mine. Lavender flooded my senses and caused me to call on every amount of reserve that I had.

Crickets chirped in the distance and the moon shined down on her, creating enough light to see every bit of hurt in her eyes.

"Because you're young. I'm ten years older than you. You've got your whole life in front of you."

Her hand came up and her fingers trailed over the scruff on my jaw, and it felt so fucking good. When was the last time a woman's touch felt this good?

"Nine years. I'm twenty-three today." She chuckled and let out a long breath and it tickled my neck. "Or maybe you just aren't attracted to me."

I barked out a laugh before reaching for her hand still resting on the side of my face and I held it in mine. "You're fucking beautiful. You're amazing with my girls. You're smart and funny and sweet."

"So, what's the problem? My parents had a ten-year age gap. Why does that matter? My mom ended up passing away young anyway. Age is just a number."

I kissed the back of her hand and squeezed it. "It matters. Your dad is my friend. We work together. He would not be happy about it, trust me."

"Because you're older than me? That's a lame excuse." She pulled her hand away and crossed her arms over her chest.

"Because I'm a divorced, single father of two. We're in different places in our lives. This is just an attraction. It'll pass. I need you to keep doing what you're doing with my girls. You're healing our family. I've never seen them happier. Hell, Hadley's finally talking. Paisley was so excited because you did her hair in some kind of space buns and painted her nails. I can't risk messing that up. Hurting them, hurting you—it's not an option."

"It was just an *almost* kiss."

"A kiss would never be enough for me," I said because it was the truth, and I reached for her chin and rubbed the pad of my thumb over her bottom lip. "Not even fucking close."

She nodded, but I saw the sadness in her gaze. "It sounds like you've made your mind up. Well, it might not have even been that good anyway." She raised a brow and smirked.

I knew she was wrong about that because this pull between us was fucking strong. The way her body reacted to my nearness had been driving me crazy these past few weeks, no matter how hard I tried to avoid her. I glanced down to see her nipples harden beneath her tank top, and I hissed out a breath.

"You can do better than me, Sunshine. I'll see you at Everly and Hawk's tomorrow?"

"Yep. Apparently, they're setting me up with a hockey player. This is your last chance to seal the deal," she said over a fit of laughter.

And damn if I didn't want to seal the deal.

Make her mine.

The thought of her with someone else had my hands fisting at my side, but I forced myself not to react. "Good for you. You deserve that. Happy birthday, Ash."

I raised a brow, waiting for her to go to her door and step inside. "Good night, Jace King. Thank you for my birthday present."

The way she licked her lips and watched me nearly undid me right there on my driveway. I held up my hand. "Night, Sunshine."

She waved before shutting the door.

"Daddy, will Ashlan be at the party? Will there be fireworks? Will there be lots of people there? Will there be food? Because I'm hungry. Will Uncle Travis and Uncle Hayden be there?" Paisley asked from the back seat, and I glanced in the rearview mirror to see Hadley watching her sister with a big smile on her face.

I loved the bond that these two shared.

But my eldest's rapid-fire questions were getting exhausting.

"How about you go easy on your old man and slow down on the questions." I chuckled and she giggled. "Yes, Niko's got fireworks. Yes, there will be lots of food. Your uncles will be there because those two wouldn't miss a free meal if their lives depended on it. And there will be plenty of people there to keep you busy."

"And will Ashlan be there?"

"She will. But it's her day off and it's a party, so don't be hanging all over her today." I put the SUV in park and climbed out to get them both unbuckled. I had Hadley on my hip and a bag full of chips and dips in my free hand, while my oldest daughter hooked her finger on the belt loop of my jeans as we walked up the driveway. There were tons of cars there already, as Hawk and Everly had volunteered to throw a big Fourth of July bash this year.

In Honey Mountain, big parties were not uncommon. Hell, I threw my fair share, but I hadn't done much of that since Karla left. Not that she helped when she was there, but I'd been drowning a bit in juggling everything since I became a full-time single parent. But hearing the music and the laughter reminded me of how much fun my oversized yard was for gatherings. It might be time to get back to adding a little fun to our lives.

"Uncle Hayden," Paisley shrieked and ran toward my baby brother. He scooped her up and swung her around, and Hadley giggled and ran the palm of her hand over my cheek.

"What's up, little dumplin'?" Travis said as he reached for Hadley who went right to him. Trav was four years older than Hayden and four years younger than me.

"What's up, dipshits," I said, and Paisley's head nearly spun off her neck.

"Daddy. I do not want to have to put you in timeout at a party." She reached for my brother's hand and raised a brow at me. I swear the girl was five going on thirty, aside from the fact that it took her a good thirty minutes to go pee.

"Yeah, Daddy. It's really uncalled for." Hayden snorted.

"You can't take him anywhere, can you?" Travis said as he winked at Paisley.

"Yeah, this is new," I grumped. "You got the girls? I need to go drop this in the kitchen." I held up the bag of snacks.

"We got the little angels," Trav said as they moved toward a group of kids playing in the oversized backyard.

Everly and Hawk's place sat right on the lake, and the girls loved to play over here. There was a fence that they'd put up after they bought the place, so it kept the kids from getting in the water without an adult. But my brothers were crazy enough to jump in there with them.

"Keep them out of the water," I shouted, and Hayden nodded, while Travis held his arm up over his head and gave me the bird.

Asshole.

"Hey, Jace. You didn't need to bring anything. I think Hawk has enough food to feed a small country." Everly helped me with the bags as we unloaded them on the counter.

"Not a problem. I figured between the firefighters and the hockey players, you'd need a whole lot of food."

"There he is," Hawk said as he strolled through the back doors that were open. It was a perfect day in Honey Mountain. The sun was shining, but there was enough of a breeze to make it tolerable to be outside. I recognized Buckley, one of

Hawk's best friends who played professional hockey with him on the San Francisco Lions. I didn't know the other two dudes who were beside him. "Jace, these are the two new rookies I told you about, Asher and Lucas. Buck and I are taking them under our wing this season, and they're going to help us get the Stanley Cup."

Everly smiled and winked at her husband. "Damn straight, baby."

"What's up?" Asher said, extending his hand. He was a few inches shorter than me, but the dude was built like a tank.

"Nice to meet you," I said as I turned to the other guy.

"Hey, I'm Lucas. Heard lots about you from Hawk." He clapped me on the shoulder.

"Ah… I see you're kissing up to her boss, huh?" Hawk said.

I looked between them with confusion.

"Lucas here has been outside gawking over Ashlan," Hawk said, shaking his head with a laugh.

"She told me she nannies for you," Lucas said with a smirk. "Your girls are adorable by the way."

The dude was about the same height as me, a bit of a pretty boy, and definitely not lacking confidence. My hands fisted at my side, and I shoved them in my pockets to hide my irritation. Of course the guy liked her. She was gorgeous and sweet, and there wasn't anything not to like about Ashlan Thomas.

He looked to be around her age, obviously very successful, and probably came with zero baggage.

This was the kind of dude she should be dating. That I should want her to date.

"Thanks. She's great with the girls." I cleared my throat, ready to end this conversation.

"She's got weekends off, right? I figured I'd stick around a few days and see if I can get her to go out with me."

"I knew you guys would be all over my sisters. But Ash is a little young for you, isn't she?" Everly said, her voice was all tease.

"She's twenty-three, isn't she? I'm twenty-eight." Lucas threw his hands in the air like the question was outrageous. "I'm just a baby."

"Ever is just a mama bear," Hawk said, moving to the other side of the island and wrapping his arms around her. "I think Asher gave it a shot with both Charlie and Dilly and struck out."

Asher snorted, but my blood was boiling because that meant that Lucas hadn't struck out. She must be into him.

Why the fuck did I care?

Her sister just all but shamed the guy for being older and I was even older than him.

This was for the best. I needed a dose of reality to get my head screwed on straight.

"I did not strike out with Charlie, thank you very much, asshole." Asher took a long pull from his beer. "She brought some dude here with her, so I'm guessing she's seeing someone. But Dilly, man, that girl is hot, but she's terrifying. She told me to go put my balls on ice and shoot my shot somewhere else."

The entire kitchen erupted in laughter just as Dylan came around the corner.

"What's so funny? Is this one icing his balls?" She moved to stand next to me and winked.

"Damn, girl. You don't mince words, do you?"

"I don't." She looked up at me as Asher and Lucas started talking to Buck while Hawk and Everly were busy pulling casseroles out of the oven.

Dylan reached for a carrot and cocked her head at me. "You look like you're sulking."

"No, I don't. I'm just in a perpetual bad mood."

Her head fell back in laughter. "I think you're sick of

sitting on the sidelines and ready to get back in the game. But you better get out there fast, because the bases are loaded, my friend."

"I have no idea what you're talking about." I reached for a celery stick because I needed something to keep my hands busy. One bite and I knew why I hated celery, stringy as shit.

"You can't stay on the bench forever, King. Because the game will be over before you know it." She chuckled and I made my way back outside.

What the fuck was with her talking in riddles all of a sudden?

Ashlan was holding Hadley in her arms as they stood there watching Paisley hop around in a sack, jumping from side to side.

My chest tightened as I took the three of them in. We'd never had family time with Karla. It had never been her thing. But seeing Ashlan with my girls made me want things I had no business wanting.

Lucas appeared beside her, and he must have said something funny because her head fell back in laughter.

Fucker.

"Ashlan sure is hot, am I right?" Hayden said, catching me off guard because I was staring.

"I don't know. I don't look at her that way. She's my fucking nanny."

Travis came up beside me and handed me a beer as he snorted. "Is that why you're standing over here gaping at her?"

"Fuck off. I'm watching the girls."

"Dude. Admit it. She's fucking hot," Hayden said as he elbowed me in the side.

"It sure is hot out here," Vivian said as she and Niko walked over with little Bee in her arms. Hayden's eyes doubled in size when he realized she may have heard his stupid ass talking. My brothers turned quickly to talk to Niko, as they knew each other well.

"Yeah, it's a warm one." I took a long pull from my water bottle and smiled down at her little angel. "She looks just like you."

"She does so far. But I think she's got her daddy's eyes." Vivian watched her sister as she gave the hockey player very little attention, and her focus was on the girls.

My girls.

All three of them.

In another world.

"How's she doing? She sure seems to love nannying for you, Jace."

"I should go get them to stop bothering her and let her enjoy the party."

She looked down at her daughter and smiled before looking back at me. "Ashlan's always been more comfortable with the little ones. I swear that girl was born to be a mother. Whenever we'd play house growing up, Ev would be the bossy teacher, me and Charlie always wanted to be the baby, Dilly insisted on being the babysitter because she said she wanted to be the rebellious teen, and Ash was always the mother. I think she's exactly where she wants to be."

The problem was that I liked her being there.

I was getting used to having her around.

And I knew better than to do that.

seven

. . .

Ashlan

THE LAST WEEK had been a bit of a blur. I'd hung out with Lucas a few times, but it felt more like a friendship. There just wasn't a spark there, but he was a super nice guy. He'd stayed in Honey Mountain and trained with Hawk for the upcoming season, and we'd hung out at the lake and at my sister's house, but when he'd gone for the kiss—all I could think about was the broody firefighter who'd been scowling at us at the Fourth of July party.

I laughed every time I pictured his face when I'd looked up to meet his gaze. He'd tried to cover it up with a forced smile, but I saw it all in his soulful blue eyes.

The man was jealous.

Whether he'd ever admit it or not was a different story. He'd made it clear that we couldn't be together, but I couldn't help myself for wanting more.

I'd told Lucas I wasn't looking for anything more than friendship, but that hadn't stopped him from being persistent. He'd asked me to dinner tonight, but thankfully, I was back on duty with the girls, and I'd missed them terribly over the past few days.

My manuscript was far enough along now, I'd started

querying agents. I knew it was all a long shot, but I was going to do whatever it took to get my story out there.

I pulled on my white cover-up over my bathing suit and piled my hair in a bun on top of my head. I'd promised the girls I'd take them to the lake to swim today, so I packed my beach bag full of sunscreen and some snacks and headed over to the main house. I knocked twice and then used my key to make my way inside. Sometimes Jace struggled in the morning to get the girls ready, and he'd told me to just come on in. I certainly wasn't going to be barging into any bathrooms, but I was comfortable here now.

I couldn't wait to see the girls.

And I couldn't wait to see Jace.

I loved when we got to spend a little time together drinking coffee when I first got here, but there was no sign of anyone.

"Hello?"

Hadley waddled down the stairs, giggling, and I scooped her up in my arms. "What's up, angel face?"

"Hi, Wuvie." She nestled her head beneath my chin, and she smelled like baby powder and French fries, if that was a thing. I loved that she called me Wuvie now, because it was her way of saying love, and I'd take that all day long.

"Where's Daddy and Paisley?" I asked as we moved toward the stairs.

She made a face and then fake coughed and pointed toward Jace's bedroom.

"Jace?" I called out because I sure as hell was not going to charge the tundra this time. Although visions of a naked Jace King still flooded my dreams.

"Hey, come on in." His voice was strained.

I carried Hadley toward his master bathroom and found him kneeling on the floor in a pair of distressed jeans and a white tee. He was rubbing Paisley's back as she leaned over the toilet.

When she turned to me, she started sobbing. "I'm sick, Ashlan."

My heart nearly shattered right there. Tears streamed down her sweet face, and she turned back toward the white porcelain bowl and heaved three times.

Hadley gagged in my arms, and I took her out and set her on her daddy's bed and turned on the Disney channel for her.

"Stay here, okay?" I asked and she nodded.

I hurried back to the bathroom, and Jace was cleaning Paisley's face with a washcloth as she sobbed.

"Are you okay? Was it something she ate?" I bent down and stroked her hair. There weren't even enough words to describe how much I loved these little girls. They were angelic and sweet and silly. I missed them when I wasn't working, and I loved spending the days that I had with them together.

"I don't know. It might be a bug. Shit. I can't leave you here to deal with this. Let me call your dad and see if he can get me covered," Jace said as he moved to his feet and scooped her up.

"Don't be ridiculous. I grew up with four sisters. I've seen my fair share of puke. She'll probably be fine in a day or two. Go to work. I've got this." I followed him into the bedroom, and he set her down on the bed beside Hadley.

Hadley was wearing a little tank top and panties, and she crawled closer to her sister and rested her head beside her. Paisley snuggled closer, and it reminded me so much of the way I was with my sisters. How many times had we been sick together and cuddled in our parents' bed? Too many to count.

"You all right for a minute?" Jace asked his oldest daughter, as he kissed her on the forehead.

"Yeah. I feel better. I want Ashlan to stay with me. But I don't feel like going to the lake today."

"I promise I'll take you when you feel better. How about I

make you some toast and a little banana, and we'll see if you can keep that down?"

"Okay," she whispered, but her eyes were growing heavy, and she looked like she was going to doze off.

"Nana, yummy." Hadley rubbed her little belly, and Jace snorted.

"This one can always eat." Jace kissed the top of Hadley's head and motioned for me to follow him downstairs.

"Did you get any sleep?" I asked as my eyes shamefully homed in on his broad shoulders that strained against the white fabric of his tee. My gaze traveled down to his narrow waist before they snapped up when we got to the kitchen, and he turned around and caught me checking him out.

He smirked. "A little bit. She woke up around three in the morning with a tummy ache. Started puking around five. It seems like she's gotten it all out because it's just bile at this point. You sure you're up for this? This is certainly not in your job description."

"Really? You think nannying is exclusive to only good times? Of course, I'm okay with it. For the record, Dilly has a weak stomach. You'd never guess it with how tough she acts, but I've held that girl's hair back more times than I can count. She gets that nasty stomach bug every year."

"You've always been a caregiver, haven't you?" he asked as he sliced up some banana on a plate.

"I guess so. I like taking care of people."

He turned and leaned against the counter, crossing his feet at the ankles. "Who takes care of you?"

His heated gaze had me shifting on my feet. "Well, I've got four overbearing sisters, one protective father, and I'm pretty good at taking care of myself."

His tongue swiped out to wet his bottom lip as his gaze scanned down my body before moving back up, his eyes locking with mine. "That's good. You were ready to go to the lake, huh?"

Was his voice gruff, or was I imagining that?

"Yeah. But we can go another time."

"Sure. They'd love that. I can't thank you enough for all that you're doing for my girls. They're different, you know? Since you've been here."

My stomach flipped at his words and the way he was staring at my mouth. Like he might kiss me.

"I love being with them. It fills something that has been missing for me, I think. I don't know how to explain it. How are they different?"

"They're calmer. Happier. Hadley's talking more and more every day, and Paisley isn't talking about how nervous she is to start school anymore. So, whatever you're doing, it's working wonders. And I'm happy to hear that you enjoy them too."

"I really do. I miss them when I'm not here," I admitted with a shrug. It was the truth. I loved getting lost in my writing, but when I was with Paisley and Hadley, it always felt like I was where I was supposed to be.

"That means a lot." He reached for the plate of bananas and studied me. "I'll just run this up to Hadley. She can eat in bed today. Do whatever makes your life easier, all right? All rules go out the door when they're sick."

"Okay. We can all just have a cuddle day." I shrugged.

He moved closer to me, the small plate in one hand, and his free hand reached for the top edge of my cover-up. I think I held my breath because it felt as if time were standing still. His fingers grazed the skin of my neck, and I closed my eyes because the feeling was so overpowering.

I'd never wanted anyone the way I wanted Jace.

Like a feral need deep within me that I couldn't explain.

"Got it," he whispered, and my eyes flew open to see the little feather in his hand.

"Thank you." I let out a breath and moved toward the cupboard to get the bottle of Pedialyte that he kept stocked at his house for moments like this. "I'll just pour this for Paisley, so she'll have it when she wakes up."

"Sounds good." He moved toward the stairs as I poured the blue liquid into the cup. "How's the hockey player?"

"Lucas?" I asked as I followed him up the stairs. Was that jealousy I heard in his harsh tone?

"Yeah. He's the one who was hitting on you, right?"

"Oh, yeah. He's fine," I said as we made our way back to the bedroom. I was about to tell him it was nothing more than friendship, but I kind of liked seeing Jace spun up about it.

It meant there was hope.

"Just make sure he treats you right," he said as he smoothed the comforter before setting down the plate with sliced banana in front of Hadley who was staring at the TV. "You deserve the best."

"Couldn't agree more," I said, and my tone was all tease. I waggled my brows at him which made him chuckle.

Because the best was standing right in front of me. Taking care of these two little angels and going off to his job serving the community.

Jace King was everything I wanted.

He'd made it clear that he'd never cross the line, and I understood his reasons, but it didn't make me want him less.

He kissed the girls goodbye. Paisley was sound asleep, and he waved at me and told me to call if I needed anything.

I climbed into bed between the two munchkins, and it was exactly where I wanted to be.

Paisley slept for several hours, and Hadley fell asleep a little while ago too. I climbed out of bed and changed out of my bathing suit while they slept and went to get my laptop. I sat in the chair beside the bed so I wouldn't disturb them, and I wrote some more. When Paisley woke up, she went running for the bathroom and I hurried in behind her. She vomited several times, and I pulled her hair back and tied it up in an elastic.

"You're all right, sweetie."

When she finished, I cleaned her face up and dropped to sit on the floor before pulling her on my lap as she sobbed.

"I feel yucky, Ash."

"I know you do, baby girl." I stroked her hair. "What if I run you a hot bath and we wash your hair and get you in some clean jammies? Would that feel good?"

She nodded, and I set her down on the floor beside me and moved to start the bathtub just as I heard a loud, strangled noise come from the bedroom. I went running out of the bathroom to find little Hadley sitting on the bed covered in vomit.

"Wuvie," she said as her shoulders started to quake and the tears began to fall.

"You're okay," I said as I scooped her up in my arms and carried her to the bathroom. I set her down next to the sink, trying to decide where to start. She was covered.

"Oh no, Hadley's got the pukes now too?" Paisley said, shaking her head.

"She does." I pulled the tank top over Hadley's head and used a fresh washcloth to clean her up. "How about two sick little girlies in the tub? I can wash your hair and we'll put on some clean clothes."

Hadley nodded, and Paisley stripped down quickly. I checked the water temperature and helped her climb into Jace's oversized bathtub. I set Hadley back on the ground and helped her out of her little unicorn panties and into the water with her sister.

"Does that feel better?" I asked, and they both nodded.

Their energy was low, because bath time was usually a little wild, but they both just leaned against the side of the tub and relaxed. I found the Tupperware that I kept under the sink with their shampoo to wash their hair with, and I took my time massaging each of their little heads. My mom used to do this for us, and nothing was better than my mama when

I didn't feel good. I was happy I could give them that comfort. Once they were both rinsed off and clean, I wrapped Paisley in a towel before lifting Hadley out.

"Does anyone feel like they need to get sick again?"

"I feel okay right now," Paisley said, and Hadley nodded.

"Okay, so we're going to get you dressed and I'll have you both wait in the playroom while I strip your daddy's bed real quick. Then we'll get you back in there and cozy, and maybe we can try a little lunch?" I quickly brushed through their hair and tied it back in elastics, just in case they got sick again.

"I am hungry," Paisley said, and her sister rubbed her belly.

"We'll try something easy like some white rice, okay? Maybe some toast. Let's see if we can keep that down."

I spent the next hour getting some food in their tummies and tucking them back in Jace's bed after I'd put on clean sheets.

When I finally sat down, my phone beeped, and I saw a few texts that I'd missed.

Jace ~ Hey, just checking in.

Jace ~ Everything okay over there?

Jace ~ You need me to come home?

Me ~ Sorry. We've been busy. Both girls slept for a few hours, but Paisley got sick again, and Hadley just got the pukes too. They seem okay now. Their fevers are gone, and they appear to be on the mend. They've both had a little rice and a half a piece of toast. They've also held down the Pedialyte, so I don't think we need to call the doctor. I'm guessing it's just a stomach bug and it will hopefully pass."

Jace ~ Damn, I'm so sorry. You want me to have my mom come over and relieve you after she gets off work? Or I can get someone to cover me here.

Me ~ Absolutely not. We're totally good. They are watching a movie now, they're bathed and clean and seem happy. I've got this.

Jace ~ Thank you, Sunshine.

My stomach fluttered at the use of that nickname again. I loved it.

Me ~ Of course. How's work?

Jace ~ Well, we had two medical calls this morning and a small house fire. Mrs. Calco was baking cookies again and set the damn oven on fire. But I'm guessing my day was easier than yours.

My head fell back in laughter. My father was always complaining about Mrs. Calco and her kitchen fires.

Me ~ Oh my gosh. Dad must be having a field day. He thinks it should be illegal for that woman to cook.

Jace ~ Yep. He had a few choice words for her husband. He told them to at the very least buy a new stove. And she gave me a plate of cookies to bring home to the girls. They were fucking charcoal on the outside.

Me ~ I do believe Paisley would ask me to put you in timeout for that one.

Jace ~ I think you're the one in timeout being stuck with two sick babies.

Me ~ We're good. I promise. As far as Mrs. Calco goes, I think she truly believes she's a good cook. But I don't think you want the girls anywhere near anything that might make them sick for a while. We're doing the BRAT diet until they can hold things down for twenty-four hours.

Jace ~ What the fuck is the BRAT diet?

Me ~ Again with the f-bombs. That's another timeout for you, Mr. King. <smiley face emoji>

Jace ~ Sorry. I'm running on no sleep. But any time you want to play teacher and put me in the corner, I'm game.

My stomach dipped.

Me ~ I wouldn't mind bossing you around. But I doubt your stubborn ass would listen.

Jace ~ I have a hunch I'd listen to anything you say,

Sunshine. A timeout with you would be the best five minutes of my life.

Wow. I didn't see this coming. He must be exhausted because he normally avoided flirting with me.

Me ~ Mine too, Jace King.

Jace ~ In another lifetime, Sunshine.

Me ~ I'm not giving up on this one just yet.

Jace ~ Can't happen. And you've got the hockey player. I can't compete with that.

Me ~ Wouldn't have struck you as a man afraid of a challenge.

I chewed on my thumbnail as the three little dots moved across the screen.

Jace ~ I'm not. Just a man who's trying to do the right thing.

Me ~ Buzzkill.

Jace ~ <laughing emoji>

Me ~ Go take a nap.

Jace ~ I love when you boss me around.

Me ~ I could make it a habit if you want. <winky face emoji>

The three little dots moved across the screen and then disappeared. Had I gone too far? I swear I couldn't read this man most of the time.

But I sure wanted to try.

eight

. . .

Jace

"LET me know if you need any help with the girls," my mom said over my Bluetooth as I pulled into the driveway outside my home.

"I will. Ashlan said they were better this morning and they haven't puked in twenty-four hours. I just feel bad that she spent two days not sleeping and taking care of them."

"She's a good girl, that's for sure. I called her a few times, and she said she had it handled. Looks like you got yourself a keeper. Those girls sure could use some consistency in their lives. God knows their own mother never provided that. Sorry, I know I'm not supposed to speak badly about her, but seeing as it's just you and me on this call, you know I never did care for Karla."

"Really, I had no idea." I groaned because my mother had despised the woman from the day we got married. She'd been a horrible wife and even worse as a mother, so I couldn't fault her for her feelings. "Just never talk about it in front of the girls, all right?"

"You don't think they are going to have an issue with their mama after she just left, gave you full custody, left you with all the responsibility, and never called again?" she hissed.

"I don't know, Mom. But I sure as fuck don't want to make it worse for them. I'm home, so I'll give you a call later."

"All right, sweetheart. I love you."

"Love you too." I ended the call. She was the only other person I said those three little words to every time we spoke, aside from my girls. My dad and my brothers and I weren't sappy bastards, but something about my mama always made me soft.

When I opened the door I didn't see anyone in the kitchen, but the house was spotless. "Hey, I'm home."

"Daddy," Paisley shouted and came bounding down the stairs. "Ash is real sick. She's got the pukies now."

Fuck.

I went charging up the stairs and found Ashlan hugging the toilet, and little Hadley was standing there in a pink T-shirt and a pair of white shorts, her hair tied up in a little knot on top of her head, and she was rubbing Ash's back and smiling up at me.

"Wuvie sick."

"Oh god. Can you close the door? It's coming again," Ashlan moaned, and I scooped Hadley up and led them both out of the bathroom and closed the door.

I heard her heaving and groaning, and I called my mom. I packed the girls an overnight bag and walked them both outside when she pulled up.

"Thanks for doing this," I said as I buckled both girls in their car seats that my mom kept in her car for them.

"You're a good man, Jace." She winked.

"Don't tell anyone."

There was no way in hell I was going to leave Ashlan to fend for herself after all she'd done for Paisley and Hadley over the past few days. She'd taken such good care of them, she'd gotten sick herself.

I hurried back inside and poured a glass of Pedialyte for

her and made my way upstairs. I knocked on the door and cracked it open. She was slumped in the corner against the cabinet, and her face was white as a ghost.

"I'm so sorry. Just give me a minute, and I'll get myself together and get out of your hair."

"Not happening, Sunshine. My mom picked up the girls and they'll spend the night with her. I'm not leaving you alone."

"Oh god. This is not how I want you to see me," she said, and two tears streamed down her face. She bent forward and groaned as if the stomach pain was unbearable. I set the drink on the counter, as I highly doubted she was going to try to get anything down right now. I dropped to sit beside her.

"Is the pain bad?" I brushed the hair away from her face.

She nodded. "Yeah. I was fine two hours ago, but it just hit me hard. I hope I didn't scare the girls."

"Are you kidding? You took such good care of them. They love you. They're just worried about you."

She crawled toward the toilet. "I've got to get sick again. Maybe you should wait outside."

"Nope. Not leaving you. Just let it out." I rubbed her back as she heaved a dozen more times.

This went on for the next four or five hours. She'd finally just dropped to lie on the floor of the bathroom, and I was fairly certain she'd emptied everything that could possibly have been in her stomach. I'd never seen someone puke that many times, at least not someone who was sober. She dozed off, and I went to get a pillow to set under her head and covered her with a throw blanket, as I continued to reply to her sisters' texts. They'd started texting me an hour ago when they hadn't heard from her, because they were all supposed to meet for dinner. Apparently, they put me on a group text so they could all pipe in.

Dilly ~ Is Ash still there? She's late for dinner. We're all here and we're wondering where she is.

Me ~ She's got the stomach bug. I think she got it from the girls. I'll have her stay here and I'll make sure she's all right.

Dilly ~ Oh, I'll bet you will, Dr. King. <winky face emoji>

Charlie ~ Dilly!! STOP!! Sorry, Jace. She just always has to go there.

Dilly ~ How did we share the same womb? You're so… proper. And annoying.

Everly ~ Oh my gosh. Why must you do this on a text chain? Is she okay, Jace? Do you need me to come pick her up and bring her home with me?

Vivi ~ You're pregnant. You don't want to get the stomach bug. I can come bring her to my house.

Charlie ~ You don't want to get the little Bee sick. She can come to my house.

Dilly ~ Ugh. He said she was fine there. Leave her alone. I'm sure Jace will take real good care of our girl. <winky face emoji>

Everly ~ Stop being inappropriate. He's her boss and a family friend. This isn't funny.

And he can read all this because he's on this text string.

I wanted to remind them that I was here, but I knew the Thomas girls well enough to know that they wouldn't care. They had nothing to hide. But I could tell Everly did not appreciate Dylan joking about me and Ashlan. Of course she didn't, I was too old for her. Her boss. And I came with a shit-ton of baggage. Trust me… I got it. But that didn't mean I wouldn't take care of her. She'd been good to my girls. Good to me. That was all this was. Maybe I'd flirted a little over texts with her the past few days, because I couldn't fucking help myself. I thought about her all the time. I couldn't get her out of my mind.

Dilly ~ Everything about this is funny. First of all, we're

all sitting in a booth together and we're arguing over text with Jace. That's fucking funny.

Charlie ~ What's second of all? And why must you be so crass?

Dilly ~ There is no second of all. That's it.

Vivi ~ You wrote first of all, which leads one to believe there's a second of all.

Everly ~ Agreed. Sorry, Jace. Call us if you need us.

Dilly ~ Or don't. <winky face emoji> <panting emoji>.

Charlie ~ <eye roll emoji>

I laughed and glanced over to see Ashlan sound asleep on the floor. She was wearing jean shorts and a black tank top. Her tan, golden skin shimmered in the last of the sunlight coming through the window. I moved to my feet and scooped her up in my arms.

"Are you taking me home? My key is in my purse," she mumbled just above a whisper.

"Not taking you home, Sunshine." I laid her down on my bed and went back to the kitchen to get a fresh glass of Pedialyte for her. When I came back into the bedroom, her eyes were open, but she looked exhausted. "Let's just try to get a few sips in you, okay?"

She nodded and pushed up a bit, and I held the glass to her plump lips. Damn, even after hours of vomiting, she was so fucking beautiful.

She took a few sips and then lay back on the pillow and closed her eyes. "Thanks for taking care of me."

"Thanks for taking care of my babies."

"Always," she whispered before her eyes closed and she dozed off. I kept the door open and moved downstairs to make myself a bagel before coming back up to check on her. I sat in the chair in my room for a few hours and watched TV beside her while she slept.

It was well after midnight when I moved across the hall to Paisley's room and dozed off myself, still wearing my clothes.

"Jace," I heard her call my name, and I jumped up and hurried across the hall.

"You all right?" The sun was just coming up, and I glanced at the clock to see that it was a little after five o'clock in the morning. Ashlan was sitting up, hair a wild mess, drinking the last of the electrolyte drink.

"Yeah. Sorry to wake you. I didn't know where everyone was. The girls are with your mom?"

I dropped to sit on the bed beside her and ran a hand through my hair. "Yeah. They spent the night there. How are you feeling?"

"Like I vomited everything that's ever been in my stomach. Otherwise, good."

I laughed. "That sounds about right."

"Thank you for taking care of me." She smoothed her hair and tucked it behind her ear. "Oh my gosh. I was supposed to meet my sisters for dinner. I need to get my phone."

I reached over and put my hand on her leg. "I talked to them. They know you were sick. I'll go get your phone. You need to take it easy. You vomited for about five hours straight yesterday. You've got nothing in your system. Let me grab your phone and a new glass of water."

"Who's the bossy one now?" she teased as I pushed to my feet.

"Trust me, Sunshine. I'm a pretty bossy dude, especially when it comes to you." Why the fuck was I going there? Why couldn't I just shake this off with her?

Desire flooded every inch of me, and I'd never had to use the restraint I'd been using lately when I was around this girl.

When I came back to the room, I handed her the glass of water and her phone and moved to sit in the chair across from her. Sitting on the bed was too close. Hell, being in the same house was too close. The same room was torture.

Lavender and sweetness surrounded me everywhere I turned.

She set her phone down and looked up at me. "Thank you for taking care of me yesterday."

"It's the least I could do. You took such good care of the girls while they were sick, and I can't tell you how much I appreciate it."

"I didn't mind at all. I love them." The corners of her lips turned up.

"I didn't mind at all either," I said. Leaving the second part off, but my feelings for Ashlan Thomas were stronger than I wanted to admit. "You have the patience of a saint when you're with them. Paisley told me that Hadley has three new words."

Ashlan's head tipped back, and she chuckled. "Yes. She has added poop, butt, and hot dog."

"Well, the girl's got her priorities straight, right?"

"Definitely."

"It means a lot. The way you're working with her. The confidence you're giving both my girls, just by being you."

She studied me for a long moment and bit down on her lip. "It's not as selfless as you think, Jace. I love being with them. It's weird, I went to school for four years, and I had this constant feeling of panic that I had no idea what I wanted to do with my life. What I wanted to be. My sisters all had a plan. I never did. And I'm thrilled to be working on my book, and it feels good and right and all those things. But being with Paisley and Hadley, I don't know. It's the most content I've felt since I lost my mom."

My chest tightened at her words. "You were young when you lost her. That had to be really tough."

"Ten years old. And trust me when I tell you, my sisters all stepped up. My dad is the most loving man, and everyone did the best they could. But being here, it's filling something that I didn't even know was missing. So, I'm the lucky one."

"It's very selfless. Don't take away from how good you are, Sunshine."

"It's not selfless. Because I'm filling something for them, and they're filling something for me." She shrugged. "It probably doesn't make sense."

"Well, I'm sure if I'd been a psych major, I'd guess that it has something to do with you losing your mama and them losing theirs. Even though your mom had no choice, it still doesn't make it easy. Loss is loss. Maybe you see something you can give them that you always wanted."

"Dr. King, you impress me." She raised a brow. "I'm sure you're on to something. Whatever it is, I'm not questioning it. I feel like I'm where I'm supposed to be, and I can't say I've ever felt that before."

"That's a good thing."

"Definitely. So, I just told you my secrets. Tell me something I don't know about you. I love your parents, you have a great family, even if Hayden's an over-the-top flirt." She snorted. "I want to know your story. Did you always want to be a firefighter? Always have a love for renovating homes?"

I scrubbed a hand over my face. I hated talking about myself. But somehow talking to Ashlan came easy. She was so open and honest that it made me want to offer her the same.

"I went away to school and did the five-year plan to stretch out the fun." I shrugged. "I came back home after an internship at a finance company and knew that wasn't for me. Sitting at a desk eight hours a day did not appeal to me. So, I signed up for the fire academy and it felt right. But I was a cocky bastard back then. Didn't have a care in the world. I bartended and saved a bunch of cash while I went through the academy and bought my first house, which I eventually flipped and was able to buy this one."

"And that's how you started the side business flipping houses," she said knowingly. "That's amazing. You're doing two things that you love."

"Yep. I'm grateful for that. The house business will help me plan for the girls' futures. I make more doing that than fighting fires at the moment, but being a firefighter is a part of me. So I know what you're saying about feeling like you're where you're supposed to be. I get it."

She smiled. "I guess we're lucky to spend our days doing what we love."

"Damn straight. So what's up with the hockey player?" I changed the subject because I wanted to know.

Needed to know.

I was a jealous bastard who had no claim to this girl, yet I wanted to claim her. Wanted to make her mine.

In another lifetime under different circumstances, I'd accept nothing less.

"You sure are worried about Lucas." She set her glass on the side table and tucked a loose piece of hair behind her ear. So fucking pretty. "We're friends."

"Does he know that?"

"I've told him. I'm not interested in more." Her eyes burned into mine, searching and seeking for answers I just couldn't give her.

"Why's that?"

"I guess I like someone else. I've always been a one-man woman. I've never liked dating much, only really had two boyfriends. Apparently, I know what I want, and I don't settle for less."

Jesus. There was nothing about this girl that I didn't like. I respected her. I admired her. I adored her. And I fucking wanted her something fierce.

I cleared my throat. "Yeah? It's good to know what you want. But you've also got to be realistic. You can't always have what you want."

"If you want it bad enough… if you're patient, I think you can." She smirked and I laughed.

Damn, she was cute.

"What if that something isn't good for you? I think it takes a selfless person to walk away when they know they aren't good for the other."

"Or he's just a stupid man who's afraid of what he's feeling," she said.

That struck a nerve.

"Or he's older and wiser. He's been kicked in the teeth enough times to know." I raised a brow.

"That doesn't mean that you're always going to get kicked in the teeth. Karla was a hot mess from the beginning. No one was surprised that she bailed. That doesn't mean everyone is going to let you down."

I leaned forward and rested my elbows on my knees and waited for her to look up at me. "Is that what you think? You think I'm resisting this because I'm afraid you'll let me down?"

"I don't know. You've been hurt, I get it."

"No, Sunshine. I'm not afraid of you hurting me. You've got it all wrong. I've just got nothing to offer. Nothing that would be good for you. A shit-ton of baggage, for starters. But if I were ten years younger, you wouldn't be walking out of this bedroom without me touching you. Tasting you. Doing all the things I wish I could. But I'm not going to. We're in different places. So, you've got to trust me on this—" I let out a long breath.

"Well, I disagree. And now you've got me all flustered thinking about what you want to do to me." She chuckled and her cheeks pinked. "How about we make a deal?"

"All right. Let me hear it."

"We can be friends. I like spending time with you. Even if it's just as friends. I won't push for more if that's not what you want. But don't avoid me, because that hurts me."

My chest squeezed.

"I'm such a selfish bastard," I said. "I've tried to keep my distance because I worried I'd fuck up and cross the line, because it's almost happened already. But of course, we can be friends. It's better that way."

She nodded and smiled. "I can live with that. So, we can go to Sunday dinner at my dad's house tomorrow and you won't insist on going separately, seeing as I live at the same address as you?"

So maybe the last few Sundays I'd said we'd meet her there and made a point to go from my parents' house first. I'd avoided her at Cap's house because if he knew how badly I wanted his daughter—he'd be done with me. The man was like a second father to me, and I'd never betray his trust. I mean, outside of my fantasies at least. Hell, he hated the way Rusty always hit on his girls, and Rusty was close to their age. Jack Thomas did not want his daughter messing around with an older man who was also a single parent.

No fucking way.

I wouldn't want it for my girls, so I understood it.

"Fine. We're friends."

"Good friends," she said, and her voice was all tease.

"Fair enough."

"Friends hang out. Most of my high school friends have moved away from Honey Mountain, and the ones that are here only like to go out and get drunk, which isn't my thing. So… I could use a new bestie."

I barked out a laugh. "I've never been called a bestie. But if it makes you happy, I'm willing to bend the rules."

"It makes me happy, Jace King."

"Then I'm all yours, Sunshine."

nine

. . .

Ashlan

"SO, were you ever in love with Karla?" I asked as I sipped my iced tea. I'd woken up hungry and after our talk about being friends, I'd convinced Jace to take me to Honey Mountain Café for breakfast. We were friends after all.

"Damn. You don't mince words, do you?" he asked after he swallowed the largest bite of pancakes that I'd ever seen fit in someone's mouth.

"I know you aren't a big talker, but when you have four sisters, there's a lot of talking *all the time.* And if we're going to be friends, we need to know more about one another. Obviously, I know the basics because I've known you for years, but I don't know anything that isn't surfacey."

I'd heard what he'd said earlier, and I respected it. I didn't necessarily agree with it. But somehow, hearing that he wanted me as badly as I wanted him, it gave me a bit of peace. So, I'd take what he was offering for now…with a smidgen of hope things could change.

I liked him.

A lot.

I liked being around him. Hearing him talk. Hearing him laugh. I knew from the years that I'd known him that he didn't do either often. So, it felt like a gift that he was comfortable with me.

He took a sip of his orange juice and blew out a breath. "I was never in love with Karla. I can't say I've ever been in love. I've been in lust. I've been stupid. And I hate saying that out loud if I'm being honest, because Paisley and Hadley are the best things that ever happened to me. Karla gave me my greatest gifts, but we never had a strong connection. I mean, our first encounter was just physical. A one-night stand. Then she showed up months later telling me she was pregnant with my child. I tried to do the stand-up thing, but there just never was anything between us. I tried—maybe she tried, I don't know. Addiction is a battle of its own and one I'm grateful I haven't had to face."

"Was she always like that? The whole time you were married?"

He took a bite of bacon and thought it over. "No. It got really bad toward the end. But I can't say it was ever really good either. We'd have moments. She was trying real hard for a little bit there right before she got pregnant with Hadley. I should have known better than to believe it would last for more than a couple of weeks. But I wanted it to work at the time, for the girls' sakes."

"I get that. You wanted them to have that traditional family."

"Yeah. I grew up with that. My parents are ridiculously in love, even all these years later. I always thought I'd have what my parents have, and this was about as far from that as you can get. But not everyone gets that, right? I mean, your parents had it, but not everyone is so lucky. And I got my girls. I'm not complaining. It's not the way I saw things going, but I made my bed, and I will lie in it the best I can. I was an idiot back then. Sleeping around and thinking nothing would happen. But at the same time—I wouldn't change a damn thing."

My heart ached for him.

"So you don't think you deserve to be happy now? Just because things didn't work out with Karla? You can still have a life of your own and be a good dad, Jace."

"Really? Have you not taken a good look at my life, Ash? I work two jobs. One of them takes me away half the week. When I am home, I'm busy raising two kids. When most people are out grabbing a beer and dinner, I'm brushing teeth and bathing babies. And I'm fine with that. I love my girls more than life. But I can't imagine bringing someone else into that. Plus, I don't want to confuse Paisley and Hadley. They've been through a lot. My life works for me."

"And when do you get to let loose and have fun?" I asked. I wanted to ask him about sex. About other women, but I didn't know how to bring that up.

But we were friends, right? He kept asking me about the hockey player. Shouldn't I be allowed to be curious about his romantic life too?

"I get by just fine." He smirked.

"Do you date? I know you don't bring women around the girls, but you must—have needs."

He snorted. "Damn, you're fucking cute, Sunshine. You worried about me?"

"I am. And this is something friends talk about. You can ask me anything."

"Yeah?" he asked, as he reached for his coffee and took a sip.

"Absolutely. I'm an open book to my bestie."

He nodded. "What happened to that dude you brought home to a family party a while back? Harry? Hank?"

"Henry." I laughed. "We dated for a few months. But I just didn't see it going anywhere, so I ended it after graduation."

"He seemed pretty into you." He raised a brow.

"You sure are paying attention to the guys around me, huh?"

"Hey, what are besties for?"

I chuckled. "Henry said that he was in love with me, and I knew I didn't feel that. I liked him a lot. As a friend. But just not in the way that I should."

"Very stand-up of you."

"What can I say? I'm a stand-up girl."

"No doubt about it. So, no Henry, and you aren't feeling it with the hockey star. You must be picky." He forked another large bite of pancakes and popped it in his mouth.

"I guess. I think you just know when you know. And you're not getting off the hook that easy. So, Karla's been gone a while." I shrugged.

"Yep. And we weren't really together for a long time before she left."

"So…"

He snorted. "Jesus, Ash. Just come out and ask the question."

I shook my head and bit down on my lip before whispering the words I was dying to ask. "How do you take care of your needs?"

"Is this really what you talk to your girlfriends about?"

"Stop deflecting, King. I told you what you wanted to know."

He set his fork down and rubbed his hands together, and it was impossible for me not to stare because they were… large.

"I've had sex three times since she left a year and a half ago. Both women were on the same page as I was, and trust me when I tell you, we practiced safe sex. But if I'm being honest, I'm a sexual dude, so I guess we can just say that I'm very well-acquainted with my hand. It's just like showering every day. It's just something you do."

My jaw fell open, and I fanned my face with the menu that was left on the table, which made him laugh. His laughter bellowed around the café, and I glanced around before leaning forward and whispering. "Wow. Thanks for the honesty. Do you watch movies and look at magazines for inspiration?"

I couldn't believe the words left my mouth before I could stop them.

"Nope. Inspiration is everywhere I look," he said as his gaze bore into me, and his tongue swiped out to wet his bottom lip.

Holy smoking hotness.

The thought of Jace King in the shower, gripping his large—

Nope. Not going there.

Was he insinuating that he thought of me?

"Well, that's good to know."

"How about you? It's obviously been a while for you as well." His lips turned up in the corners, and I couldn't stop staring at his mouth.

"It has been a while if I'm being honest. I'm just fine though."

He leaned forward, his face so close to mine that I sucked in a breath. "Do you touch yourself when you're in my bed, Sunshine?"

I reached for my water and guzzled it. Taking a minute to process his words and waiting for him to lean back in his seat. "I mean. There's inspiration everywhere, right?"

He nodded. "There sure is."

Thankfully, we were interrupted by Hawk and Everly, who showed up unexpectedly. They slid right into our booth and ordered breakfast.

I was thankful for the reprieve so I could pull myself together.

"You sure you're feeling better? Your face is flushed," Everly asked.

That's because of all the sexy talk with my new bestie.

Who also happened to be my boss.

"Yes. I'm just a little warm because it's blisteringly hot outside," I insisted.

Jace's gaze locked with mine and he smirked.

Cocky bastard.

Jace ~ I'll meet you at the school in thirty minutes, just need to catch a quick shower because we just got back from that house fire.

Every time he talked about taking a shower, I wondered if he was going to be *taking care of business.* I swear he mentioned the shower often just to get under my skin. We'd fallen into a good routine the past few weeks. We texted and talked all day. He'd text me from the firehouse at night long after the girls went to bed. We'd speak on my days off all day as well. He'd tell me about things the girls had done or ask me about my day or how the book was coming along. I spent a lot of time with Jace and the girls when I wasn't working these days, because I missed them on my days off.

Me ~ Perfect. We're going to walk, but I'm putting Hadley in the stroller because she looks like she's ready for a nap.

Jace ~ See you soon, Sunshine.

Hadley was already asleep before we made it to the corner. Paisley had been quiet all day and I knew she was nervous about meeting her teacher. She didn't end up in Charlotte's class, as she taught kindergarten at the same school, probably because Principal Peters knew we were close family friends. But her teacher, Mrs. Clandy was a beloved teacher at the school, according to Charlotte.

"You look so pretty today, sweetie," I said as I pushed the stroller and she walked beside me.

"Thank you for taking me to get a new dress and shoes."

She smiled up at me. "Do you think everyone is going to come to meet the teacher with their mamas?"

There it was.

The elephant in the room.

This sweet girl had been angsting for months about being called out for not having her mother there. I knew that kids could be cruel, but I also knew the way that you responded to it would make or break it continuing.

I came to a stop and bent down to meet her eyes. "You don't owe anyone an explanation. Do you remember I told you my mama got sick when I was young?"

"Yeah." She put her hand on my cheek and smiled. We'd put her hair up in two buns on top of her head, and her blue eyes were shining in the sunlight. She was so adorable that my chest squeezed. "I remember, and you were sad for a long time, right?"

"Yes, I was. But guess what?"

"What?"

"Well, you've met my crazy sisters. Every single one of them stepped up. There was always someone that came to school with me, or brought treats on my birthday, it really doesn't matter who it is, as long as you have your tribe, right? And you've got me, Paisley. I will be here for anything you need, okay? And you'll be surprised that when you stop worrying about it, no one will question you."

She smiled so wide and then wrapped her little arms around me. "They'll probably all think you're my mama anyway. You don't have to tell them that you're not if you don't want to."

She pulled back and chewed on her thumbnail while she waited for me to answer.

"I won't be saying a word. This is your day, and I can't wait to see your classroom."

"Thank you, Ash. I'm so glad you're coming too. I love Daddy, but he brought store-bought cupcakes on my birthday last year, and all the mamas make real treats for the birthdays, so everyone knew that Daddy got them."

"Well, guess what?"

"What?" she asked, as we started walking again.

"You know Vivi makes the best treats. Your birthday is in a couple weeks, so maybe we can talk to her about some ideas for the best cupcakes, and you, me, and Hadley can make them ourselves."

She clapped her hands together and her smile spread so wide across her face that it actually made my heart hurt. It's the little things that matter so much when you're young. I'd do whatever I could to help calm her nerves.

"I can't wait to bring the best treats on my birthday. You don't think it will hurt Daddy's feelings if we make the treats this year, do you? Even when our mom lived with us, she didn't make treats. Daddy always got them. But in kindergarten, the kids care what kind of treats you have."

"Of course, they do. It's a big deal. You're in big girl school now. And I'll talk to Daddy, and we can see if he wants to help. Maybe he could just add some sprinkles on top or something easy so he feels like he's involved," I teased.

"Yes. We will give him an easy job, but we won't tell him that because I don't want to make him sad."

So sweet.

"I think that's a perfect plan." We arrived at the school and I looked down at her. "You ready for this?"

"I am. Let's do this." She giggled.

"Hey, hey, hey," a voice shouted from behind us, and we whipped around to see Jace jogging toward us, looking like something out of every woman's fantasies. He wore a white tee, a pair of jeans, and his hair looked like he'd been tugging at it per usual. He was so sexy that my heart always raced in his presence. No matter how much time we spent together. "There's my girls."

My girls.

I knew he meant Paisley and Hadley, but for just a minute, I wondered what it would feel like to really be his.

A girl could dream, right?

"Hi, Daddy. You don't smell like fire," Paisley said as she sniffed the air around him before hugging him tight, and he chuckled.

"Good to know. I took an *extra long* shower," he said, and his gaze locked with mine and winked.

He winked.

He was messing with me.

And the fact that he'd accentuated the words *extra long*—was he telling me something in code? I could vouch for the fact that he had every right to boast about his size after my sneak peek at his goods. Or maybe I was just too used to getting lost in fiction and reading into every word that he said.

"Hey, Sunshine. You look pretty, and Paisley looks like a little princess. Thanks for getting her ready." Jace had given me his credit card and asked me to take Paisley to buy a special dress for her for today. When I'd checked her closet, she had clothes in all different sizes, very few being anything that would fit her. He'd bought a few dresses for her before I'd come to work for him and they were a size 10, but he'd said he didn't know how the sizing worked, and they'd looked tiny to him, so he'd bought them, which had made me laugh. I'd insisted he come with us last weekend, and I showed him how to purchase clothes in the correct size for both girls. We'd loaded up on panties and summer clothes and some school outfits for Paisley.

"Of course, it's a big day."

We walked down the hallway, and Paisley stopped outside her classroom. "Should I take the teacher her gift now?"

"Yep," I said, handing her the pastry box from Honey

Bee's Bakery. Jace looked at me with confusion as I handed them to Paisley.

"We had Vivi make a few cookies that are decorated like red apples, and some say *best teacher*, you know, just some fun treats for her to give to Mrs. Clandy."

"That was really sweet of you. Thank you for thinking of that. Hell, I don't know half of this stuff," Jace whispered.

"Daddy," Paisley hissed, and his eyes widened. "We're in school. Behave."

I covered my mouth with my hand to mask my laughter. Paisley led the way into the classroom and Jace leaned close to me. He smelled like mint and sexy man. I didn't miss the way several of the mothers all turned their attention to him when we walked in.

"I'm more afraid of Paisley scolding me than I am Mrs. Clandy."

I chuckled and nudged him with my shoulder. "Behave, Mr. King."

"Yes, ma'am, Sunshine." He waggled his brows, and I shook my head.

Mrs. Clandy walked toward us, holding the gift box in one hand and Paisley's hand in the other. "Hello, I'm Mrs. Clandy. It's so nice to meet you all. I've heard amazing things about Miss Paisley here, and I was thrilled to find out she would be in my class."

Paisley's cheeks flushed pink, and her eyes widened as she looked at me with the biggest smile on her face.

"Nice to meet you," Jace said, extending his hand.

I did the same, and Paisley pointed at Hadley in the stroller and told her teacher that she was her baby sister. She thanked us for the cookies and told Paisley to take us around the room and show us where her cubby was and to pick something out of the treasure box.

We thanked her and she turned back toward us and shook

her head. “Such a beautiful family. Thrilled to have you in my classroom this year.”

My heart raced at her words. Should we correct her?

I glanced at Paisley who was beaming up at her teacher, and Jace looked over at me and smiled.

Okay then.

Maybe in our own weird way, we were a family.

It sure felt like it.

ten

. . .

Jace

SCHOOL HAD STARTED and Paisley was thriving. I'd been so nervous about it going well, that it had been such a pleasant surprise that things had gone so smoothly. She loved her teacher, she loved learning all the things, and she came home telling us everything that she learned each day. Ashlan had made a huge difference in my girls' lives. There'd been an empty space that she was filling for my kids, one that had been missing. Hell, she was doing the same for me. I hadn't even realized how much I'd missed the company of a woman. The talks, the laughter, the teasing, and flirting.

We were friends—but it was so much more.

I knew it.

She knew it.

But we accepted that this was how it needed to be. I'd tried hard to set boundaries, but every day grew more challenging.

This girl was seeping into every bit of my being.

When I was away at the firehouse, I fucking missed her like mad. It made no sense. I'd been married to Karla for a few years, and I couldn't ever remember a time that I'd missed her. I always had this panicked feeling when I was working, that my girls weren't okay. I'd hired babysitters, had my mom or my brothers stop by the house constantly when I was on duty to check on them.

I felt none of that now. My girls were in good hands. The best hands. They were with someone who loved them and cared for them, and it gave me an unexplainable peace that I hadn't realized had been missing.

"Hey, you get any sleep last night?" Cap asked. Jack Thomas was one of the best people I'd ever known. Hell, I watched him with his girls and hoped like hell that I could be half the father that he was to his daughters.

"Yeah. A little bit. That was a hell of a fire, huh?" I said as I laced my shoes before pushing to my feet.

"Yep. But we got it under control. For a minute, I thought we might need to call in a backup crew. The boys rallied."

"They did. Rook and Tallboy are really stepping up. They took charge last night for the first time that I've noticed."

"Agreed. Our team is strong." He cleared his throat. "So, how's my baby girl doing over at the house? She seems really happy taking care of the girls."

"She's amazing with them. Hell, she brought a teacher gift to meet the teacher, and she packs these amazing lunches for Paisley to take to school. I used to just stick a sandwich and some chips in there. But Ash, she's writing notes and puts in special treats. Making sure she's got a balanced meal. She and Paisley and Hadley worked so hard making these little heart cupcakes to take to school for Paisley's birthday treat last week. They barely let me sprinkle the tiniest bit on top because they wanted them to be just right. I just, I don't know." I scrubbed a hand down the back of my neck. "I didn't realize how much they were missing even before Karla left. I know that she didn't make them feel safe. From what I've learned from Paisley since she left is that they were afraid of her, I think. But Ashlan, she's changed them. Paisley loves school, Hadley won't stop talking—even if penis is her favorite word."

Cap snorted. "Ashlan has a gift for spreading goodness, that's for sure. The girl is a caregiver and a bleeding heart."

I knew there was a *but* in there, but he hadn't said it yet.

"She is."

"Is this a friendship or something more?" He leaned against the wall and crossed his arms over his chest.

I ran my hand over the scruff on my jaw as I took a minute to think how to best answer the question. "We're friends."

"I noticed at dinner on Sunday night that you two just seem, I don't know, like more than that. And I'm not here to judge you, Jace. It's not my business. But you're one of my closest friends, and she's my baby girl. I'd hope like hell that you'd proceed with caution. She's got a tender heart, and I don't want to see her get hurt."

"That's why I won't cross the line. We've discussed it. I knew you wouldn't be okay with it, and I understand why. I'm not okay with it either, so I get it."

He studied me with a puzzled look on his face. "You think I have a problem with you having kids?"

I let out a long breath. "Among other things. Single dad. One failed marriage already. I'm nine years older than her. I don't have a lot to bring to the plate for a girl who's got her whole life ahead of her."

"You're talking to a guy who married a girl a decade younger than me. Age doesn't mean shit. That's not my issue. Nor am I concerned about you being a single dad. Hell, she probably finds that to be a plus. She loves your girls. My concern is that she's young and she's tenderhearted. Always has been. And she seems like she's all in, and I just don't know if you are. We won't have a problem unless she gets hurt in all of this. If there's no room for her in your life, I'm asking you as a friend not to go there. I understand you're dealing with a lot, having two young kids and trying to do it all on your own… so you either make room for someone in your life or you don't. Take it from someone who's been single since he lost the love of his life, I get it."

"I know how hard that's been, Cap. The one thing I will say is that you at least got to experience that kind of love. I didn't have that with Karla. So, it's not heartache that I feel, it's just—"

"What?"

"I don't want to bring Ashlan down. She's so… good. And she deserves the fairy tale. You know… the dude on the horse who isn't strapped down with two kids. She deserves the white picket fence, the husband who dotes on her and has lots of babies of her own."

His eyes doubled in size, surprised by how much I'd thought about this maybe. Hell, I was surprised by it too—but it consumed my thoughts. Wanting and needing this girl in a way I'd never experienced. But knowing at the same time that she could do better. That she deserved more.

That she deserved everything.

"Fairy tales are bullshit. Look at Ever and Hawk and Vivi and Niko. They went through lots of ups and downs to find their way to one another. Life's messy. I speak from experience. I loved Beth in a way I can't describe, but our time together wasn't drama-free. Hell, her parents hated me when we first met. I was ten years older than her, and I didn't have a pot to piss in. But we figured it out. One thing I've learned in life is that none of that matters. Not other people's opinions or what you think is the fairy tale for another person—it comes down to the basics. If you love someone, there's no running from it. And when you find it, it sure is worth the fight. But if you aren't sure, or you don't think it's the real deal, don't be playing games with someone's heart. Especially someone as special as Ashlan."

"I would never take that lightly."

"I know you wouldn't. You're a good man, Jace. I think

you just might be the only one who doesn't know it." He clapped me on the shoulder. "Come on. Breakfast is ready, and we've got a full day ahead of us."

I was still thinking about what he'd said when I moved to sit at the oversized table beside Niko.

"You guys coming over this weekend?" he asked as he handed me the platter of scrambled eggs. We'd spent all last weekend finishing up final details on the Elm Street house, and we'd put it on the market two days ago. It would be nice to finally have a weekend off.

"Yeah, I think so. The girls loved swimming in the lake at your house last weekend."

He nodded. "Yeah. I can't wait until our little Bee can run around and play in the water."

"Don't rush it. It goes by too fast as it is," Cap said as he sat beside Big Al across from us.

"Well, I'm not rushing it, but I sure as hell won't mind when she stops having explosive shits. I mean, who'd think a little angel like that could drop a bomb?"

I barked out a laugh. "Fuck. Paisley had the shits all the time. Apparently she had a sensitive stomach."

"Oh my god. What is happening here? I just lost my appetite." Rusty was pinching the bridge of his nose dramatically.

"Toughen up, you big baby," Big Al said. "You put out fires for a living and you've seen plenty of shit on some of the medical calls we've gone out on. Baby poop is not a big deal. Hell, I've got a grandson that shits bigger than your head, Rust."

The entire table erupted in laughter.

"I'm never having kids. That's disgusting," he hissed.

"That's the crazy part. You don't even care. It doesn't make me sick, it's just that every time I'm watching a game, the girl has a little explosion, and the smell is pretty horrific. It's as bad as Rusty smells after we workout."

"Ewww… I can't imagine having to change Rusty's diaper," Tallboy said over a mouthful of bacon.

"What the fuck are we talking about? How did we get to this? Come on now, guys. Let's talk about women and sex and beer." Rusty pounded on his chest and let out a long burp.

"I have something I'd like to say," Rook said, and I looked over to see him smiling nervously at Niko.

"Well, go ahead, kid. You've got our attention now," Gramps said, and the old man was moody as hell, but he sure loved our team.

"I, uh, I'm going to ask Jada to marry me. I was hoping you all could help me out with a proposal."

Everyone turned to look at Niko, who was Jada's older brother, and he rolled his eyes. "He already asked my permission. I gave him my blessing. What can I say? I'm a big softy these days."

"You ready to be a husband and a father?" I asked, because Jada had a daughter, and I wondered if he realized how much responsibility came with that.

"Hell, yeah. I love Jada and Mabel more than anything."

"Well, you got Niko's blessing, which is probably the toughest nut in our crew… so why the hell do you need us to help propose?" Gramps grumped. "You going to ask us to give you the birds and the bees talk next?"

Rusty slapped the table and fell over laughing. "The birds and the bees talk from Gramps would be priceless."

"Shut up, Rusty." Gramps shot him the bird.

"I want to do a grand gesture when I propose. I was wondering, Cap, if maybe we could take the fire truck over to the bakery and call her outside, and I could propose to her on top of the truck."

"Oh, for god's sake. Kids these days are so over the top. I just asked Lottie to marry me while we were eating a burger. And guess what, assholes. She said yes."

"Hey, I proposed to Vivi in a canoe on the water." Niko shrugged. "I put thought into what she'd want. I think Jada would like this. It's a little over the top, but she'll remember it forever."

Gramps groaned. "Canoes and fire trucks, hell, Cap, didn't Hawk propose at the goddamn Stanley Cup?"

"He did." Cap snorted. "I don't have a problem with grand gestures, especially when they're for my girls."

I thought about how I'd proposed to Karla. I hadn't. She'd informed me that she was pregnant, and I moved her in, and I'd agreed to a quick courthouse wedding. I was a man who would always take responsibility for my actions, and that's what I'd done. But, it hadn't been right from the start. Neither of us were excited about it, and we barely spoke on the way home from our wedding. Maybe a grand gesture meant you were actually excited about spending the rest of your life together.

"I like it," I said.

"Another goddamn softy," Big Al said with a laugh.

"All right. Let us know when you want to do it, Rook." Cap pushed to his feet and moved to the sink.

Everyone started their own conversations and I turned to look at Rook. "You got a ring yet?"

"Yeah, Niko and Vivi helped me pick it out." He smiled.

"You know taking care of a kid is a lot of work, right?"

"I'm with Mabel every day, and I love that girl something fierce. I can't wait to be her daddy." He shrugged. "I plan on adopting her after we're married. I'll be proposing again, I guess, when I ask Mabel if she'll agree to it."

"That's great. Do you think you guys will have kids of your own?" I don't know why I was so curious about this, but Rook was Ashlan's age and I was surprised he was willing to take on all this responsibility.

"If we're lucky. I'd like to have a big family and give

Mabel siblings of her own. But we're not in a rush. We just want to start our family and make it official."

I pushed to my feet and clapped him on the shoulder. "Good for you, buddy. I'm happy for you."

"Thanks, Jace. I hope I'm half the dad you are someday."

I cleared my throat, surprised by his words. Hell, most days I just felt like I was surviving. So hearing him say that—it meant something to me.

I glanced over to see Cap watching me, and he smirked. "Told you. You're the only one who doesn't know it."

The alarm sounded, and we were all scrambling to get into our gear. And in no time, we were off. Sirens blaring, we piled in the truck and Cap filled us in. There was a big fire out at the hotel on the outskirts of town.

It was going to be a long day.

When we arrived at the scene, there was a slew of people sitting on the curb coughing and crying and flailing their hands as they filled us in.

"All right, there are still a few people in the building. They're trapped on the west side. Let's go." Cap waved his hand over his head for everyone to follow.

Niko and I took the lead and made our way into the blazing building. I glanced over at him, and he nodded. We always had one another's back. There was no other way to walk into a situation like this unless you were with someone you trusted.

Tallboy and Rusty held the line and made a path for us, and the heat blazed as we moved deeper into the building. The structure quaked as the fire breathed through the large space. I'd been in a few bad fires in my day, but this one felt different.

The heat.

The smoke.

Even with all of our gear—it was almost overpowering.

I tried to listen as I headed toward the west side and motioned for Niko to follow.

"I don't think I can hold it back," Tallboy shouted, and Rusty moved closer to him as they both attempted to clear a path for us.

I moved toward the stairs that were barely visible in the heavy gray cloud that consumed the space. I heard shouting, but oftentimes that sound could mess with your head. Fire had a way of speaking as well, but I knew the people trapped in the building were in the direction we were moving, so I followed my hunch.

I moved first. Testing the stairs as I hurried up the shaky path. The only one leading to where we needed to go.

"It's not stable," Niko shouted as he moved behind me.

I knew it wasn't, but I also knew it was our only chance at getting the people trapped in the building out of here.

"Spray the stairs, and then go call for the ladder," I shouted at Tallboy who did what I said. "Rusty, you hold the line, brother."

"Got it," he said as he cleared a small path for me again. The stairs beneath my feet started to shake, and before I realized what was happening, part of it crumbled. I reached for the banister as I heard Niko shout my name.

I swung on the metal banister and flung myself up to stable ground, as I motioned for Niko to follow my path and Rusty to keep it as clear as he could. He wouldn't be able to come any farther with us, and we all three knew it. But I had Niko by my side, and I knew that Tallboy would have that ladder ready for us.

"You crazy son of a bitch," Niko shrieked as his feet landed beside mine.

"Go, Rusty. We'll need you outside." I motioned and he continued hosing the path for us before he ran out to help Tallboy from the other side.

The cries for help grew louder.

The heat stronger.

The smoke thick and heavy.

"You hear that?" I shouted to Niko.

"Yes. I think they're in that back room."

I moved quickly, keeping my breaths calm even though I knew we were not in the best situation.

The building creaked, the fire warning us to get out.

But the cries for help were stronger.

I thought of my girls.

Paisley and Hadley.

Ashlan.

I'd get out of here no matter what. Because they were counting on me.

I checked the door and looked at Niko, as he charged through. We found four people huddled on the floor, and relief flooded me. Time was not on our side. There was no turning back.

I moved toward the window, kicking out the glass and motioning for the ladder. Tallboy and Rusty were there. Samson and Rook were working the ladder and waving their hands for us to get out.

Firemen could speak without words most of the time.

Hand signals. Body language. Simple motions.

We knew what one another needed.

That's the only way we survived. Working as a team.

I hoped that Cap and Big Al had swept the downstairs where we'd heard one person had been trapped. Niko and I stayed the course. I couldn't think about anything else. Not right now.

One by one, we hurried them out the window.

The flames were spreading through the room as Niko and I both looked at one another. I motioned for him to go first, and I was right behind him.

eleven

. . .

Ashlan

HADLEY and I were at Honey Bee's Bakery having lunch while Paisley was at school.

"Donuts," I said, pointing to the far corner of the display case.

"Donuts." She smiled. This girl had melted my heart over the past few weeks. She was making so much progress. She liked when I taught her new words.

"Cupcakes," I said, motioning to the other side of the display case.

"Cups… cupstakes."

"You're doing so great with this, sweetie," I said, covering her little hand with mine as she sat beside me. She popped a little bite of pastry in her mouth and smiled.

Cherub cheeks.

Big brown eyes.

Sweet as sugar.

Vivi walked over to us and set down two sugar cookies. "How are we doing over here?"

"Vee Vee," Hadley said, and Vivian smiled so wide.

"That's the first time you've said my name." She kissed

Hadley's forehead as Jilly walked out from the back of the kitchen holding Baby Bee in her arms.

"Bee Bee," Hadley said, which was sort of a mix of Bee and Baby and I'd call it a win.

I scooped her up on my lap and wrapped my arms around her. "I'm proud of you. You just keep going, baby girl."

"Um, I don't want to scare you, but my mom just called and said there's a big fire at the Honey Mountain Hotel."

Vivi's back went ramrod straight and her gaze locked with mine. "Okay. How bad is it?"

"I don't know. My mom said it was a doozy though."

"Can you take Bee up to the office and see if she'll go down for her nap? I'm going to go call Busy Betty."

"Of course," Jilly said as she hurried back through the kitchen and Vivi stepped behind the counter to call Busy Betty, Rusty's mom, who was always in the know.

"I'll call Lottie," I said, my heart racing. My father was a firefighter along with Niko and…

Jace.

My heart raced so fast I couldn't think.

"Hi, darling." Lottie picked up on the first ring. "I think they've got it almost contained, but they're going to be there a few more hours."

"Okay. Everyone's all right?"

"Yep. I just drove out here. They're going to be exhausted, but they seem okay so far."

I let out a long breath and hugged Hadley a little bit tighter.

"Thank you so much. Do you think me and Vivi should head out there?" My heart raced and worry flooded me. I'd grown up with my dad being in this profession, but it never got easier.

"No. They've got the area taped off. But Al saw me and told me they were okay. He said for me to head home, but I'll keep you posted if I hear of any changes."

"Thank you, Lottie." Lottie and Al were the two sweetest people around. She'd experienced her husband's close calls a number of times and she'd always been there to support us and help us navigate through the stressful situations that arose when someone you loved was a firefighter.

"Love you, sweetheart. They'll be okay."

I nodded even though she couldn't see me. "Love you."

I ended the call and sent a text to Charlotte, Everly, and Dylan with the update. Fire families always kept one another in the loop. We'd been doing this for years.

Vivi walked toward me and let out a breath. "It sounds like they've got it under control. This never gets easy, does it?"

I shook my head, and Hadley pointed at the display case and I set her on her feet so she could walk over and look at all the treats.

"You okay?" I asked.

"Yeah. I'll feel better when they're home. How about you?" She studied me before dropping to sit in the chair across from mine. The bakery was quiet which was rare.

"I'm good."

"How are things going with Jace? You two sure seem to be spending a lot of time together."

I shrugged. "Yeah. I mean, I do work for him."

"Right. But when you aren't working, you're together quite a bit, right?"

"I guess. I like hanging out with them. You know I love the girls," I said, glancing over at Hadley as she repeated all her new words as she took in the pastry case.

"I do. And you're so good with them, Ash. But I see the way you look at him. The way he looks at you. The way you just freaked out because you were worried about him in the fire."

I rolled my eyes. "Dad and Niko are in that fire too."

"I know. But I saw the same panic that I was feeling when I looked at you. You're in love with him, aren't you?"

I shook my head. "That's crazy. We're friends. Sure, I care about him. But he doesn't want more with me. He's made it clear."

"Well," she said with a chuckle. "Niko was pretty adamant that way as well. I see the way he looks at you. Everyone does. It sure doesn't look like friendship to me."

I told her she was imagining things and we sat there talking for a while, as Hadley played a game running from table to table and then back to me. We hadn't heard anything more about the fire and I figured it was probably all under control, and I started to relax.

"Wuvie." Hadley waddled in my direction and laid her head on my lap. That was her way of telling me she was tired.

Vivian looked from Hadley to me and smiled. "I guess she's ready for a nap, huh? I'll keep you posted on the fire, but I think it's going to be okay."

I had a sick feeling in my stomach. I wished Jace would just come home now. I kept checking my phone and he hadn't texted yet, which meant he was still out there. "All right. Love you. I'll call you later."

The door flew open, and Dylan came storming into the bakery. "The wind shifted, and it's not in their favor."

"Where did you hear that?" Vivi jumped to her feet, and I stood holding Hadley in my arms.

"I drove down there. I got your text, and I was on my way home from class, and I drove straight there. They had it partially contained, but not anymore. They're calling in backup from Westberg." The fire crew from the next town over.

My heart sank. Wind could take things from bad to worse. I checked my phone just as two texts came through on my phone. The first one was Lottie telling me exactly what Dylan had just said. The wind had shifted and it wasn't good. The second one was from Jace.

Jace ~ We've got a big one building here. I know I'm supposed to pick Paisley up from school, but I think we're going to be late. My mom could pick her up if you aren't able to, but I thought I'd check with you first.

I typed frantically.

Me ~ Of course I'll get her. Are you okay? I'm worried.

Jace ~ Don't be worrying about anything, Sunshine. Everyone is fine. Thank you for being with the girls.

I had this strong urge to tell him that I loved him. I'd learned a long time ago that life was precious, and you should never hold back on what you feel. But I'd been holding back for weeks. I couldn't even admit it to my sister. I most definitely couldn't say it to him. I'd scare him off.

Me ~ Okay. Be safe, bestie. Xo

It was lame, but the least I could do was tell him to be safe. It wasn't the time to pledge my love to a man who had made it clear he didn't want anything more than a friendship with me.

The three little dots danced across the phone, and I stared at it as if I were waiting for something big. But they disappeared.

Wasn't that how it always went with him? He'd give me a little bit of himself, only to pull back any time things got heated.

"Hello. Earth to Ash. What's going on?" Dylan asked as she threw her arms out to her side.

"Oh. That was Jace. He asked me to pick up Paisley from school. They are going to be there for a while." I shook my head. "Should we go out there?"

"No. The damn police have it taped off. There was no sneaking by this time. I even tried flirting with Brady Townsend and he still told me no. He said it was too dangerous, and Dad told him not to let anyone close." She rolled her eyes. "And the girls shouldn't go anywhere near that. It could be traumatizing."

I nodded. "Okay. I'm going to let Hadley fall asleep in the car and go pick up Paisley. I'll have my phone on me. Please call me the minute you hear anything."

"No way, girl. You go get Paisley, and I'll call Ev and Charlie and meet you at Jace's house. Vivi, have Jilly close the bakery, and bring little Bee over there. We can wait this out together."

"Always so bossy, Dilly." Vivi laughed as she wrapped her arms around me. "But she's right. I'll see you in thirty minutes. We can order takeout for dinner and just be together."

"You're welcome." Dylan waved as she typed into her phone, most likely bossing around the rest of the Thomas girls. It's what she did best. "See you in a little bit."

I drove in silence to the school and the sky overhead was hazy and gray, reminding me just how big this fire was. I texted Charlotte because Hadley was asleep in the back seat, and I'd normally just carry her in, but I knew we were going to have a long night and I wanted her to sleep now while she could. My sister came walking out with Paisley's hand in hers and hurried to the car.

"I'll see you in a few minutes," Charlotte said as she buckled her into her car seat. "Love you."

I waved. "Thank you. Love you. See you soon."

When I pulled away from the school, I looked in the rearview mirror and my gaze locked with Paisley's. So similar to her father's eyes, it made my chest squeeze.

"How was your day, love bug?"

"It was good. Where's Daddy? I heard my teacher say something about a fire. Is Daddy fighting a fire right now?" she asked, and I glanced in the rearview mirror to see her fidgeting with her hands.

"Yes, but I just talked to him and he's doing great. He's

just got to stay and help for a bit, so I thought we'd get takeout and everyone's going to come over and hang out. Is that okay?"

"Who's going to take care of us if something happens to Daddy? We don't have a mama, so if something happens to Daddy, we won't have any parents."

I could physically feel the weight of her words sitting on my heart. I glanced in the rearview mirror again and saw a tear moving down her cheek. I pulled the car over on the side of the road and hurried out of my seat. I unbuckled Paisley and lifted her up before sliding her car seat over and settling her on my lap. I hugged her tight. I knew that fear. I also used to wonder what would happen to us if Dad got hurt after our mom passed away, but I was older than Paisley. This was a lot for a little girl to worry about.

"Nothing is going to happen to your daddy. And you will never be alone, Paisley. I love you so much." We just sat like that for the longest time and then Hadley woke up and started giggling.

"Wuvie? No dwive?"

Paisley and I both burst out in a fit of giggles because drive was a new word for her, and the three of us sat in the back seat of my car laughing so hard I had tears running down my face.

I swiped at my cheeks. "Okay. I need to get us home. We've got Dilly, Charlie, Vivi, and Ever coming over."

"Bee Bee," Hadley said.

"Yep. Baby Bee is coming too."

"I like when your sisters come over," Paisley said as I buckled her back in her car seat and moved up front again. "It's like one big family."

I drove the short distance to the house and got them inside and settled with a snack at the table so Paisley could start her homework, and Hadley was attempting to color just as the doorbell rang. My heart had been racing since I got home, but

I did the best I could to hide my anxiety from the girls. The moment they realized just how dangerous their daddy's job was, the worry would be all-consuming. I hoped we could shelter them from that for a while, especially Paisley, as she had a lot of worries as it was.

There was a knock on the door and Paisley hurried to her feet, pulling the door open. "Hi! It's Dilly, Charlie, Ever, Vivi, and little Bee," Paisley said as they strolled inside.

They each hugged her one at a time, and Dylan was already on the phone ordering takeout for everyone.

"Any news?" I asked Vivi, careful to make sure Paisley wasn't listening. My sisters all understood the importance of putting on a brave face in front of the girls.

She shook her head and her eyes watered as she kissed little Bee's forehead.

"Give me that baby," I said, kissing Vivian on the cheek and pulling my sweet niece into my arms. She was getting so big now. Her head popped up and it sort of wobbled as she took me in. She was so gorgeous and sweet just like her mama.

I cuddled her close and she tucked her face in the crook of my neck. Paisley piled her homework into her folder. "All done. I'm going to run to the bathroom. Save my seat, Dilly."

"Oh, girl, you know I'm all about seat saving." My sister winked as she ran off to the bathroom.

"How's she doing?" Everly asked after she got off the phone with Hawk. He was back in San Francisco meeting with his trainer Wes, but as soon as he heard about the fire, he'd hopped back in his truck and was on his way home.

"She's a little nervous, but otherwise okay. She's thriving at school. I'm so proud of her."

Everly nodded as she studied me. "You were made for this, you know that? Some people are born to be mamas. Me on the other hand… I've got indigestion, my feet are swollen, and I still have a ways to go."

We all chuckled, and it felt good to laugh when we would rather cry, knowing the danger the guys were in.

Vivian got a call from Lottie letting us know the crew from Westberg had arrived. They were from the next town over, and they'd called in the Honey Mountain fire crew more times than I could count for backup, so they were always happy to rally and help when needed. A sense of relief washed over me, just knowing that they had double the manpower now.

The doorbell rang, and Everly laughed when she saw how much food Dylan had ordered. Pizzas and wings and some sort of cinnamon treats to dip in icing.

"No one orders food like you do, girl," Everly said to Dylan as I set the plates and napkins out.

"That's just how I roll." She waggled her brows. "Should I go check on Paisley? She's still in the restroom."

I smiled. That girl sure did take her time. "Yep. Let her know that the food's here."

"Mmmmm mmmmm," Hadley shouted, and my sisters burst out in laughter at how animated she was as she rubbed her little belly.

"I'm very interested in this," Dylan said as she and Paisley returned to the table.

I'd pulled a few chairs from the dining room into the kitchen so we'd all have a seat at the farmhouse table.

"You don't do that when you go potty?" Paisley asked as I set a slice of pizza on her plate, along with some celery and carrots that we had in the refrigerator.

"Ummm… no, ma'am. I didn't know that was a thing. Did you know about this, Ash?"

"What?"

"She takes all her clothes off, because apparently it keeps your clothes from smelling like a poopy," Dylan said over a mouthful of cheese and crust.

"I knew about it. It is rather brilliant." I winked at Paisley, and she beamed.

"I'm seriously implementing this plan. Plus, think of the freedom of sitting on the toilet with your Kindle app open, buck naked. I am totally here for it. And your clothes won't be polluted."

"Of course, you're here for it," Everly teased. "Any chance to be naked."

Paisley was laughing now, and all that worry had been washed away. Even if just for now. I checked my phone several times under the table, and I still hadn't heard from Jace or my dad.

The wait was brutal, but being surrounded by the people I loved made it tolerable.

"They've got it under control," Vivi shouted, pushing to her feet as she read her phone.

My phone beeped just then with a text from Jace.

Jace ~ Everyone's fine, Sunshine. That fire was a bitch. Don't tell Paisley I said that because if she puts me in timeout tonight, I'll definitely fall asleep. I'll be home soon. Can't thank you enough for staying with the girls.

Tears of relief ran down my face.

"Wuvie." Hadley reached for my hand and I laughed.

"I'm just happy, baby girl." I swiped at my cheeks as my gaze locked with Paisley and I smiled. Her lips turned up in the corners of her mouth and all that worry washed away.

Me ~ I'm so relieved. Take your time. We have plenty of food here if you're hungry. I can stay as long as you need me to. I'm sure you're exhausted.

Jace ~ There is something I wanted to talk to you about.

My stomach dipped at his words.

Me ~ Are you giving me my walking papers?

He knew I was teasing, but I chewed on my thumbnail as I waited for his response.

Jace ~ Not even close. I'll see you soon.

I sent him a heart eyes emoji, because I was corny

that way.

"What's going on? You look all flushed," Dylan said as she waggled her brows and Everly cut up some more pizza for Hadley. Charlotte and Paisley were deep in conversation about the Halloween parade at school next month, and Vivian left the room to change Bee's diaper.

"I'm not flushed. Jace just said he had something to talk to me about," I whispered, making sure no one else heard me.

"Oh, I see. I hope he wants to discuss introducing you further to his giant schlong." She fell back laughing and I slapped her shoulder.

"You have a one-track mind."

"I'm kidding. I see how he looks at you, Ash. And I promise you, that is not friendship. Maybe the fire knocked some sense into him," she whispered in my ear.

The doorbell rang and Everly jumped up. "Please tell me that you didn't order more food."

"Nope. This is it for tonight." Dylan chuckled as I leaned over to wipe the sauce from Hadley's cheeks.

"What are you doing here?" Everly's tone was harsh, and it had my head turning in her direction.

"The question is, what are you doing here? This is my house," Karla said as she stormed past my sister and moved into the kitchen. Her blonde hair was shorter than it used to be and rested on her shoulders. She was a little bit taller than me and looked older than she was. She'd always worn a lot of makeup, and I think her lifestyle had just taken a toll on her. Paisley jumped from her chair, but she didn't move toward her mother, she hurried over to stand beside me. Her hand found mine, and I pushed to stand, tucking her behind me. I don't know why. As far as I knew, Karla wasn't a physical threat to the girls, but every instinct I had kicked in.

My stomach dipped and I nearly lost the air in my lungs when my gaze locked with hers.

Because I knew that everything was about to change.

twelve

. . .

Jace

HELL, I couldn't remember the last time I'd been this tired. I was fucking thankful that the crew from Westberg had arrived. Once the wind shifted, we knew we were in trouble. They'd taken the rear end of the building while we'd continued to attack the blaze head-on. Together we'd finally gained power over that son of a bitch and gotten the fire under control.

I pulled into my driveway and saw a bunch of cars, which didn't surprise me. I knew the Thomas girls always got together when there was a big blaze like we'd faced tonight. It was good for my girls to see family rally around one another. I'd received no less than a dozen calls from my mother, and she said she'd been on the phone with Ashlan several times over the last few hours.

I felt a contentment wash over me, knowing that my girls were in good hands no matter what. Ashlan was a fierce protector, and my mother was very similar. I knew they'd be there for them at all costs and I was fucking thankful.

When I pushed the kitchen door open, all of that peace washed away.

Just as quickly as it came—it was gone.

Paisley was crying as she stood behind Ashlan, and Charlotte had Hadley in her arms as Everly stood beside her. Vivian was holding little Bee and glaring at my ex-wife who was flailing her arms and making a scene. Dylan stood beside Ashlan protectively, as Karla's anger seemed to be aimed at the girl protecting my babies.

"She's the fucking nanny?" Karla spun around when I came through the door. "She thinks she can keep my kids from me?"

I let out a long breath and moved toward Ashlan, studying her to make sure she was all right before I dealt with this mess. I ran my hand through Paisley's hair and winked at her.

"Not sure what you're doing here." My tone was harsh as I took in the woman who'd walked out of our kids' lives without so much as a second glance.

No thought.

No accountability.

"This is my house, and these are my children." She crossed her arms over her chest as she raised a brow, daring me to challenge her.

She had no clue how badly I'd like to throw her ass out of here.

I didn't want to do this in front of my girls.

"All right, I've got this. Ash, do you mind taking the girls upstairs and getting them in bed?" I scrubbed a hand over the back of my neck. "Karla, let's take this outside."

Ashlan's sisters all hugged her quickly and mumbled something that was probably Thomas girl code because she nodded. Charlotte handed Hadley to Ashlan, and my baby girl held on tight, knowing something wasn't right. Each of Ash's sisters paused to hug me goodbye as they made their way through the kitchen and out the back door. Dylan took her time, glaring at Karla and letting out some sort of growl before she stepped outside.

My gaze locked with Ashlan's as she held Hadley in her arms and reached for Paisley's hand. I didn't miss my eldest daughter's tear-streaked cheeks and my blood boiled.

Rage and anger and frustration coursed through my veins.

This woman's level of selfishness never ceased to amaze me.

She just took and took and took and didn't give a damn who she hurt in the process.

But I'd made sure she'd never be able to hurt them again, and I'd do whatever I could to honor that.

"What the fuck do you think you're doing?" I held the door open for her to step outside.

"I don't need an invitation to come to my own home, Jace. These are my babies. This is my home." She stormed out to the darkness, which is where I wished she'd stayed.

We stood on the porch, and I crossed my arms over my chest. "You actually do need an invitation. We're divorced. This is not your home. And the girls, fuck, you gave that up without so much as an ounce of thought. You signed over sole custody to me. Do you remember that? And now you think you can just show up here unannounced and pull this shit?"

"I know I messed up. It was a mistake to leave with Zee. He was an asshole."

I snorted. "Why the fuck are you telling me this? Listen to me loud and clear… I don't give a fuck who you're with or what you do. The girls are what I care about."

"Well, I've met someone. We're here to see the girls, and we plan on buying a house here. He's from the city, but he knew I was missing my girls. He's got a son, too."

"So, what now? You've met some random dude with a kid, and now it's cool to be a mother? It doesn't work that way, Karla. You can't keep coming in and out of their lives." My hands fisted at my sides as I spoke, because I was trying hard to control the building anger. The hatred I had toward this woman was something I couldn't explain. What she'd done to them—it was unforgivable.

"I know I messed up. I just want to see them. Are you that spiteful that you won't even let me see them?"

My jaw clenched. "Spiteful? Are you fucking kidding me? You're so fucking delusional. I'll need to speak with my lawyer. You need to leave. If you're still interested in seeing the girls tomorrow, I'll have him reach out to you."

"Jace. Come on. We don't need to call our lawyers, do we? We're friends?"

Friends? Was she for fucking real?

"You've got my number. You haven't used it in a year and a half. Not once have you checked on them. You missed birthdays and Christmas and first days of school. And if you notice, those girls were not rushing toward you. They barely know you at this point, and that's on you. You can't blame me. You can't blame the kids or your parents or your attorney. This was your choice." I moved toward the door. "Don't come here uninvited again. I'll have my attorney reach out."

"Are you fucking that so-called nanny?"

I pointed my finger at her as she walked backward on the driveway with a twisted smile on her face.

"Don't fucking go there. She's been more of a mother to those girls than you ever were. Leave."

"She's a little young, don't you think?" She chuckled.

I stepped inside and slammed the door behind me before I sent a text to Winston Hastings who had handled my divorce and custody agreement. He responded immediately and asked me to meet him at his office first thing in the morning.

This shit just never stopped.

Hell, maybe this was a sign. I wanted to speak to Ash about my talk with her father, about the way I couldn't stop fucking thinking about her, but this was an example of the shit show that was my life these days.

She'd be smart to run for the hills.

Hell, I'd be smart to set her free. This shit was endless, and she didn't need to be involved in it.

Fuck me.

Every time I thought I deserved a shot at happiness—Karla was there to remind me that I didn't.

I moved upstairs as the house was quiet and I checked on Hadley who was lying on her side with her hands in the praying position beneath her neck.

So fucking perfect.

I leaned over and kissed the top of her head before walking out of her room. I found Ashlan lying with Paisley and she looked up to see me in the doorway. She held her finger up to give her a minute, and then she carefully climbed out of bed, and I kissed Paisley's forehead as well.

The fire had freaked me the fuck out today. I'd nearly fallen three stories when the floor gave out beneath me, but luckily that metal banister had been within reach, and I was able to grip that and climb over to the other side. Niko had blasted me later for taking that risk. Shit like that had a way of making you look at your mortality. I'd thought of my girls.

And I'd thought of Ashlan.

When I reached for that banister, she'd been right there at the forefront of my thoughts along with Paisley and Hadley. And that had been a wake-up call.

But then I'd come home to find Karla here. Man, sometimes it felt like the hits just kept on coming. Reminders of why I needed to keep my head on straight. Focus on the girls. Continue to show up for them.

Getting selfish now would be a mistake.

For everyone.

Ashlan followed me out and across the hall to my bedroom. She sat on my bed, and I closed the door and studied her. The crease between her eyes was deep with worry and I wanted to kiss all that concern away.

"Is everything okay?" she asked, her eyes searching mine.

"I don't fucking know. I don't know why she's here. She said she ended things with the first dude she ran off with, and she met someone new who has a kid? Now she's interested in knowing her daughters. She's out of her fucking mind showing up here like that."

She reached for my hands as I dropped to sit beside her. "I'm sorry for letting her in. She just sort of caught us off guard."

"It's okay. She doesn't take no for an answer, so she would have come in one way or another. I'm just sorry that you had to deal with that. I'm glad you had your sisters here."

"I'm not fragile, Jace. I can handle myself. I'm not afraid of Karla if that's what you're worried about," she said, and I interlaced my fingers with hers before I could stop myself.

"Yeah. I know you're strong, Sunshine. But that doesn't mean I want you to deal with my shit."

"What if I want to?" Her eyes were wet with emotion as she studied mine.

"Fuck. My life is a mess. But I'm so fucking thankful for you." I ran a hand through her silky hair, the way I'd been dying to for so long.

"Is that what you wanted to talk to me about? The fact that your life is a mess? Or did you know Karla was back in town and you wanted to discuss that with me?" she asked.

"I didn't know she was here. I would have given you a heads-up. I don't even fucking remember what I wanted to talk to you about now, because I've got to meet with my attorney tomorrow morning and try to figure this shit out."

She nodded. But she knew I was lying. I was going to talk to her about us.

About the possibility of us.

But it died before we even had a chance.

Just like I knew it would.

"Although Paisley will be at school, I can stay with Hadley tomorrow while you go meet with him."

"Thank you. I can bring her with me if I need to," I said as my hand moved to her cheek.

The room was quiet, the smell of lavender wafted around us, and I couldn't help myself. I stroked her soft skin, and she ran her fingers through my hair.

"I'm happy to stay with her. I'm glad you're okay. I was so worried about you tonight," she whispered. "I was so scared you'd get hurt."

"Yeah? I was thinking about you during that fire too."

Her eyes widened and her breaths were coming hard and fast.

"What were you thinking?"

"About your beautiful eyes. Your perfect mouth." I inched closer, my nose grazing hers. "I think about you all the time. I have nothing to offer you, Ash, but I fucking want to kiss you right now."

Her lips skimmed across mine and my dick shot to attention. "Kiss me."

"My life is a shit show." I gave her one last warning.

"I'm not asking you to marry me, Jace. I'm asking you to kiss me."

That was all it took. My mouth crashed into hers and I fucking loved the little gasp that escaped her mouth when I actually did it. Her lips parted, inviting me in. My tongue found hers, hungry and needy, and searching for more. This girl was like a lifeline I didn't even know I needed.

My hand tangled into her silky hair, and I lifted her, settling her on my lap so she was straddling me. I took the kiss deeper, and she met me every step of the way. Her hips started moving, as she ground against my erection as it strained behind the zipper on my jeans. I'd kissed plenty of women in my life, but this kiss—nothing had ever compared.

She moaned into my mouth, as she found her rhythm. It was the most erotic thing I'd ever experienced and probably the most selfish thing I'd ever done, but I couldn't stop it if I wanted to.

Faster.

Needier.

She ground up against my throbbing cock and I wanted her so bad I thought I'd lose my fucking mind.

"Please don't stop," she whispered against my mouth as her head fell back and my lips found her neck. She bucked against me with a need I recognized because I felt it too.

Both of my hands gripped her hips as I tugged her even closer, moving her up and down in perfect rhythm as her eyes fell closed and she let herself go. The friction of my jeans rubbing against all her sweetness had my dick ready to explode like a fucking teenage boy who couldn't handle himself.

"Jace," she cried out, and my mouth found hers to keep her from waking the girls. I kissed her hard as she rode out every last bit of pleasure.

I'd never seen anything hotter.

Sexier.

She pulled back to look at me, her eyes wild as they searched mine in the little bit of moonlight coming through my windows. Her breaths were still out of control, hair wild, and I stroked her cheek as I gave her a minute to process what had just happened.

"Um. Wow." She chuckled. "Sorry about that."

"Don't ever be fucking sorry for letting yourself go with me," I said as I nipped at her bottom lip.

"I've never orgasmed while making out with someone." She shook her head, and her cheeks were flush. She looked fucking gorgeous.

"Well, then you've been with the wrong guys." I shouldn't have said it. Because I was most definitely not the right guy. But I knew what she wanted. What she needed. And I could damn well make her body sing if she wanted me to.

"What if the right guy doesn't want me?" she asked as she searched my gaze and my need to flip her onto this bed and take things further was strong, but I put my hands on each side of her face instead.

"There isn't a fucking man on this planet that doesn't want you, Sunshine. I'm sure you can tell how badly I want you right now." I shifted just enough to let her feel how hard I was beneath her.

"You're wrong about me, you know that?" She kissed me once more, hard and fast before climbing off my lap. "I don't give up that easily. This isn't just an attraction for me."

"What is it then?"

She held on to my hand as she looked down at me. "It's everything. But if I'm the only one that sees it, there isn't much I can do about it. Text me and let me know what time you need me here in the morning for Hadley."

And just like that, she walked out of my bedroom and down the stairs.

Served me fucking right.

I lay back on my bed and groaned before internally cursing myself for going there with her.

Because now that I'd had a taste of her—anything less would never be enough.

Ashlan acted completely normal when she arrived this morning at the house. The girl just continually showed up for me. I'd never had a relationship like this. And it wasn't even an actual relationship. We were friends. She worked for me. We'd had one moment of weakness and made out like horny teens. The irony was not lost on me that the most mature relationship I'd had to date with a woman was with the one who was almost a decade younger than me.

Clearly, age didn't mean shit.

Hell, maybe I was just scared to actually let myself be happy, because it had been so long since I had been. I mean, sure, my girls made me happy. But this was different. I struggled with giving myself the permission to put my guard down. To count on someone.

To love someone.

But I fucking loved Ashlan Thomas.

Again, what were the chances that the woman I loved would be the one I'd never even slept with? I couldn't even imagine what would happen if I allowed myself to cross that line with her. To feel all the things that were right there calling out to me every time I was around her.

Just kissing her brought something out in me. Something feral. Something I didn't know how to stop.

I shook it off as I stepped off the elevator at Winston Hastings' office.

"Good morning. Can I help you?" the woman behind the front desk asked.

"I'm Jace King. I have an appointment with Mr. Hastings."

"Yes. He's expecting you. Follow me." She pushed to her feet and led me down the hallway.

The door was open, and Winston looked up just as we arrived.

"Thank you, Lydia. You can close the door and hold all my calls please," he said, as he pushed to his feet and motioned for me to come in. He extended his hand and guided me to the seat across from his desk. Last time I'd been in this office had been a happy day. Karla had walked into this office with Zee and hadn't retained a lawyer or put up any kind of fight to retain custody of the girls, agreeing to give me sole legal custody. She'd simply asked to relinquish all financial responsibility and barely looked at me before leaving.

It had been a win for me.

Today felt different. I hoped I was just being paranoid.

"So, she's back, huh? I hoped she'd just stay away, unless

she truly has her act together? I mean, that is always the hope too. That both parents can be in their children's lives." Winston sat in the chair behind his desk and clasped his hands together.

"I don't think she's got her act together. She was over at the house acting like a lunatic last night. The girls appeared scared. Neither ran to her. Claims she's got a new boyfriend who has a kid and now she wants to play the part of being a mom. She can't though, right?" I rested my elbows on my knees and let out a long breath.

"I'll be honest with you, Jace, this is not a black-and-white issue. It can get tricky with custody. A mother without custody rarely loses all rights to their children. She can file for joint custody if she proves to the court that she's turned her life around."

"What the fuck?" I groaned, running a hand through my hair. "She gave that up."

"Now, hold on. Don't go flying off your rocker just yet. It's not a guarantee, that's not what I'm saying. She hasn't filed anything or hired an attorney as far as I know. No one has reached out to me. I'm guessing this is just another Karla move. It most likely won't last. She wants to breeze into town and play mama in front of her new boyfriend. She doesn't have a permanent residence in Honey Mountain, right? As far as you know, she doesn't have employment or anything like that?"

"No. I think she just got here. I'm sure I would have heard about it if she'd been here long. She claimed they were looking at homes here, but I think she's probably full of shit. She has no family here and not really any friends that would actually help her out at this point."

"Okay. So, let's play this right. Let's be cooperative," he said, and he put his hands up as I started to protest. "Just hear me out. You having full legal custody means you make all decisions for the girls, and she agreed to that. But that does not mean that she doesn't have visitation rights. We don't want to make this ugly. Don't force her back against the wall, because if she decides to fight you, Jace, this could go bad fast. There are many variations of child custody laws, and in the state of California, the main focus is to allow both parents to be in the lives of their children if possible, pending there are no outside factors such as abuse or drugs and alcohol."

"She fucking abandoned her children. We haven't heard from her in a year and a half," I hissed as I pushed to my feet and paced around his office.

"I'm on your side. None of that will please the court. But what I'm saying is, if she makes an effort, if she decides to fight for them, the court will always consider it. So I advise playing nice with her. Her track record shows that she never sticks around for long. We can request to have a court-appointed chaperone present during visitation for now, and you can be there as well. It can be at a public place, a park or a restaurant, and someone will be there to make sure they're safe. Let her put on a show for a week or so, and then she'll hit the road again."

"Do I have a choice?" I asked as I sat back down.

"You always have a choice. You can take the gamble and refuse her visitation, but if that makes her angry and she decides to fight you for it, things could get tricky. Listen, the court will still frown upon her leaving. She abandoned her children in the eyes of the court. You have been their steady, their constant. You could win even if she fights you. But this is my advice. Keep it civil. We'll keep the visitation short. Throw her a bone, and hopefully she'll show off to her new boyfriend and then be gone in no time."

"And my girls just have to deal with this shit?"

"I know it's not fair, but I've been doing this for a long time, and I think if you show a little good faith, it will go a long way. Let's just see what she does."

"All right. I'll do what you think is best." I really didn't agree with this shit at all because it played with my girls' heads. Paisley was all-knowing and could sense things, so I needed to make sure the visitations were supervised by not only a chaperone but me as well.

"I think that's the move. I'll request Evelyn Richards as the court-appointed chaperone. She's the best, and she'll make sure the girls are in good hands. You can take them to the meeting point and stay nearby. I'll handle setting this up with Karla, and this might just be a one and done."

I agreed and sat by as he made the calls to both Karla and Evelyn Richards. A sick feeling settled in my stomach, but I hoped like hell he was right.

And she'd walk away just like she had before.

thirteen

. . .

Ashlan

IT WAS A QUIET MORNING. Paisley was at school, and I'd just put Hadley down for her nap. Normally I would be writing today as it was technically my day off, but I was a ball of nerves waiting for Jace to get back from his attorney's office. So, instead, I found myself scrolling through a Halloween catalog. The girls were trying to come up with ideas about what to be, and I said I would look at the pages that Paisley tabbed.

The door opened and I looked up to see Jace walk in. He looked so freaking good. He wore a white button-up that was completely wrinkled but managed to look sexy as hell with his faded jeans. His hair looked like he'd been tugging on it, per usual. His light blue eyes found mine, and he pulled his hand from behind his back and handed me a fistful of wildflowers.

I laughed. "What's this?"

"I picked them for you on my way home. It's a peace offering for last night. I didn't handle it right."

"You're mad that you kissed me?" I rolled my eyes.

"Nope. I'm mad that I stopped." He set the flowers on the

table and lifted me off the chair, before settling in the seat and holding me on his lap.

"What does that mean?" I asked as my hands came over his as they wrapped around me. He nuzzled his nose into the crook of my neck.

"I don't fucking have a clue. And with Karla back, things are messy. Winston thinks we should play nice and let her see the girls with a court-appointed chaperone present. He thinks she'll go away again, and we can just keep the peace."

I turned a little bit in his arms and looked at him. "Are you okay with that?"

"No. But he thinks if I force her hand, she could fight me. Apparently, me having sole legal custody does not mean that Karla can't have visitation. She could also decide to fight me for joint custody and make things very uncomfortable for everyone." He tucked my hair behind my ear. His calloused fingers grazing the skin on my neck sent goose bumps down my arms.

"How do you feel about that?" I ran my fingers through his hair.

"I don't have a choice. I was driving home thinking about what exactly I can control in my life. I'm ready to start living again. It's been so fucking long since I let myself do that, you know?"

"That's a good thing." I smiled.

"You're a good thing, Sunshine. I've been stupid to push you away. I talked to your dad about it."

My jaw fell open. "What? You did? What did he say?"

He snorted. "You sound so surprised."

"Well, I can't even get you to admit that you like me, so going to my dad seems like a leap."

"Of course I like you. I like you a lot. Probably too much." He cleared his throat. "I didn't go to him, he came to me. He sees it. Hell, I think everyone sees it."

"Sees what?"

"This…" He motioned his hand between us. "This connection. This pull."

"What did he say? Was he mad?"

"No. He just said that I shouldn't go there unless I was all in. It's fair. I get it. We're family friends, and if it's not the real deal, we shouldn't entertain it. If it's just an attraction, we need to walk away."

"And what did you say?" I asked as my heart raced with every word that left his mouth.

"I said I didn't think I was good enough. I still don't. But I don't know how to walk away from this. I don't fucking want to."

I bit down on my bottom lip and shook my head. "It's about time."

He barked out a laugh. "Sorry I made you wait."

"Well, you're old, right? I can't expect you to be quick."

He wrapped a hand behind my head and tangled his fingers in my hair, holding me a breath from his mouth. "Old, huh? I think that means I'm more experienced."

"Well, after that kiss, I can't argue with that."

"If you knew the things I want to do to you, Ash? The number of times I've thought of you," he whispered.

"Is that why you always talked about taking a shower?" I chuckled.

His tongue swiped out to wet his lips, and I squirmed on his lap because I needed his mouth on mine now.

"I thought about you everywhere." His mouth covered mine and I got lost in the moment. His tongue dipping in. Tasting and exploring and needing me as badly as I needed him.

I shifted so I was straddling him, and he pushed to his feet, taking me with him. My legs wrapped around his waist, and our mouths never lost contact. He moved up the stairs and into his room as he kicked the door closed before he dropped me on the bed.

"You sure you want to do this? This is your last chance to stop this before we cross the line," he said, his voice gruff as he settled above me, looking at me like he was trying to memorize every curve of my face.

"I want everything with you, Jace."

"Fuck. You're going to kill me, Sunshine," he whispered. "What time did you put Hadley down?"

"Just a few minutes before you got home."

He nodded as he sat back on his knees, one leg on each side of me. "That means we've only got about half an hour."

My eyes widened. "You need more time than that?"

"I plan to take my time with you. Taste every inch of you. Make you come on my fingers and my tongue and then my cock."

My jaw fell open at his words.

"What? Your hero doesn't talk dirty in your books?" He laughed as his fingers grazed my lips and then moved down my neck and over my tank top, settling between my boobs.

"No, but you're giving me a lot to work with. I like hearing what you want to do."

"Yeah? What do you want, Sunshine?"

"Just you. I've wanted you for a long time." My eyes watered because I was overcome with emotion. This was finally happening. There were many times I thought it would never happen.

"You're so fucking sweet. I don't want to do anything to rush you. We can take this as slow as you need."

"I'm tired of waiting." I tugged at his dress shirt and yanked him closer. "I want you."

His mouth crashed into mine, his knee moving my legs apart so he could settle between them. He ground all his hardness up against me and I writhed beneath him like a freaking cat in heat.

I'd never wanted anyone or anything more.

My fingers fumbled with the buttons on his shirt as he

kissed me senseless. He leaned back and gripped each side of his shirt and yanked it open, buttons flying all over the bed and the floor.

I laughed and shook my head. "Definitely putting that in the book."

He smiled and yanked the shirt from his arms and tossed it to the floor. "That little girl is going to wake up early just to fuck with me. I've had a bad case of blue balls for months. Since the day you started invading my thoughts."

"Well, we can't have that, can we? I think we'll have to save your dirty thoughts about all the ways you're going to make me cry out in pleasure and stick to the basics," I said as I waggled my brows. "Because I need you right now, Jace King."

He reached for the hem of my shirt, and I sat forward just enough for him to tug it over my head. His fingers skimmed over the white lace of my bra before he tugged the fabric down on one side and his mouth came over my hard peak.

Air rushed from my lungs as desire ached between my legs. His tongue teasing and tasting, and my back nearly arched off the bed. He reached behind me and unclasped my bra before giving the other side equal attention. "Do you know how many times I've thought about these perfect tits?"

"Tell me," I teased.

"Every day for months. Every night. Every shower. Every time I slipped into bed after you'd been here. Smelling you on my sheets and gripping my dick and imagining these perfect tits."

I closed my eyes because it was almost too much.

The need. The desire.

I'd had sex with two people before. It was fine. Nothing to write home about. I'd figured the good sex only lived on the pages of fiction in the romance books I read.

But Jace King was the real deal. Manly and sexy. An amazing father. Loyal and fiercely protective.

But the man was burning hot.

Like nothing I'd ever experienced.

"Please," I whispered. "She's going to wake up soon."

He pulled back, his heated gaze taking me in. "Fuck. Okay. But you need to know that we will only be jumping ahead a few steps because I need to be inside you now, and I will not be cockblocked by a toddler who wants lunch."

I giggled as he reached for the nightstand and grabbed a condom from the top drawer. He pushed back and slowly unsnapped my jean shorts and slipped them down my thighs. He stunned me when he leaned forward, and his mouth covered my lace panties and he kissed me there right over the lace before pulling back.

"I'll be back for more when we have more time."

I nodded as he slipped the lace down my legs. I lay there completely naked as I watched him shove his jeans and boxer briefs down his muscular body. His tongue slipped out to wet his lips, and I watched as he sheathed his large erection. His muscled chest and chiseled abs had my mouth going dry.

Damn.

Was I intimidated by his size? By his beauty? By his desire?

No. Because it was Jace. I knew we'd be perfect together.

He moved forward and settled between my legs. "When you walked in on me in the shower when you first started working here—fuck, I've thought about that moment a million times. How badly I wanted you back then and every day since. The way you looked at me then, the way you look at me now—I don't deserve it. But I'm going to fucking try hard not to mess this up."

I smiled. So sweet. "You couldn't mess it up if you tried."

"You sure about this?"

"I've never been more sure about anything," I whispered as he moved closer. His tip teased my entrance and my eyes closed with anticipation.

"No. Eyes on me. I want to see you."

My eyes flew open at his demand, and his hand found both of mine and pinned them above my head. Our fingers intertwined as he inched his way in slowly, his gaze never leaving mine. Watching me to make sure he wasn't hurting me.

"You okay?" he whispered.

"Yes. Don't stop."

"I'm never going to stop, Sunshine," he said, as his mouth covered mine and he filled me completely. I gasped into his mouth.

Both pleasure and pain.

The best kind of pain. His hand still holding both of my hands above my head as he pulled back and started to move.

"So fucking beautiful," he whispered. "I'm fucking crazy about you."

I couldn't find words, as the sensation was so great. I couldn't think straight. My back arched as my hips moved with his.

Perfectly synced, just as I knew we'd be.

"I'm crazy about you," I finally said, as my body heated in a way I'd never experienced.

He chuckled. "That's it, baby. I'm going to make you feel so fucking good."

He already was. My entire body tingled with anticipation. We moved like this for what felt like forever. My gaze never leaving his. His mouth came over mine, just as his hand moved between us. He kissed me softer this time, his tongue moving in and out slowly, and I was so turned on I couldn't see straight.

"Jace," I whispered, as his hand found my most sensitive spot, touching me exactly where I needed him. He moved faster, following my lead. I was panting and gasping.

"Come for me, Sunshine," he whispered against my ear, and I exploded.

Bursts of light and heated flames erupted behind my eyes as my body quaked with need. I continued to buck against him, and he moved again.

Once.

Twice.

And he went right over the edge with me. Calling out my name, as our bodies slapped together, riding out every last bit of pleasure.

I'd never felt anything remotely close to this.

And I never wanted it to end.

He fell forward, letting my hands go as he braced himself so he wouldn't crush me. He rolled onto his side and pulled me with him.

"You okay?" he asked as he tipped my chin up to meet his gaze.

"I've never been better."

"Don't fucking bite down on that bottom lip, Sunshine. I'm already hard again." He pulled out and moved to the bathroom to dispose of the condom.

He came back to bed and climbed in next to me. His fingers ran down my back and I settled against his chest.

"That was amazing," I whispered. "It's never been like that for me."

He wrapped his arms around me tighter. "Trust me when I tell you, it's never been like that for me either. Not even fucking close."

"Wuvie?" Hadley called out from her room. The girl always took a minute to wake up, but she'd let me know she was starting the process. I startled and jumped up, rushing to the bathroom. Jace chuckled behind me and made his way in, carrying my clothes.

"This is fucking torture. I just got these off of you, and now you're going to put them back on."

"You can take them off again real soon," I teased as I

cleaned myself up before pulling on my panties and bra as he watched.

He groaned before slipping his clothes back on, but he went to his dresser for a T-shirt seeing as he'd destroyed his dress shirt in the heat of the moment.

"I'm going out first. You stay in here," I said as I hurried past him, but he grabbed my hand and tugged me back.

He backed me up against the dresser. "Am I your dirty little secret?"

I laughed. "You're dirty, that's for sure."

He nipped at my bottom lip, and I tugged him closer. I wanted more.

How was that possible?

"She's three. She just learned to poop on the potty. She's not analyzing us." He caressed my cheek.

"Well, we need to sit down and discuss how we're going to handle this." I shrugged. "Paisley's old enough to understand."

He smiled and shook his head. "Fucking adorable. You want to make it official, baby?"

My head fell back, and his lips found my neck. "Yes."

"Wuvie?" Hadley called out again, and I pushed Jace back and hurried for the door.

"Wait five minutes. I'm going to make her lunch."

He lifted his chin and winked. I fanned my face with my hand as I hurried to Hadley's room. She was sitting up in her bed, her two little buns we'd put in earlier were barely hanging on, with one down by her ear and the other almost completely out of the elastic. She held out her arms and I scooped her up and carried her downstairs. "Are you hungry?"

"Wunch?"

"Yep. That's a new one for you." I set her in her chair and bent down and opened my mouth so she could see my tongue, and I pressed it to the back of my top teeth and slowly rolled the L sound for her. "Lllllunch."

"Wuuuuunch."

I pointed to my tongue and showed her again. We'd been working on it every day. I had a lot of speech delays as a kid, so I was empathetic to the importance of being understood. I wanted to help her with it.

I turned to see the wildflowers that Jace gave me sitting on the table and I picked them up and put them in a small vase. My stomach fluttered with thoughts of what had just happened.

I covered my mouth with my hand and closed my eyes as I thought about the way he'd touched me. The way he'd made me feel.

A hand covered my bottom and I startled when his lips grazed my ear. "You thinking about what we just did?"

"Daddy," Hadley called out, and I slapped his hand off of my ass and gave him a look that was a reminder that we hadn't decided how to handle this just yet.

He chuckled and kissed my cheek before moving toward his daughter and scooping her into his arms.

I just watched him.

I was completely and hopelessly in love with this man.

fourteen

. . .

Jace

I SAT on the park bench watching Evelyn Richards push Hadley on the swing while Paisley kept looking over at me. I was only about twenty feet away, and it pissed me off that I had to even allow this. Karla came walking up with a dude that was not much taller than her and not at all what I expected. He was wearing a collared shirt and dress pants and looked like a clean-cut guy. There was a boy walking beside him, but he looked a couple years older than my girls. What the fuck was this? She brought her insta-family with her, and that's how she was going to spend time with her daughters?

Evelyn stood beside Paisley, who looked uncomfortable, and I nearly jumped off the bench. His kid looked to be around ten years old, and I didn't know what the fuck was going on.

Evelyn appeared to be lecturing Karla, because her shoulders were squared, and she didn't look pleased. She pointed at me, and they all turned to look over. The dude held his hands up before leading the boy away.

In my direction.

What the actual fuck?

I was in no mood to meet and greet Karla's latest flavor of the week.

"Are you Jace?" he asked, and his kid smiled.

I pushed to my feet. "I am."

"Hey, I'm Calvin. This is my son, Dawson." He extended his arm and I followed suit and forced a smile at his kid. I wasn't going to make a scene in front of the boy, but I had no desire to get to know the guy. My concern was my girls. I sat back down and watched as Paisley continued to ignore Karla. Hadley waddled her way over to Karla and though she seemed unsure, she was definitely more receptive. But keep in mind, the girl was still searching for her penis every day in the bathtub, so she wasn't the most aware of what was happening around her.

"Thanks for letting Karla have this time with the girls," he said as he sat down beside me on the bench. Temperatures were dropping as fall in Honey Mountain had arrived.

His son pulled a soccer ball out of the backpack that Calvin had been carrying and he moved a few feet away to kick the ball around.

I cleared my throat. "Yep. Not sure it's such a great idea, but I'm trying to keep the peace."

"That's kind of you. She's working hard to get her life back," he said, and the dude seemed far too nice to be running around with Karla.

"How long have you two been together?" I asked.

"Two months."

There it was. She was pretty damn good at putting on a show for a few months at a time. But after years with this woman, I'd never seen her stick to anything very long. Not when it came to saving her marriage. Not when it came to being a mother. So, I had my doubts.

"You share time with your son?" I asked.

He cleared his throat. "No. My wife, his mama, she passed away when he was only three."

Damn. I didn't see that coming. I certainly wasn't about to ask how or what happened, but I did feel bad for the guy.

"I'm sorry to hear that."

"Yeah, that's what I'm trying to tell Karla. Family is most important. Life is short. I encouraged her to get herself together and come talk to you. So, if you're angry, you can steer all that toward me." He smiled.

Fuck me. This guy was too much. How the hell did he fall into her web?

"Are you from around here? How'd you guys meet?"

"We live in San Francisco. Karla came to work for me about eight months ago." He held up his hands. "I know. Office romances are frowned upon, but we just clicked. She'd just gotten out of a relationship with Zee, and she was a bit of a mess. It was just a friendship between us at first, and then it turned into something more a few months ago." He smiled again.

"What do you do for a living?"

"My family owns Trident Market," he said, and I glanced over to see his discomfort with what he'd shared.

"The largest grocery store chain on the West Coast?"

"Yeah. My grandfather started it, and now me and my brother run all seventy-three stores."

Motherfucker.

The dude had money.

He could afford an attorney if he wanted one.

I was suddenly putting together the reason Karla was with him. She always had a motive.

"Impressive," I said, rubbing my hands together as I deciphered the information.

"Karla tells me you're a firefighter. That's much more admirable work." He shrugged. "Listen, Jace, I've been a single father for a long time. I know how tough it is. We're not here to hurt you. Just trying to give her a chance to get her life back."

I let out a long breath that I hadn't even realized I'd been holding in.

"What was she doing at your grocery stores?"

"She was just a checkout girl when she started, but she stopped drinking and is a manager of one of the branches in the city now."

"I'm glad to hear she stopped drinking." But the erratic behavior I saw the other night in my house was not supportive of that.

"Yeah, Zee had her messed up in a lot of stuff when I met her. But she's really worked hard to turn things around."

I doubted that was true, but a part of me would be happy for her if it was. Hell, I hated that my girls didn't know their mother. The way she'd behaved, it had always been for the better. But if she was really turning her life around, and she wanted to see them a few times a year, that might not be the end of the world. There was a lot of hurt to heal still as far as Paisley was concerned, and I'm sure there was a lot of underlying abandonment issues for Hadley as well, but if Karla was willing to do the work, I wouldn't stand in her way.

"She does have a pattern of blaming everyone around her for what goes wrong in her life. I'm not saying that Zee was a stand-up guy. I didn't know him at all, and I heard he was a pretty bad dude. But she's the one who happily gave *me* legal custody. She's the one who left her babies and never checked on them in a year and a half. Would you be okay with someone doing that to your son?"

He looked up at me and I saw the empathy there. This guy was not a bullshitter. He was a good guy. There was no denying it. "I would be upset too, Jace. She'll have to work hard if she wants forgiveness from all three of you."

"How long are you guys staying in town?"

"It sort of depends on how things go, I guess. Karla wants to maybe look at a summer house here, you know, so she could see the girls sometimes."

My hands fisted at my sides. They'd been together for two months and he'd come here with her, and they were looking at houses now? Clearly, she had this guy wrapped around her finger. That scared the shit out of me. Not because he wasn't a good guy—but because she would not last long with this dude if she was still the girl that I knew all too well. She was using him for something, and money was at the top of her list most of the time. It used to get beat out by alcohol and drugs, at least that's what I learned after she'd left, and I'd realized she'd drained most of our savings account on her addiction. But he had the financial resources to take this as far as he wanted. Would he hire her an attorney? A sick feeling resided in my stomach. She'd found her meal ticket, and he had the resources to complicate things.

"You sure she's not drinking or doing anything else?"

"She spends most of her time with us. Dawson likes her. And she's never had a drink in front of me."

That did not answer my question.

He had no idea who he was dealing with.

Or maybe I was just a jaded asshole who didn't believe people like Karla could change.

Evelyn walked my way with Paisley's hand in hers and Karla pushed Hadley in her stroller. I was thankful for the chaperone right now because I would've lost my shit long before. Paisley let Evelyn's hand go when she saw me, and she started running my way. "Daddy."

She ran right into my arms, and I scooped her up. She didn't do that a lot anymore, and I knew it was because she was upset.

"You're all right, Buttercup."

Karla smiled at Calvin and then gave me one of her typical sneers. "Thanks for this, Jace."

I nodded and glanced at Evelyn for direction.

"All right. That's enough for today. If you want to discuss

anything further, you'll have to reach out to Mr. Hastings." She handed Karla a business card.

"I don't know why we have to make this so formal. Can't we just work this out between the two of us?" she asked.

Paisley buried her face in the crook of my neck, and I felt her tears on my skin. "No. Not this time."

"You're such an—" she hissed just as Calvin interrupted.

"Come on, sweetheart. Don't let your temper control you. This was kind of Jace to agree to this today. And it was nice to meet you." He extended his hand to me, and I took it once again.

I wanted to warn him. He was clearly blinded to who she was. But she wasn't fooling me.

"You're right, baby. My bad. It was great to see you, Paisley." She patted the back of my little girl's head and then leaned over the stroller to kiss Hadley goodbye. "You need to get this one talking, Jace. She's far too old to be like this."

Yeah, don't take any accountability for all the shit you've put these little girls through. Just keep pointing the finger. She hadn't changed at all.

Calvin motioned for her to walk with him, and they headed toward the parking lot. Evelyn glanced over her shoulder and waited for them to get all the way to their car before she spoke.

"All right. I think you've got some tired little girls." She smiled. "Shall we walk them to your car and then we can chat for a minute."

"Of course." I patted Paisley on the back. "You okay?"

She pushed back and swiped at her cheeks and glanced around to make sure they were gone before wiggling to get down. "Yeah. I don't want to see her again." She reached for my hand.

Evelyn shot me a look when we got to the car.

"Let's get you two buckled and we can talk about it at home."

I shut the door and faced the woman who'd just observed their visit. "How was it?"

"I can't quite read her, Jace. She only talked about how rich her boyfriend was. How she was going to be looking at big houses here. She didn't really make much of an effort to talk to the girls, outside of offering Hadley a piece of chocolate, which she gladly took."

I snorted. "That one is far too easy."

"Paisley wasn't receptive. I think there's been a lot of damage there, and it's going to take time. I'm not sure I see her sticking around for that, if I'm basing it on my gut and experience."

"Yeah. Calvin's actually a decent guy. I'm not sure what he's doing with her."

"Well, let's just hope things die down. She didn't request another meeting. Maybe this is a one-and-done deal," Evelyn said.

"All right. Let Winston know I'll check in with him later. Thank you for doing this."

"You have real sweet girls, Jace. You're doing a great job." She smiled.

I held my hand up. "Thank you."

I climbed in the car and buckled up, meeting Paisley's gaze in my rearview mirror. "You okay?"

"Yeah. Can we go get lunch? I'm hungry."

"Sure," I said.

"Wuvie wunch. Wuvie wunch." Hadley clapped her hands together and smiled. The girl was so damn cute my chest squeezed.

"Can we call Ashlan and see if she wants to come with us?" Paisley asked.

Ashlan and I hadn't told Paisley yet about the fact that we were dating. We planned to sit down with her this weekend, but then Winston had called and set up the meeting with Karla for this morning. We'd been sneaking around this past week, and it had been fucking amazing. Every second with her. But we hadn't had much alone time between my shifts at the station, the girls, and searching for the next flip house with Niko while we waited for the Elm Street house to close. We'd received a full price offer on the property.

But Ashlan had been the one to turn my mood around this morning before I left for the park. She'd dropped off some muffins because she'd promised to braid Paisley's hair for her this morning, as she was nervous about the meeting. And she'd managed to make everything better when I'd pulled her into the bathroom while the girls were coloring and kissed her senseless.

Ashlan Thomas was everything that had been missing from our lives, and none of us could get enough now.

We hadn't had sex since the first time, and it's all I fucking thought about. We talked on the phone all night, with me alone in my bed and Ashlan just a few feet away in my guesthouse. It was torture in a way, and we needed to get this out in the open.

"I think that's a great idea." I called her quickly from the car phone, and she said she'd meet us at Honey Mountain Café in twenty minutes. I was taking Ashlan out tonight on our first official date, and my mom was keeping the girls overnight at her house. "You guys are good with going to Grammy and Pop's tonight?"

"Yes," Paisley said. "Pops said he'll get us donuts in the morning."

"Gram, Pop." Hadley clapped. She was talking more and more each day. Though they'd both been a bit traumatized by seeing their mother after all this time, especially Paisley—now that we had left the park, they seemed to relax, which was a relief.

"So, how did it go with your mama?" I asked, glancing in the rearview mirror, watching their reaction.

"Karla just talked about her new boyfriend and her new kid." Paisley shrugged and stared out the window.

Hadley reached over to pat her sister's arm as if she understood that she was upset but didn't have the words to communicate about it.

"Yeah. How do you feel about that?"

"I don't know them. And I haven't seen her in a long time. She didn't ask me about school. Or about Halloween."

"Well, it's been a long time and maybe she just didn't know where to start." I wanted to make the best of a shit situation. Karla had always been selfish, so this wasn't a surprise. But I could imagine for a six-year-old who hadn't seen her mama since she was four, this was a lot to absorb. I didn't like that my daughter had all this anger, nor that she had to deal with this at such a young age. But I couldn't take it away no matter how hard I tried, so I'd do my best to help her manage it.

"Ashlan and I have it down to two costumes." She changed the subject, and I didn't push back.

"Yeah. What are you thinking?" I pulled into the lot outside of the restaurant.

"I'm either going to be a teacher or a firefighter."

I put the car in park and our eyes locked in the rearview mirror. "That sounds great. Both are good choices. How about you, Sweet Pea?"

"Ruff, ruff," Hadley said before her tongue hung out of her mouth and she panted.

Ashlan had been taking Hadley over to the Wilson's farm in the mornings after they'd dropped Paisley at school over the last few weeks. She was convinced that Hadley was talking more because of the animals. She said my baby girl connected with them and that's where she was the most vocal. Never would have thought of that, but Ashlan had witnessed it firsthand. I'd agreed to go with them on my day off this week.

I'd talked to Jack and let him know that I was all in with his daughter, and he'd given me his blessing. He did tell me that if I ever hurt her, he would hunt me down and kill me slowly. Otherwise, we'd kept what was happening between us fairly quiet, but I was done with keeping it a secret. She deserved more.

We walked into the restaurant, and it looked like we'd just missed the lunch rush. Hadley and Paisley hurried over to Ashlan when they saw her standing by the hostess stand and rushed her for hugs. After she set them down, the hostess led us to a table.

"Hi," Ashlan said as her gaze locked with mine and she smiled.

"Hey, Sunshine." I tipped my chin up and winked.

The girls quickly took their seats, and Hadley announced that she wanted to sit in a normal chair and was done with the high chair. I didn't fight her, and Ashlan took the seat beside me, and I found her hand beneath the table. The server came over to take our lunch orders before walking away.

"How was the park?" she asked, and her attention was directed at Paisley who was definitely more distracted than normal today.

"It wasn't fun."

"Ah, I see. I'm sure it's hard because it's been a long time. But the good news is that your mama is trying, right?" she pressed. The girl was all goodness. Most people had nothing nice to say about Karla anymore, but Ashlan was still trying to help mend the relationship.

"I guess. She has a new kid and we saw him." Paisley huffed.

Ashlan's head spun in my direction, and she didn't hide her confusion that he'd been at the park too.

"She's got a new boyfriend and he has a son. He's quite a bit older though."

"I didn't realize they'd be coming with her today. Were they nice?" Ashlan asked my daughter.

"I only met them for a minute because Miss Evelyn didn't think they should be at our playdate." Paisley smiled up at the server when she set her chicken fingers down in front of her. Ashlan helped Hadley manage her noodles from across the table.

"Her boyfriend Calvin is a nice enough guy, and Dawson seemed well-mannered." I raised a brow at Paisley.

"I don't want to talk about Karla anymore today," my daughter said, and I snorted. The girl did not mince words. She'd been that way since she'd started talking.

"Fine. How about this," I said as I reached for a few chips and popped them in my mouth. "I like Ashlan and she likes me."

Ashlan coughed over the sip of water she'd just taken and looked at me with wide eyes. I don't think she thought I'd follow through with doing this today because of all that was going on with Karla. But I was done letting that woman take anything more from us. This was happening. It took me a long time to get here, and I wasn't waiting anymore.

"I like Ashlan and I like you too," Paisley said over a laugh.

"This is different, Buttercup. I want to date her." Jeez. I felt like a teenage boy talking to my parents about a girl. I was the dad here. Why the fuck was I nervous?

Her eyes grew wide, and she looked between us. "Like boyfriend and girlfriend."

"Yep. Is that all right with you?"

I glanced over at Hadley who was stacking her noodles on top of one another and giggling at herself.

"Yeah. That's all right with me. Does that mean Ashlan can come over even more?"

"I hope so," I said, waggling my brows at the beautiful woman beside me.

"I do too. I'm so glad you're okay with it." Ashlan squeezed my hand beneath the table.

"You like Daddy, huh?" Paisley smiled, and Hadley started clapping.

"I wike Daddy," Hadley said.

"Yeah, I do too." Ashlan laughed and leaned her head against my shoulder as her cheeks flushed pink.

Just like that, we were finding our new normal.

And I was fucking happy about it.

fifteen

. . .

Ashlan

I WORE A YELLOW SUNDRESS, a jean jacket, and sandals. Dylan and Charlotte came over to help me get ready. Jace and I weren't doing things in the usual order, as we'd had a lot of hurdles we'd had to overcome to get here. But it was still our first date, and I couldn't wait to be alone with him. To be able to say that we were together.

The girls knew. My family knew. And that's all that mattered to me.

No more hiding my feelings.

"Where is he taking you?" Charlotte asked as she sat on my bed, reading her phone.

"I don't know. He said dinner and a surprise."

"Oh, I know what the surprise must be. Sounds like big daddy's coming out to play," Dylan said and we all burst out in laughter. She ran her fingers through my hair after she'd put in a few beach waves for me.

"Okay, enough big daddy talk." I glanced down at my phone to see the text from Jace. "He just dropped off the girls and he's on his way to pick me up."

"That's our cue. I need to head over to Jilly's. She wants me to help her go through some catalog for bridesmaids' dresses." Jilly had gotten engaged last weekend, and we were all so happy for her. She and Garrett had been together for a long time.

"I'm guessing Ledger Dane will be coming in town for that wedding." Dylan smirked, because we liked to give Charlotte a hard time about her secret crush on her best friend's older brother.

"I assume you're right, seeing as he's her brother and he's paying for the wedding." She smirked, knowing we were going to have a field day with this news.

"That's nice of him to pay for the wedding. I'm guessing you'll both be in the wedding party? How do you feel about that?" I bumped her with my shoulder as I reached for my purse on the table.

"It's no big deal. We're friends. Nothing more. Have you forgotten that I'm dating Lyle? Things are going well for us."

Dylan groaned. "Things are going well if you're into snooze fests. That guy talked my ear off about bugs. Black bugs. Brown bugs. Creepy crawlers. I mean, who wants to talk about that?"

Charlotte laughed. "He's an exterminator. It's his thing. Everyone has their thing."

"Well, he better have an impressive penis if all he talks about is bugs." Dylan snorted.

"Come on, dirty bird. Let's go get some pizza, I'm starving. Call us later and let us know how it went," Charlotte said as they made their way out the door.

"Better yet… don't call us. Just have fun with that hot man of yours," Dylan shouted as they made their way down the driveway.

Jace pulled in less than a minute later, and I stepped outside. He put the car in park and got out and made his way to me. "You look so fucking pretty."

He backed me up against the passenger door and kissed me breathless. My fingers tangled in his hair, and I moaned into his mouth. I couldn't stop thinking about the day we'd had sex, and I couldn't wait to do it again.

"Thank you," I said when he pulled back. His baby blues danced with pops of amber and gold from the last of the sun shining down on us.

"Let's go or we'll never get out of here." He helped me into the car and made his way around to the driver's seat.

"So where are we going, Mr. King?"

I couldn't wait to be alone with him.

"It's a surprise." He glanced over at me as we pulled out on the road.

"So, the girls seem okay with everything? Did Paisley say anything else?"

"You know how she is. She asked me five hundred fucking questions when I drove her to my parents' house." He pulled down a side street that led to the lake.

"What did she ask?"

"If I'd kissed you. If I'd held your hand. If I thought we'd get married someday. If you'd ever sleep over at the house when I was home. If I'd ever tried your spaghetti and meatballs." He barked out a laugh. "And those were just the first few."

"I'm glad she didn't ask me because I've thought about kissing you nonstop," I said, laughing because I could feel my cheeks heat.

"Yeah? You thinking about the way I touched you, Sunshine?" His voice was gruff, and his hand landed on my thigh.

"All day, every day," I admitted as I bit down on my bottom lip and looked out the window to avoid his heated gaze.

He pulled the fabric of my dress up my leg and his hand slipped beneath. My head whipped in his direction, and he smirked before putting his eyes back on the road.

"Me too. You want me to take the edge off?"

My breaths were coming fast as his fingers inched beneath the lace of my panties. Touching me exactly where I needed him.

"I'm certainly not going to stop you," I whispered as my head fell back from the sensation of his calloused fingers against my most sensitive area.

"You're so fucking sexy. I'm sorry I made you wait this long. I promise that won't happen again." The car came to a stop, and he turned to face me, his mouth crashing into mine as he slipped a finger inside me, and my hips started moving of their own volition. My hands were in his hair, and his tongue explored my mouth. He slipped another finger in and I started to see stars behind my eyes. The friction was too much. The sensation of his mouth. His fingers. His tongue.

He took his time, and it was a sweet kind of torture.

I tried to hold on, but I was too far gone.

"Jace," I said, as my head fell back.

"Come for me, baby." His lips grazed my ear and that's all it took. My body exploded. He continued working me until I rode out every last bit of pleasure.

He pulled his hand out and slipped his fingers in his mouth, smiling at me as he groaned.

"So fucking sweet."

"Holy shit," I said, because this man was so sexy, I was going to lose my mind.

"Off to a good start?" he asked as he caressed my cheek.

"Best date I've ever had, and we haven't even gotten out of the car." I chuckled as I glanced out at the field leading down to the water. "Where are we?"

"This is a place I've always come to think. To clear my head. It's the best hidden secret on Honey Mountain Lake." He climbed out of the car and came around to help me out.

"I don't think I've ever come to this side of the lake."

"Yeah. I found it when I was a teenager, and I've never brought anyone here," he said, reaching for my hand as we moved toward the water through the grass and brush. He walked backward with my hand in his as he watched me.

"I'm honored that I'm the first you've brought here."

"Never had any desire to share it with anyone before you." He came to a stop and there was a large blanket set up in the sand with a picnic basket sitting on top of it. There were four rocks set on each corner of the blanket to keep it in place, along with a blanket folded up on the side as well, which I imagined was for when it got colder tonight. He'd set up a little bonfire that wasn't going yet, but all it was missing were the flames. I nearly lost my breath as I took it in. There were wildflowers that he'd picked sitting beside the basket and a bottle of wine was lying there as well.

"This is amazing," I said. The water lapped against the shore, and the smell of pine and jasmine surrounded us. Honey Mountain Lake was the deepest blue water I'd ever seen in my life. "Thank you so much for bringing me here. When did you set all of this up?"

He nodded and we both dropped to sit on the blanket. "I snuck over here after I dropped the girls off." He opened a package of wipes and handed me one before washing his own hands as well.

"Nice manners. I like it," I teased.

He opened the basket and pulled out a charcuterie board covered in clear wrap and set it down. There was French bread and meats and cheeses. He opened the bottle of wine and poured us each a glass, and we sat there eating and drinking and laughing. He had nuts and chocolate and berries too.

"I had no idea you were such a romantic." I tucked my hair behind my ears as the breeze moved around us. Without saying a word, he reached for the blanket and wrapped it around me. The man just always knew what I needed. I didn't know how, but I wasn't questioning it.

"I'm not. But it's different with you. It always has been. Even if I didn't want to admit how I felt."

"It's different with you too," I said, leaning into him.

"I know I can't give you everything, Ash. But being with you, it's showed me that I want things for myself too."

"What kind of things?" I whispered.

"You. Being with you. I just don't want to drag you down with my shit. I don't know what's going to happen with Karla. It's out of my fucking control. Are you sure you want to go here with me? Because I swear to fucking god, if this is too much for you, I'll understand. Most days it's too much for me. My life is messy. I didn't think I'd ever make room for anyone, but I fucking can't walk away from this unless you want me to."

My heart ached and I moved closer, reaching for his hands. "I've known you a long time. This isn't an insta-love thing for me. This has been building for a while now. And being around you and the girls all the time—I love it. It's exactly where I want to be. Where I feel content. Messy doesn't scare me. Karla doesn't scare me."

A wicked smile spread across his face. "Insta-love? What's that?"

"You know. Where someone falls hard and fast. They jump in without thinking. But at the rate you've pushed me away over the past few months…" I said, raising my brow at him. "I had plenty of time to think about things. I live in your home half the week, your life is not a mystery to me. I'm in it. I want to stay in it."

"I don't know what I did to deserve you, Sunshine. But I'm so fucking grateful." He pulled me onto his lap and wrapped his arms around me. The sun was just going down and we sat there staring out at the water. It was the most intimate, romantic moment I'd ever shared with anyone. Baring our souls during the sunset. We sat there talking about our childhoods and my sisters and the firehouse. We talked about how hard it was for him when the girls were younger and Karla was checked out. The stress he lived with. He got up and started the fire before pulling me back to sit between his legs and wrapping his arms around me.

"That had to be lonely, huh?" I asked, tipping my head back and looking over my shoulder at him.

"I think I got used to it in a way. Felt like it was my cross to bear for the way Karla and I got together. There was no thought. I think when you're young, you don't look forward enough to realize that this person could be your wife or the mother of your children. In the moment, you just don't think. And I am not proud of that, because it hurt my babies."

I turned around so I could face him. "You couldn't predict that, Jace. Most people grow up when they have kids. She's selfish. And maybe she'll change now or someday, but that's not on you. You've stepped up for those girls and no one can take that away from you."

"You always see the good in people, don't you?" he asked, pushing the hair away from my face.

"I try, but I'm not blind to who people are. The only way Karla deserves a second chance with your girls is if she is truly trying to change her life. But the way she acted the other night when she came over—she didn't act like someone who has turned things around. But time will tell, right?"

"Yeah. I agree. It just really bothers me how upset Paisley was about seeing Karla after all this time. There must be some consideration in the court when the child is clearly afraid of her mother. Calvin said she hasn't had a drink in front of him in months, but the woman is as sneaky as they come, so that doesn't mean much to me. I think she's probably up to something, but we'll see."

"I hate that Paisley is upset by it too. She's so young to have to deal with this. But she's a strong little girl, Jace. And we'll be there to help her through it." I tilted my head and smiled. "One day at a time."

"If it gets to be too much, you just say when, okay?" he said, reminding me once again that I didn't need to stay. Did he not know how crazy in love I was with him? I wanted to tell him, but I didn't want to scare him away.

"It's not going to happen." I leaned my forehead against his. "You're the one who isn't used to making room in your life for anyone outside of the girls. Maybe you'll tire of me first."

He flipped me onto my back and hovered above me. The wind was blowing, the sun had just disappeared behind the mountains, and the water lapped against the shore in the distance. There couldn't be a more perfect setting or a more perfect man for me.

"Not going to happen, Sunshine. I wouldn't have gone here with you unless I was all in." His tongue swiped along his bottom lip, and I squeezed my thighs together in response. "I'm. All. In. And I'm a man of my word."

"Looks like we're both all in then." My words sounded breathy and full of need.

His mouth crashed into mine, and we stayed right there for hours. Laughing and talking and kissing under the stars.

The connection I felt to this man was indescribable.

I felt content and safe and loved all at the same time.

And that was a first for me.

sixteen

. . .

Jace

"YOU REALLY THINK a puppy is a good idea?" I groaned. We'd just dropped Paisley at school, and Ashlan had convinced me to come out to the Wilson's farm to see Hadley with the animals. She'd also mentioned that they had a new litter of pups and she thought that might be something the girls would like.

The thought of puppy training and cleaning up poop and being responsible for something else—it wasn't something I was dying to do. But I'd agreed to keep an open mind.

"I think you should just consider it." She smiled as I unbuckled Hadley and set her on her feet. My little munchkin took off running like this was her second home.

"How often do you bring her here?" I chuckled as I reached for Ashlan's hand. I'd never been a guy who was big on hand-holding or public displays of affection—but everything was different with this girl. I couldn't keep my hands off her, and it wasn't just about sex. Not by a long shot, even though the sex was fucking phenomenal. I just liked having her near. She'd started sleeping over, but she still snuck out before the girls woke up because she thought we should give them a little more time to adjust to everything.

"We come every day that I'm with her." She chuckled.

I glanced down at my phone to see a text from Winston. "Fuck. Karla must still be here because she just reached out and requested another meeting."

Ashlan glanced over at Hadley who was standing a few feet from us babbling to the goats like they were her best friends. She returned her attention to me. "Well, maybe she's getting ready to leave and wants to see them once more before she heads back to the city."

I nodded, but the sick feeling in my stomach knew it wasn't going to be so easy. If Karla wasn't sticking around, she would have already left. I returned my attention to my little girl. "Maybe. Why is she talking to the goats?"

Ashlan's head fell back in laughter. "This is what I'm telling you. She's so vocal here, Jace. She must just feel comfortable with them."

Hadley bent her knees and put her hands there, moving her face right in front of the goat. "Daddy and Wuvie." Then she pointed at me and smiled. I'll be damned if the goat didn't look completely entertained by her. He leaned forward and started sniffing the flowers on her sweater.

"No, Gigi." She pet the goat's head and stepped back.

"She named them?" I whispered.

"She did. She has names for all the animals here. But her favorite is the golden retriever who just had a litter of pups a few weeks ago. Her name is Goldy and Hadley calls her Dee Dee."

"Hey there, angel face." Mrs. Wilson came walking out of the barn and scooped up my daughter like they were old friends. "Hey, Ashlan. Hi, Jace. Good to see you out here. Your little girl sure loves the animals."

I nodded. "That's what I hear. Thank you for letting her come hang here all the time."

"No worries at all. The animals love having visitors, and I think Hadley King just might be their favorite. You all want to come in and meet the pups? They just got their shots, so I think they'd love some visitors."

"Yes, please. Hadley is dying to see the babies," Ashlan said as she smiled up at me.

"Why do I feel like I'm being set up?" I whispered against her ear, and she chuckled.

"We're just looking at them. I want you to see how cute she is with Goldy."

Hadley talked nonstop as she waved at the different animals as we entered the barn.

"Daddy see Dee Dee?"

"Can't wait, Sweet Pea." We stepped inside one of the stalls and six little pups played in the center while their mama slept in the corner. They were fucking cute, no doubt about it. White and gold and full of spunk.

Mrs. Wilson set Hadley down on the ground layered in a bit of hay and bent down to meet her gaze. "Their teeth are sharp, sweetie. So just be careful."

"Yep. We talked about that, right, Hadley? Baby teeth hurt."

"No bite," Hadley said as she pointed her finger at the pups and then squealed with excitement about seeing them. She bent down and they all rushed her. Her little head with the ponytail sitting on top fell back in a fit of giggles. She hugged them one at a time, and I'll be damned if they didn't seem to understand her direction. They took turns cuddling her and Ashlan was bent down on the hay, taking photos of her on her phone.

It struck me once again that Ashlan Thomas was what had been missing from my girls' lives. What had been missing from mine. The love I felt for this woman was something I'd never experienced.

It was strong and constant and intense.

It grew with each day.

Ashlan pushed to her feet and moved beside me as she beamed down at Hadley. I was overcome with emotion.

She'd brought so much light into our lives.

Into my life.

Sunshine.

"Thank you," I said as I kissed the top of her head.

"For what?"

"Everything." Wasn't that the fucking truth?

Most of the pups had tired out and dozed off on the floor around Hadley. But one puppy, in particular, sat on her lap looking up at her as she whispered to him over and over. "Wuv, Buddy."

And goddamn, if my chest didn't threaten to burst. Watching the way she soothed and loved on the little guy did something to me. Since Ashlan had come into our lives, we'd all been healing in a way. She'd helped Paisley adjust to school and now she was thriving. She'd found something that inspired Hadley and gave her joy, and now she was thriving too.

And me… there weren't enough words to describe how much she'd healed me.

"Daddy wuv Buddy?" she asked, looking up at me with those big brown eyes.

"Yeah. Daddy loves Buddy. Is that his name?"

She nodded and continued petting him, and Mrs. Wilson chuckled as she stepped up beside me.

"That one's not spoken for just yet, so let me know if you're interested." She winked and clapped me on the shoulder.

"I'll give you a call later." I wrapped an arm around Ashlan as we both watched Hadley sing the little guy to sleep.

Her eyes were growing tired as we'd spent most of the morning out here and she was ready for a nap. I scooped her up after she said goodbye, and we thanked Mrs. Wilson again on our way to the car. We were quiet on the short drive home because Hadley immediately fell asleep in her car seat, and I was still processing all the feelings that I had for Ashlan.

We both got out of the car and when I made my way around to her side of the car, I pressed a hand on each side of her sweet face as my gaze locked with hers.

"What are you thinking?" she asked as she studied me.

"I love you. I love you so fucking much."

She smiled. "I love you too, Jace King."

My mouth came down over hers and I kissed her. It wasn't the most romantic place to tell her that I loved her, but it was our place. We hadn't followed any rules so far—and that seemed to work just fine for us.

Halloween had been the best mix of perfection and shit show. Hadley had been a golden retriever because she wanted to look just like Buddy, her puppy that we were getting in two weeks. Yeah, I'd turned into a big pussy and agreed to get the dog. We'd taken Paisley out there to meet him, and she was crazy about him too. Ashlan had found a dog costume that was about as close to looking like Buddy as one could get. Paisley had dressed as a firefighter, which made my chest ache that she'd ever want to be anything like me—because the girl was already so much more. She looked cute as hell with fake soot on her cheeks and all the gear.

We'd taken them to just about every house in Honey Mountain, or at least it felt that way. Niko and Vivi had brought over Baby Bee and pushed her in the stroller. Ashlan had pulled Hadley in her little wagon, and Dylan and Charlotte had come by with water bottles filled with wine and laughed the entire time watching the girls run from door to door. Hawk and Everly were back in the city as hockey season was crazy busy now.

We'd just gotten the girls to sleep when Ashlan's phone rang, and she held her finger up to let me know she needed to take the call. She'd just finished her manuscript two weeks ago and had been sending out queries to agents, all while telling me every day what a long shot it was. I'd been reading her manuscript, and I'd never been much of a reader, and most definitely had never read a romance novel—but damn, if the girl didn't have a gift. Sure, it didn't hurt my ego that the dude was a rock star firefighter with the same build and eye color as me. He was a fucking stallion in the sack, and I'd teased the hell out of her about it. But the truth was—I couldn't put the damn thing down. The girl could write. This couple had overcome all sorts of crazy shit to find their way back to one another, and I'd teared up more times than I was willing to admit. So, I plopped down on the couch and pulled the book up on my phone because I wanted to see if Jade had told her mom to fuck off after she found out she'd hidden all the letters he'd written her over the years. I got choked up at the emotional speech as her character laid all her shit out there.

"Jace," Ashlan whispered and my head sprung up.

"This is good shit, baby. Fuck Maria Balson for doing that to them." I shook my head and realized her eyes were wet with emotion. I jumped to my feet, and she charged me. Lunging her body into mine and hugging me.

"That was Willow Cowles," she croaked.

"Who is Willow Cowles?"

"The agent that everyone wants to work with. The most unattainable. I wasn't even going to query her, but Dylan gave me the whole Rocky Balboa speech and I just went for it. And she loved it. She requested the full manuscript but told me she is going to sign me regardless. She sees big things in my future." Her words broke on a sob, and I pulled her into my arms.

"You're a fucking rock star, baby. I'm so proud of you."

"She said she thinks she has a publishing house that will want it. I'm just shocked."

"And she works on Halloween, so you know she's a fucking workhorse, right?" I said as I pulled back to see the tears streaming down her face before swiping them away with my thumbs.

"Yep. I'm so glad I was with you when I found out. You're my good luck charm, Jace King."

"You're mine, Sunshine." I wrapped her up in a hug and just held her there.

Wondering how the hell I existed before this girl came into my life.

The next two weeks were a blur, and Thanksgiving was just around the corner, as was the arrival of Buddy. He was all the girls were talking about these days. Hadley had expanded her vocabulary a lot over the past few weeks. She was talking about the dog and how he needed to go on walks, how he would probably miss his mama, how he was going to sleep with her, and she was starting to list all the things she wanted for Christmas. I'd never been so grateful for a long list of shit before—because it meant she was talking.

The excitement of the week was that we had all showed up at Honey Bee's Bakery yesterday to see our young Rook propose to Jada from the top of the fire truck. She'd gasped and cried and it was a beautiful fucking thing. Ashlan had brought Paisley and Hadley to the bakery so they would all be there to see it, and now it was all Paisley could talk about, which was a good thing seeing as she'd been very quiet since her last meeting with her mother.

Evelyn had met us at the park for another visit with Karla this past weekend, and neither of the girls spoke about it after. Calvin had been there, but he'd looked a little less happy than he'd been the last time I'd seen him. My guess was that Karla was starting to show her true colors, but maybe I was just pulling that out of my ass because she hadn't convinced me that anything had changed. Evelyn swore she smelled booze on her this last visit, and she'd gone quiet since—so I'd assumed they'd left town for now. Winston was documenting everything that Evelyn had shared, building a case against Karla if it came down to that in the future.

Ashlan had submitted her completed manuscript and her agent was already shopping it to different publishing houses. I didn't know much about the book world, but I'd sat in on a few calls with the infamous Willow Cowles and knew that this was a big deal. Apparently, it was really tough to break in as a debut author, but she'd done it.

Tonight I was taking her out for dinner to celebrate.

"Daddy, why can't we go with you guys to dinner? Ashlan likes us as much as she likes you," Paisley said, with her hands on her hips.

"Don't get all bossy on me. She's my girlfriend and I want to take her out. You get plenty of time with her when I'm at the firehouse and you don't see me whining about, do you?"

"Well, sometimes you get grumpy when you miss us." She crossed her arms over her chest.

"I always get grumpy when I miss you," I said, scooping her into my arms and rubbing my scruff on her neck.

She giggled and screamed, and Hadley came running across the hall with her stuffed pig in her hands. She tossed her pig on the bed and lunged toward me and I scooped her up as well. I dropped them both down on the bed and bent down.

"I want to talk to you about something."

"It's not about Buddy, right? We're still getting him?"

I rolled my eyes. "Of course. I gave you my word, didn't I?"

"You did. So, what do you want to talk to us about?" She raised a brow.

"I like daddy talk," Hadley said with a smile.

"Well, I wanted to see what you guys would think about Ashlan moving in here with us all the time. I know she stays with you when I'm gone, but I wondered how you'd feel about her staying here when I'm home?"

"Yes." Paisley fist-pumped the sky and Hadley mimicked her.

"Yeah? That would be all right with you?" I asked. "I was going to ask her tonight."

"Billy Graber says that I don't have a real mommy because I only live with you. So maybe Ashlan can be like a real mommy?"

That little fucker was on my last nerve.

"That kid sure does talk a lot, doesn't he? Listen, Karla is your mother. I know she's not perfect, and I know what she's done has been really hard on you girls, but she's still your mother. But Ashlan has definitely been there for you, and if that helps you feel like you've got a mama at home, I'm sure she'd be happy about it too."

"I want her to be here all the time, Daddy," Paisley whispered and reached for my hand.

"Wuvie home." Hadley leaned on her sister, and I ruffled the top of her head.

"Yeah. Me too. All right. Let's get you over to Grammy's house." I grabbed their bags and bundled them in their coats because it was getting cold outside, and the first snow was due any day. I dropped them off at my parents' house before heading to pick up Ashlan.

The thought of asking her to move in with me had me a little on edge. I didn't know if she was ready for all that. We spent all our time together when I wasn't working. I'd even set up a desk for her at the house so she could work over there as well.

When I got to her door, she was wearing a white turtleneck sweater and a pair of skinny jeans that hugged her slight curves in all the right places. She was stunning. Hair pulled back in some sort of elastic and a few pieces falling around her pretty face. I tugged her close to me and kissed her before pulling back to look at her.

"I missed you," she said with a smile.

"Yeah? I missed you too." I moved toward the car and opened the door for her.

When I got in the driver's side, I cranked up the heat as the temperature was dropping the minute the sun went down. Winter was definitely on the way. Ashlan talked about the shower they were going to throw for Everly, and then we talked a little bit about how it would work when we brought Buddy home.

"I'm not big on picking up dog shit," I admitted as I put the car in park.

"Oh, yeah? What are you big on?"

I hopped out of the car and helped her to her feet, before pressing her back against the passenger door. "I'm big on *you.*"

"Is that so?" She ran her fingers through my hair, and I ran the pad of my thumb over her bottom lip.

"That is so. In fact, there's something I wanted to talk to you about."

"You're not getting out of getting that puppy, Jace King."

I barked out a laugh. "Not trying to. Hell, I feel like Buddy's more popular in that house than I am, and he hasn't even moved in yet."

She smiled and nodded. "You may be right. So, what do you want to talk to me about?"

"Move in with me, Sunshine."

Her eyes widened and they looked like they were glossing over in the glow of the streetlight a few feet away. "You want me to live with you?"

"I do. I want you with me all the time."

"What do you think the girls will say?" she asked.

"I got two fist pumps and a lot of cheers. I already talked to them. They want you there all the time."

"Me too," she said as she wrapped her hands around my neck.

"Just like that?" I asked, fucking happy that she'd said yes.

"Just like that. Now kiss me, roomie."

She didn't have to ask me twice. My mouth was on hers. Her lips parting just like they always did for me. We'd fit together from the moment my lips first touched hers. And I'd craved her ever since. Wanting and needing in a way that had been so foreign to me at first, but I'd embraced this thing between us, and I was fucking thankful for her every day.

"What the actual fuck is this?" a voice shouted behind me, and I pulled back to see Karla standing there with Chelsea Peters, a girl she'd been on and off friends with throughout our marriage.

"This is none of your business," I hissed, pulling Ashlan against my side and wrapping an arm around her protectively.

"So, I have to hear my girls talk about the goddamn nanny on the two visits I got with them, and now I find out you're fucking her?"

"You better watch the way you speak to me and to my girlfriend," I warned.

I glanced down to see Ashlan glaring at my ex-wife, and even Chelsea looked a bit horrified by Karla's outburst.

"Come on, Karla. You've had a little too much to drink. Let's get you home." Figured as much all along.

"I thought you weren't drinking anymore? Does Calvin know about this?"

She let out a maniacal laugh and crossed her arms over her chest. "He understands that I like an occasional drink with friends. I don't drink in front of him or his son. He's going to marry me soon, Jace. So I'd watch yourself."

What the fuck did I need to watch myself for?

"You threatening me, Karla? You leave your girls and think you can stroll into town and see them twice and that gives you the right to judge me? You don't have a fucking clue who I am or who they are, and you only have yourself to blame for that."

"Fuck you, Jace. Those babies love me," she snarled. The woman was so twisted. She had no clue that her actions had consequences.

I turned around and pointed at her. "You have some fucking nerve. You're too selfish to even realize what you're missing out on."

"Come on, Jace. Don't even engage anymore with her," Ashlan said.

"And you shut the fuck up, little girl. You aren't involved in this. You're just the babysitter and apparently a whore as well."

My hands fisted and I was ready to tell her to go to hell, but Ashlan squared her shoulders and faced my ex-wife, remaining completely calm as she spoke. "I actually feel sorry for you. You have the most amazing family, but you're too blind to see it. But that's okay, it worked out well for me."

Damn. She didn't shout or cuss her out. She stood there as confident as ever, unfazed by the ugliness that had spewed from Karla's mouth as she faced her head-on.

Karla laughed. "This will last about fifteen minutes. Jace doesn't know how to love anyone but himself. Sure, you're probably impressed by his big dick—but even that will wear off."

My blood boiled, and I wanted to punch a wall, but Ashlan put her hand on my arm and turned me to face her. "Come on, baby. Let's go get dinner."

And just like that, we walked away, leaving an intoxicated Karla standing there begging for a fight.

She hadn't changed a bit.

seventeen

. . .

Ashlan

MY HANDS WERE SHAKING, but I did my best to get myself in check. I wouldn't give Karla the energy she was begging for. I'd known girls like her my entire life, and I'd made a point to avoid them. But a heaviness sat on my chest because this woman was Paisley and Hadley's mother. At least biologically. And if I wanted to be in their lives, which I very much wanted to be, I had to do what I could to keep the peace. And keep those two little angels unscathed.

Jace checked in at the hostess stand and we hadn't said a word since we'd stepped inside, as we were seated at a table in the back.

"I'm sorry about that," he said before clearing his throat. I could feel his discomfort the minute she'd approached.

"Don't apologize for something you have no control over."

He studied me before reaching across the table to take my hands in his. "She shouldn't have said that to you. She was definitely drunk. So much for making this huge effort to get her life back. To fight for the girls."

"Yeah, I could smell the booze on her. But I'm fine. Karla hates me because I have what she wishes she had." I shrugged. "She's looking for a fight, but she won't find one here."

"She's thirty-two fucking years old and acts like she's in elementary school. She's always fought dirty. When we were married, I would try not to engage, to walk away, but she'd just keep coming. I didn't even realize how bad it had gotten with her until she was gone, and I didn't have that stress surrounding me all the time. The woman is toxic. Even though doing it alone at first wasn't easy, it's been so much better for all three of us. She only seems to be getting worse. But when she doesn't get her way, she usually just ups the drama. I'm just hoping like hell she goes away. I don't want the girls exposed to this."

I nodded. "Yeah. They deserve a lot better than that. And so do you."

"So how about we don't give Karla any more of our time, and we focus on us."

"I like the sound of that," I said as he pulled his hands away when the server walked over to take our order.

Once she stepped away, he smiled. "You look fucking gorgeous."

"Thank you. You've got the whole hot fireman thing going yourself," I teased. "So, I wanted to run something by you. Paisley had asked me a bunch of questions about our family dinners that we have at my dad's on Sundays."

"What about them?" he asked as he tore off a piece of bread from the basket that was between us.

"Well, she asked if we could start doing them sometimes, and I was thinking, it might be fun to host Thanksgiving this year. The girls could help me cook. My sisters could come over and help, and everyone will bring stuff. But I think she'd really like that, and I would too."

He studied me for a long minute. "Look at you, bringing life back into our home. Sounds good to me. You think your dad will mind if we take it over this year? Now that you're moving in, it would be both of us hosting."

My stomach dipped at his words. Even though I spent all my time over at Jace's house, it meant something to me that he wanted me there full-time. Because that's exactly where I wanted to be.

"It would. I think he'd be just fine with it."

"Let's do it."

"I think I'm going to like living with you, Jace King," I said, waggling my brows.

"Because we're cooking a turkey together, or because you can have your way with me whenever you want?" His voice was gruff, and I squeezed my thighs in response.

"A little bit of both, I guess." I chuckled. "So, whenever I want, huh?"

"Whenever you want, baby. I'm all yours."

"Well, then, I guess we better eat quickly and get home."

"Check, please." He held his hand up, and I burst out laughing before leaning over the table to pull his arm down. "Fine. But we're definitely going to eat fast. I've got a taste for something sweet."

Holy hot fireman.

This man could get me going any time he wanted.

"So do I."

"Don't tease me, Sunshine. I'll have your ass thrown over my shoulder and out the door before the food gets here." His tongue slowly grazed along his bottom lip as his heated gaze held me captive from across the table.

"Don't threaten me with a good time," I teased, and a wide grin spread across his handsome face.

"You're all mine tonight. We don't even have to be quiet. And then I say we start moving your stuff in tomorrow."

My chest squeezed. I couldn't imagine a time in my life that I'd ever been happier.

"Let's do it. So, I have something important to tell you."

"Tell me." He studied me.

"Willow called right before you picked me up."

Our server arrived at our table and set down our food. Soft music moved through the dining room, and the smell of warm bread and cheese had my stomach growling. Jace ordered the sea bass, and I ordered a steak, but we'd agreed to share because I was torn between the two.

"What did she say?"

"She has a publisher who wants my book. I'm just completely blown away because I never in a million years thought this would happen with this book, nor did I expect it to happen this quickly."

"And you're just telling me now?" He laughed as he reached for my hand and brought it to his lips. "That's fucking amazing, baby."

"Well, I wanted to tell you over dinner, and then we ran into Karla, and you know… I was waiting for the perfect moment."

"This is the perfect moment. And I'm not surprised at all. I know it's a competitive industry, but I don't even fucking read, and I couldn't put it down."

I smiled. "Thank you. Anyway, they'd like to meet with me in person after the holidays."

"Where? In New York?"

I bit down on my bottom lip because I could barely contain my excitement. "Yeah. And I thought maybe you and the girls could go with me. What do you think about New Year's in New York? There's so much to do there and… I don't know. Would that be too much?"

"No. I think they'd love that. We can take them skating and to that famous toy store. Let me just clear my schedule with your dad and request the time off."

"Just like that, huh?" I teased, because he always said it to me.

"Just like that, Sunshine. I'm proud of you."

"Thank you. Do you think your family would come to your house for Thanksgiving too?"

"Our house." He raised a brow in challenge. "And yes, my mom would love to have a year where she doesn't have to cook, and you know that Travis and Hayden never miss a free meal. Obviously, we'll include all the guys from the firehouse that don't have a place to go."

I laughed. "All right. We've got a plan."

"We sure do. Eat up. I want to get you home." He reached over and set a piece of sea bass on my plate before cutting off a piece of steak.

We spent the next half an hour talking about where my things were going to fit in his house.

Our house.

"You can use the spare bedroom for your office. Hell, that room hasn't been used for anything in years. I can even build you custom bookshelves if you want."

Was there anything sexier than a man who wanted to build you shelves for all your books?

Not in my world.

The server stopped at the table to check on us and asked how everything was and we both said we'd really enjoyed our meals.

"Can I get you any dessert?" she asked.

"Nope. I've got dessert waiting for me at home." Jace winked at me, and I could feel my cheeks flush.

The waitress glanced over at me and smiled before handing him the bill.

We were out the door in no time, and I couldn't wait to get home.

To start living my life with the man that I loved and the two little girls that owned my heart.

We'd spent the next day moving all my things over to the house aside from the furniture, which we'd leave for now in the guesthouse. The following week was a blur as I'd been helping my sisters plan Everly's baby shower. Hawk and Everly had just found out that they were having a boy, and we were all thrilled. After growing up in a house full of girls, we were all looking forward to a little boy joining the family. We'd also been adjusting to our new addition, with little Buddy coming home two days ago. We hadn't heard a peep from Karla, and Jace was convinced she had gone back to the city and we wouldn't hear from her again for a while. I wasn't quite certain. Not after the way she'd raged the last time we saw her.

Dylan had just arrived to help me put together the favors for Everly's shower, while Hadley sat in the little play area we'd gated off for Buddy. She loved this puppy so much. His name was the first word she spoke when she woke up and her last word before she fell asleep at night. She talked up a storm while she sat in there playing with him just a few feet from where Dylan and I had set everything up on the large kitchen farm table. Jace was encouraging me to put my own touch on the home now that I'd moved in. But it already felt like home to me, so there wasn't much I'd change aside from more throw pillows and a few decorative touches and some family pictures.

"She sure loves that little furry thing, doesn't she?" Dylan asked as she scrunched her nose.

"He's the cutest puppy on the planet. How can you not find him adorable?"

"You really want to know?" She raised a brow in challenge.

"I really do."

"Well, for starters, when I picked him up to say hello, he bit my nipple," she said, shooting her best glare at Buddy, the eight-pound ball of fluff.

I snorted and shook my head. "He's a baby. He's just saying hi."

"By literally piercing my nipple? I haven't checked it yet, but I'm guessing I could put a hoop earring in there now. The damn thing nipped me so hard."

Hadley started giggling. "Wipple. Wipple. Wipple."

Dylan laughed and I shot her a look. "Thanks for that. Trust me… *your girls* will be just fine."

"Just saying. Teach that boy some manners."

We continued stuffing the hockey sticks with candy as the baby shower was a hockey theme. We found these favors with a paper blade on the bottom and clear plastic sticks that we filled with candy. The pucks were two round cookies that Vivi had made that we slipped into a clear bag, with a label that read: Hawky Pucks. The centerpieces were vintage skates that I'd found online, and Charlotte had been busy attaching pucks to the bottom so the skates would stand on their own. She'd tucked a mason jar inside each skate, and we would be filling those with fresh flowers. Vivian was hosting the party at her house, and we all had our jobs for the big event. We still had several weeks until the big day, but we were busy prepping things now because we knew with the holidays, life would get very busy for all of us.

I made the three of us lunch while Dylan and I kept busy with the favors. Thankfully Buddy had fallen asleep, and Hadley was yawning as she finished eating her noodles and cheese.

"You ready for bed, little bug?" I asked, and she held her little arms up in the air. I took her upstairs and cleaned up her hands and face before lying her down in bed.

"School, Wuvie?" she asked as her hand found my cheek. God, I loved this girl and her sister more than I'd ever thought possible.

"Yep. I talked to your daddy about it, and you'll be starting school soon." We had plans to take her over to see it next week. She'd been asking about going to school these past few weeks when we'd drop Paisley off in the morning. She was ready for the socialization, and Jace hoped it would help with her delayed speech as well. The plan was for her to start in January after the holidays.

"Buddy school?"

"No, honey. They won't let him come to school, but I will take care of him until you get home." I kissed her forehead. She'd only be going two and a half hours a day, three days a week in the beginning to allow her to get adjusted. I felt an odd pang of sadness about losing my days with her because I enjoyed that time we spent together. But I knew in my gut that it would be good for her, and it wasn't full-time, so we'd still have time to go out to the Wilson's barn a few days a week even after she started.

One thing that I struggled with was the fact that my boyfriend still insisted on paying me, but this definitely didn't feel like a job anymore. I loved the girls so much, so it was something we definitely disagreed about. But he didn't want me to go get another job, and after a long argument about me not feeling comfortable with him paying me, I'd agreed to keep things as is… for now.

"Wuv," she whispered, and her little eyes closed.

I covered her with her throw blanket and made my way back downstairs to find my sister sitting in the play area, lecturing a sleeping puppy. "No one likes a man to be that aggressive," she said as she stroked his soft fur.

My head fell back in laughter. "I knew you liked him."

"Aside from the piercing? Sure. He's fine." She climbed over the gate and joined me back at the table. "So, no word from Karla, huh? I wonder if it was the growl?"

I'd told my sisters what had happened that night at the steakhouse with her, and Dylan had somehow managed to run into her the following night at Beer Mountain when she was out with Charlotte. Apparently, Karla had made a snide comment about me loud enough for my sisters to hear, and that would never fly with them. Dylan had gotten in her face, they'd exchanged a few words, and Dylan had ended it with her infamous growl. The girl never backed down, and Karla had been escorted out of the bar as she'd thrown a glass at the bartender when he refused to serve her after the altercation.

"It must have been. She's obviously drinking again, and her boyfriend, Calvin, thought she'd stopped, so I'm not sure what's going on there. And it's weird that we've both seen her out and he wasn't with her. Jace said Calvin was actually a pretty nice guy."

"The poor guy has no clue who she is. She's unstable. Always has been. I know she's Paisley and Hadley's mom, and under normal circumstances, I'd be sending her all the girl power vibes to get better, but she's just hard to root for, you know? She's so selfish. I look at the way you are with those little girls, Ash, and that's how it should be. She's always put herself first. But it does worry me the way she reacted to you."

"Why?"

"Because she sounded jealous. She may not want Jace and the girls, but it sure as hell doesn't sound like she wants you to have them either. And that is a recipe for disaster."

My stomach twisted. "Well, let's just hope she's gone for a while. She doesn't have custody rights to the girls, so if she comes to town every year or two and just wants to see them at the park, we can live with that."

"Let's hope so. You guys have a good thing going." She bit off the end of one of the blue bubble gum cigars we had in a pile on the table. "I'm happy for you."

"Thanks. I can't remember a time I've ever been happier."

She cocked her head to the side and smiled. "Well, all the good lovin' is definitely helping, I'm sure."

I shook my head and chuckled. "You always have to go there, don't you?"

"Of course. Where else would I go?" She winked as she filled another bag with cookies.

"Charlie broke up with the bug guy. I think she couldn't handle one more conversation about creepy crawlers. The man was obsessed."

"His name is Lyle. And they did not break up because of his profession. They broke up because she didn't see a future with him."

"Because he's obsessed with insects, obviously." She rolled her eyes. "Of course, she told you all the deets. You definitely hold a lot of secrets in that head of yours, Ash."

My lips turned up in the corners. My sisters all called me *the vault* when we were growing up because no one could keep a secret better than me.

"I take them to the grave. You know that."

"Come on. Tell me the truth about her and Ledger Dane. Every time I bring up his name, her face flushes. I know she crushed hard on him back in the day. Did something happen between them? I've always thought it did."

"Everyone crushed on Ledger in high school. And Charlie would never do anything to hurt her friendship with Jilly. That's what I know." That was not all I knew, but it wasn't my story to tell. I was happy she'd confided in me. It wasn't that she didn't trust our sisters, it was that she wanted to get it off her chest and not have to keep talking about it after she did. Everly would have asked too many questions to count. Vivian would have thought it had to do with Ledger every time Charlotte was upset. And Dylan would have never let it go.

She was like a dog with a bone when it came to protecting her sisters, especially her twin, Charlotte.

"You're suspect, girl. I've always known you know more than you say. But, since you're the one I share my deepest secrets with, I can appreciate that you take them to the grave. You're who I'll come to if I ever commit murder."

I chucked a candy cigar at her and gasped. "Don't say

that."

"Why? Everly would definitely be the one to bust me out of the slammer. Vivian would be baking me treats and keeping me well fed behind bars. Charlotte would visit me every day and cry about how sad life was without me. And you'd be keeping the biggest secret of all. You're the vault." She clapped her hands together once and smiled. "We've all got our roles in life."

"You're the murderer?"

"I'm the protector. The muscle. The intimidator, if you will." She raised a brow, daring me to challenge her.

"You're also the one who got bit in the nipple by a tiny puppy and had a meltdown."

"Semantics. I can throw down with the best of them."

I spent the next hour laughing at her craziness. No one was more entertaining than Dylan Thomas. We finished making the favors and got them all packed up to take to Vivi's house.

"You're all so domestic now. Everly keeps hosting barbecues. Vivi's having the baby shower. You're hosting Thanksgiving. And me and Charlie just get to eat all the food and reap the benefits. *Hashtag winning*," Dylan sang out.

Just then the door flew open, and Jace walked in. "Hey, Dilly." He sauntered past her and pulled me to my feet. "I missed you, Sunshine."

Dylan broke out in a fit of laughter. "And that's my cue. You're nauseatingly sweet together, but also super hot… which makes me very uncomfortable. Love you."

She kissed my cheek and clapped Jace on the shoulder before walking out the door.

"Do you know how happy it makes me that I get to come home to you every day?" he whispered as his lips grazed mine.

"I do. Because I feel the same way."

No truer words had ever been spoken.

eighteen

. . .

Jace

ASHLAN AND PAISLEY were busy in the kitchen making pies, and Hadley and I had just gotten back from taking Buddy for a walk. The little dude was pretty awesome, considering he was still a pup. He was almost potty trained, and he slept through the night. But the best part of getting this puppy was what was happening with my little girl. Hadley was talking nonstop now. I no longer kept a list of her vocabulary because there were too many words to count. She talked nonstop about her new four-legged bestie. How many times he ate. How many times he pooped. How many times he kissed her a day. She was counting. She was talking. She was singing.

She was happy.

I knew in my gut it was a combination of everything. Ashlan coming into our lives the way that she did—there was no way to explain it, other than the fact that she'd brought life back into our home.

Happiness.

Consistency.

Fun.

Love.

And my girls were thriving because of it. Hell, I was thriving because of it. I couldn't remember a time that I'd felt this at peace in my life. There was no drama. I didn't come home wondering what disaster would be waiting for me. I didn't wonder if she'd come back every time she went somewhere. And don't even get me started about the sex.

Fucking phenomenal.

I couldn't get enough of this woman.

Falling asleep next to her. Waking up next to her. And all that happened after the girls went to sleep.

I still couldn't get enough.

I finally understood the way my father felt about my mother. Like she hung the moon. Because she did in his eyes.

And Ashlan Thomas hung the fucking moon.

I came up behind her, wrapped my arms around her middle, and kissed her neck as she turned into me.

"Ewww… Daddy, don't be gross in the kitchen," Paisley shouted, and Ashlan laughed.

"Yeah, Daddy." Ashlan waggled her brows, and I gave her a chaste kiss just as the back door flew open.

"Damn, it smells good. What time's dinner?" Hayden said as he scooped up Hadley, and Buddy started jumping on his leg and barking.

"Dinner's not for three hours. Why are you here so early?" I asked as Travis walked in next, holding a case of beer.

"We're hungry, douchedi—" Travis paused as he looked at my girls and quickly covered his ass. "Shmoopie-pie."

Paisley's head fell back in laughter and the corners of Ashlan's lips turned up.

"Yeah. I called Ash and she said she was making us some appetizers and we could watch the game." Hayden smirked. The cocky bastard.

I glanced over at my girlfriend, and she moved to the oven to pull out two pans full of pizza rolls and taquitos. My brothers had no shame. I was fairly certain they'd called her and convinced her to cook for them because they were sure coming around a lot more lately.

"She's already making you dinner, you jack… *potatoes,*" I said as I shot Paisley a look that dared her to challenge the fact that I'd corrected what would have come next normally, all while trying to sound annoyed with my brothers, but even I couldn't hide my smile. This house felt like a home now. I loved having my family come around. They'd always stayed away when Karla was here because you never knew which Karla you were going to get. The girls and I usually went to my parents' house on our own, as Karla wasn't a fan of my family. So us all being together—it was nice.

"I invited them. I thought you guys could watch the game before everyone gets here," she said.

"Yeah, jack potato." Travis snorted. "She invited us."

After she set the tray down on the counter, I tugged her close and whispered in her ear, "I love you."

I'd never been big on the sentiment, but saying it to Ashlan Thomas all day, every day, still didn't feel like enough.

This girl had healed me in ways I couldn't begin to wrap my head around.

She'd taken the broken and damaged pieces and made me whole again.

"I love you," she said, her gaze locking with mine.

No doubt.

Pure faith.

Faith in a man who didn't have a whole lot to offer her.

And like a greedy bastard, I was taking what she was offering.

"I think Paisley wants to talk to you before you go watch the game." Her grin spread clear across her face like she couldn't wait for what was coming next.

Paisley looked at her uncles and then back at me, as I let Ashlan go and leaned against the counter, crossing my feet at the ankle. My daughter looked to Ashlan again and started giggling.

"Billy Graber put flowers in my cubby yesterday and he wrote me this note." She handed me the piece of paper that read: *Do you want to be my girlfriend?* He gave her two choices, which were yes and maybe, and told her to check the box.

This little prick didn't offer her the option of saying no.

And don't even get me fucking started about the fact that she was only six years old.

I glanced over at Ashlan, and she used her hand to cover her mouth to keep from laughing.

Hayden grabbed the paper from me, and he and Travis burst out in laughter.

Was no one taking this shit seriously?

This little dude was barking up the wrong tree.

He'd been fucking with me since pre-K and I was done.

"I don't think this is funny at all," I said, sending my brothers a pointed look. "For starters, he gave you two choices, neither being no."

"Daddy," she groaned. "I'm six. I don't want a boyfriend. But me and Ash are trying to figure out how to let him down easy. We don't need to hurt his feelings."

I grasped my chest and shook my head, wondering how I had any part in creating someone so… good. I didn't give a fuck about Billy Graber's feelings at this point. He'd taunted my little girl about not having a mama, he'd gotten me put in timeout for swearing more times than I could count, and he'd told my daughter that he had a penis. I wouldn't mind her hurting his feelings enough that the kid stayed the fuck away from her. But at the same time, I was proud as hell that she took the time to consider how it would make someone feel to reject them.

"All right. So what do you want to do?"

"Well, I can see that you'd like to kick his little… can I say arse?" Travis paused to look at Paisley and she giggled. Of course, she gave her uncles a pass. "But I think beating up a six-year-old might be a bit much, even for you."

I rolled my eyes. "I'm not touching the dude. But he needs to know that no means no."

"Yes," Hayden said over his laughter. "Power to the woman. You've got a voice, little girl. Now go out there and use it."

Ashlan shook her head at all three of us. "He's six. Let's take it down a notch. Paisley actually likes him as a friend, and that's what she's going to tell him."

Paisley moved closer to Ashlan, seeking all that kindness and wisdom.

"Yes. I am going to tell him that I'm not allowed to date until I'm sixteen years old, but we can be friends." I'd told her that she couldn't date until she was sixteen when she'd asked about me and Ashlan dating and had wondered when she would be at an age where she could do that too.

"I just changed my mind. You tell that little pri—pretty boy, that it's twenty-five."

Ashlan snorted and handed me a platter of goodies. "You've got time to make that decision. I think it's a little soon to be throwing that out there. Go watch the game. We've got cooking to do."

I glanced at my daughter. "I'm proud of you for putting thought into it before you broke the little dude's heart. You're pure sweetness, Paisley King."

"I don't know where I get it from. It must be from Ashlan," she said dryly. The girl could deliver a one-liner like an adult. My brothers' laughter filled the kitchen as we made our way to the family room to watch the game.

I walked past the dog play area and saw Hadley sound asleep in there, curled up next to her puppy. My girlfriend had put a pillow and blanket in there for her this morning as Hadley wanted to be with Buddy and was feeling sleepy.

"Damn, dude. Your ass is getting a second chance," Travis

said as he sat down on the recliner, knowing damn well that was my favorite seat.

"A second chance at what?" I set the platter down on the table before dropping my ass on the couch.

"Life. Happiness. All of it, brother. You deserve it after the shit you've been through." Travis stared at the TV, avoiding my gaze because we didn't do sappy bullshit.

"Yeah. How'd you get so fucking lucky? She's sweet and gorgeous and smart. Great to your girls. And for whatever fucking reason, she seems to be crazy about you," Hayden said over a mouthful of taquito.

I snorted. "I don't have a fucking clue."

"Don't question it," he said. "Just don't fuck it up."

I nodded. That was the goal. And things had gone quiet with Karla, so all was peaceful in our household right now, and I was—happy.

"Hey, hey," Dylan said as she sauntered into the family room with a beer in her hand. "How are the King brothers today?"

"A lot better now." Hayden winked. The dude had swagger, no doubt about it. But Dylan Thomas was not easily wooed.

"Good one, Hayden." She chuckled and leaned over to grab a few taquitos and piled them on a plate.

"Looking good, Dilly," Travis tossed out as he waggled his brows at her.

"You boys are full of it today, aren't you?" She laughed. "So, Jace, I heard your baby girl got asked out already." She couldn't hide the smile. "I hear you took it very well."

"Oh, yeah. He's super mature about this stuff. He wanted to go kick the little dude's ass," Hayden said.

"It sounds like Paisley's got it all handled. You need not worry. You're raising strong girls." She winked before walking out of the room just as her father, Big Al, Gramps, Rusty, Tallboy, Samson, and Rook walked in.

"Good Christ. Did you come together on a bus?" I joked as I pushed to my feet to greet them.

"We thought we'd catch the game before we ate," Jack said as he cracked open a beer and took a seat on the oversized sectional.

My dad showed up just a few minutes later, and my mom was helping Ashlan in the kitchen.

Hadley came running over to me, her hair a mess from her nap and her arms up for a cuddle. "Daddy, hug me."

The guys laughed as I scooped my little angel into my arms. She showed me where Buddy had scratched her, and she proceeded to tell all of us about it. My father beamed, my gaze catching his, and he smiled. She was doing better.

Hell, we were all doing better.

We watched the game, and Niko showed up wearing some sort of backpack on his chest with little Bee asleep there, which led to everyone giving him a ton of shit.

"Dude, the next thing that's going to happen is you're going to have a dad bod and start wearing polo shirts," Rusty said over his laughter.

Gramps smacked him on the back of the head. "Hey. I like polo shirts, you little shit."

Hadley gasped and covered her mouth with her chubby little hands.

"Ah, shit. I mean poop. Sorry, Hadley."

She just giggled, and Hawk walked in. Ashlan hadn't thought Hawk and Everly would be here, with him having a game this weekend.

"You made it," I said, pushing to my feet and giving him one of those half bro hugs. We'd grown close over the past year. The dude was family.

"Yeah. My girl would have been devastated not to be here, so we made it work. Hell, I can play hockey on very little sleep. We'll head back to the city tomorrow night." He laughed. "So, what's the story on that new house? How about we go take a quick look tomorrow before I head back to the city?"

Hawk had asked about getting involved in the house flipping business I'd been doing with Niko. He wanted to throw in money for now, and after he retired, he would join us in the labor aspect. Niko had found the old Kelly estate on the foreclosure list. It was a massive project, but with the money Hawk was offering to throw in, we'd have the funds to do it right. We'd make a boatload of cash if we could flip it for what I thought we could.

"Let's do it."

He nodded. "Perfect. I saw the photos you sent online. It's going to be a ton of work, but the payoff will be massive."

"It'll definitely be our largest project to date, but I'm down for it," Niko said. We all held up our glasses. I was the only one having a beer, Niko and Hawk drinking water because Niko didn't drink and Hawk was in the middle of his season. We clinked them together and took a sip.

"If we're going to make this official, maybe we should come up with a name," Hawk said.

I laughed. The dude always thought of the big picture.

"I like that. How about three badass dudes renovating homes one at a time," Niko said with a laugh.

"Not bad. A little lengthy." I snorted.

"Honey Mountain Homes," Jack said as he pushed to his feet. "It's got a nice ring to it."

"I like three badass dudes renovating homes one at a time more, but I think Jack's name will fit better on a business card." Hawk slapped Jack on the back as he made his way to the kitchen.

"Done. Honey Mountain Homes it is." I chugged my beer, feeling good about it.

Paisley and Hadley sat on the family room floor playing with Buddy, and I just sat back and took it all in. Last year at this time, I'd been solo parenting. Karla had been gone for months, and I was at the Thomas' house for dinner feeling like I was drowning.

And today—I was living.

We were living.

And it felt damn good.

nineteen

. . .

Ashlan

I UNZIPPED Hadley when we got to Honey Bee's Bakery as the girl was completely covered in winter gear outside of her eyes and nose. She giggled when I pulled her coat off, and I kissed her little nose which was bright red. She wore a pink turtleneck sweater, jeans, and snow boots today, and she was quite possibly the cutest thing I'd ever seen. As was her sister, who we'd bundled up to take to school. Poor Mrs. Clandy had to get all of this gear on and off these little kids every time they went out to recess and came back inside. Christmas was only a week away, and the snow had taken over Honey Mountain. Jace and I had gotten the girls up on skis for the first time last weekend, and they'd loved it. He'd thought they were too young, but I'd assured him that my parents had gotten us up on that mountain shortly after we started walking. And skiing those slopes was my passion. I loved this time of year, aside from clearing the snow off my car.

"Coooold," Hadley said, and I took off my coat and pulled her close to me, rubbing her back and waiting for the warmth of the bakery to hit her.

There was a long line and Vivi and Jilly were working

hard to fill the orders. I pulled Hadley in my arms and made my way behind the counter.

"You need help?"

"Could you run upstairs and check on little Bee and see if she's up from her nap?" Vivi asked.

"Bee Bee." Hadley clapped her hands together.

"Of course." We made our way upstairs, and my niece was just starting to stir. I set Hadley down at the craft table and pulled out the crayons and paper that Vivi kept up here. Her first bakery had been burned to the ground by Niko's crazy father, who was now serving time in prison, as Vivi and Niko's niece Mabel had been trapped upstairs. But she'd found another bakery not too far from the original Honey Bee's and had gotten it up and running in no time. The kitchen was much larger as was the upstairs area which she used for storage and a play area for when little Bee got older. She kept all the crafts upstairs, and my girls loved coming here to play.

My girls.

They sure felt like they were mine. In every sense of the word. I loved them something fierce, and now that we were together every day, I'd grown very attached.

I knew their tired voices, their happy voices, and their sad voices. I loved the way they smelled like baby powder and sweetness. I'd grown comfortable with getting them ready and knowing what they liked to wear, without allowing them to leave the house in Halloween costumes. Hadley was a girly girl, and she liked wearing a lot of pink, rainbows, and anything that sparkled. Her brown hair with pops of gold was getting long, and she loved having me style it in all the fun ways. Paisley was more of a tomboy. She liked her clothing kind of neutral, nothing flashy, but she loved when I braided her hair in fancy styles. I loved the way they greeted me first thing in the morning, and the way they hugged me super tight before they fell asleep at night.

"Bee Bee awake?" Hadley asked as she hovered beside the Pack 'n Play and peeked over.

"Yes. Hi, sweet Bee." I scooped my niece up and hugged her against me. Everyone said that she looked like me as a baby, but that was only because Vivi and I looked so much alike. People always assumed we were the twins because Charlotte and Dilly looked nothing alike. I ran my fingers over her back, and she cooed.

She had just started crawling and we were all so excited to see her moving around. I kissed her cheek before setting her in her little saucer, and I made my way to the cupboard to get her some Cheerios. This little girl liked to eat as soon as she woke up. I set some of the cereal on the tray just as Vivi made her way upstairs.

"Awww… thank you for getting her up and giving her a snack. How'd you sleep, angel pie?" Vivi asked, and Hadley had her knees bent as she studied the little girl.

"Yummy," Hadley said.

Vivi and I laughed, and I poured a little bowl for Hadley and set her up at the table.

We let the girls hang out for a little bit before moving everything downstairs so we could look at wedding ideas for Jilly's special day. She'd asked me to come give my opinion. Even though she was Charlotte's bestie, we were all close. She'd asked me all sorts of questions about bridesmaids' dresses and centerpieces. I enjoyed designing and planning events, so I was happy to help.

We had little Bee set up in her saucer while Hadley sang to her and entertained her.

"Oh my gosh, these dresses are so gorgeous. This one is so elegant and would fit your color scheme perfectly," I said, pointing to the champagne-colored gown. She was having a June wedding and wanted to keep it very traditional in décor.

We spent the next hour eating cookies, drinking hot chocolate, and looking at floral arrangements, centerpieces, and cakes.

"It's funny, I've thought about my wedding for years, yet now that I'm actually getting married, I just don't know what I want."

"That's okay. You've got plenty of time." Vivi popped the rest of the cookie in her mouth as Jilly moved to her feet.

"I totally forgot. I've got to go meet Garrett to look at a few locations. We need to lock in a venue before we start decorating it, right?" She chuckled as she hurried to get her coat, hat, and mittens on.

"I can't wait to hear about the old lodge at Honey Mountain Lake that they renovated. I heard it's going to be amazing for summer weddings because the whole backside is windows, and all that natural light will flood the space." I said, biting the head off of a gingerbread man cookie.

"I'll send you photos. Love you both." She waved as she headed out into the blistering cold.

Hadley had moved to sit on my lap and sip her hot chocolate, and I looked down to see that she'd dozed off.

"This is going to be such a pretty wedding," I said as I stroked Hadley's hair and my sister studied me.

"Do you and Jace talk about getting married?"

My mouth fell open. "What? No. We're just living in the present, you know?"

She nodded. "I get that. But what do you want? Would you like to get married and have babies? I know that was always your plan, but I wondered how you felt about it now."

"I mean, of course, I'd love to get married someday. I'd like to have more children, as long as it wouldn't make the girls feel insecure at all."

"Well, keep in mind that lots of people have multiple children. This situation wouldn't be any different, would it?" she asked me, concern flooding her gaze.

"I don't know. I mean…" I looked down to make sure

Hadley was asleep before whispering the next sentence. "Their mama left, and that complicates things. I want to make sure they feel completely secure and loved, you know?"

A wide grin spread clear across her face. "You're so good for them."

"They're so good for me," I admitted, my voice cracking a bit as the words left my mouth. "I didn't even know what was missing from my life until these three entered it. So for now, I'm super happy."

"I'm glad, Ash. But it's a talk you should definitely be having with Jace."

I nodded. "Yeah, there's just been so much going on with me moving in and the whole Karla situation. We haven't talked much about the future."

I did want to get married someday. I was afraid to bring up the topic because I didn't know if it was something he'd ever entertain again.

And honestly, I didn't know if I was ready to have such a heavy conversation with Jace just yet. I wasn't in a hurry. We were happy. Things were really good.

Really, really good.

I knew it should have been something we discussed before moving in together, but we hadn't done anything right. We'd gone on our first date months after spending endless time together. We'd moved in together, even though I had already lived there half the time when he hadn't been home.

And I could be happy living with Jace and raising Paisley and Hadley with him for the rest of my life, if that was the most that he could give me.

He was enough.

They were enough.

"Hey, he might surprise you. We all see the way he looks at you."

"Oh, yeah? How's that?" I smirked.

"Like you're the only girl in the room. Like a man who's crazy in love."

I couldn't help but smile. "I feel the same way."

"I know you do. You have the biggest heart and when you love someone, you love them with all that you have. I think me, Dilly, Ev, and Charlie can attest to that. But it's okay to want things for yourself too."

I nodded. "I have everything I want right now."

My alarm went off on my phone and I quickly turned it off before moving to my feet. "All right. I've got to go pick up Paisley. It's her last day of school before winter break. We're going to decorate our tree tonight. I love you."

"Love you." She hugged me tight, with Hadley sound asleep in my arms between us.

I got out to my car and buckled her up, chuckling at the fact that she remained sound asleep even as the burst of cold hit us hard. I turned the heat on high and made my way to school to pick up Paisley. The girls were looking forward to decorating the tree, and so was I.

We had spaghetti, garlic bread, and salad for dinner before decorating the tree. I'd had some ornaments of my own, as my mother had bought us an ornament every year from the time I was born. There was the cheerleader ornament, my driver's license ornament, and the braces off ornament, and all the fun ones in between. The girls loved the sentiment and were thrilled that I'd bought them each one of their own to start our own tradition.

"Mine is a firefighter girl with my name on it," Paisley shouted as she hung it on the tree.

Jace helped Hadley remove hers from the bag and they chuckled when they saw the cute little girl with her dog that looked just like Buddy, and their names were painted on the front. They hung it on the tree together, and Hadley yawned.

"Is the last one for Daddy?" Paisley asked.

"Yep." I handed him the little bag and he raised a brow.

He pulled out the ornament and stared down at the house which was a construction site, and *Honey Mountain Homes* was written on the front. He cocked his head to the side. "You really are all sunshine, aren't you? Thank you, baby." He kissed my forehead and let Paisley hang it on the tree.

"Time for bed," Jace said, and we hurried the girls upstairs. They'd already had their baths, so they brushed their teeth and we tucked them in one at a time, just like we always did.

"This is going to be the best Christmas we've ever had." Paisley hugged me extra tight.

When Jace and I made our way downstairs, he insisted I sit by the tree while he made us each a cup of hot cocoa and brought some cookies over as well.

"How'd I get so lucky to find you?" he asked as he pulled me onto his lap.

I smiled and he studied me.

"Hey, something on your mind?"

"No, I'm fine." I shook my head, pushing thoughts of my conversation with Vivian away.

He used his thumb and finger to turn my chin, forcing me to meet his gaze. "Talk to me."

I looked off at the tree for a minute while I gathered myself. "I was just thinking about the future, you know? It's something we never talk about."

"Well, I see you in mine, if that's what you're asking. I can't imagine a future without you, Ashlan."

I nodded. "Me too."

His gaze locked with mine. The prettiest blue eyes I'd ever seen. Pops of gold and amber sparkled in the light from the tree. "But you want to know what that looks like."

How did he know me so well?

"I mean, not today. I'm twenty-three years old. I'm not in a hurry. I just want to know that it's a possibility someday."

He cleared his throat, tucking the hair behind my ear. "I'm thirty-two years old, and I never thought I'd be divorced and raising two kids at this age, but here I am. I've got to be honest when I tell you that I never thought I'd marry again. In fact, if you'd asked me six months ago, I would say it would never happen."

"I get it, Jace. I do. And I'm not here to pressure you, because what we have is enough if this is all that you can give me."

"So fucking sweet," he whispered as his lips grazed mine. "But since I met you, things have changed."

I nipped at his bottom lip, and he tugged me closer, shifting me so I was straddling him. "What's changed?"

"Well, Sunshine—I'd never say never when it comes to you. I see marriage in our future. I see a lot of things."

"That's all I needed to hear. I don't want to rush things. We've got forever to figure it out. I just wanted to make sure we're on the same page."

"We're on the same page." He tangled his hand in my hair and covered my mouth with his.

twenty

. . .

Jace

SUNSHINE ~ **We're on our way to drop Paisley off with your mom to do some Christmas shopping, and then Hadley and I are bundling up to head out to the Wilson's farm if you want to meet us there?**

Me ~ I'll meet you there, baby. I miss you.

Sunshine ~ Miss you more. Xx

I'd just finished a three-day shift, and I was fucking ready to get home to my girls. Niko and I were starting renovations on the house that we'd just bought with Hawk, and Honey Mountain Homes was off and running. I was going to take Ashlan over this afternoon to see it, as she was going to help us choose some of the finishes. She had an eye for design, and I was looking forward to getting her input.

"Hey, dude, there's some guy in a fancy suit here looking for you," Rusty said when I was on my way down for breakfast.

Jack's head shot up and his gaze locked with mine. Ashlan's father was more than just captain of this firehouse. He was one of my closest friends, and we were all family. He followed me down the hall to find Winston Hastings standing there in a three-piece suit looking at his phone.

"Winston?" I asked, surprised to see him there.

"Hey, Jace, hi Jack, good to see you." He cleared his throat. "I'm not here with great news and hoped we could go somewhere and talk."

My shoulders stiffened. I turned to Jack, who clapped me on the shoulder and said, "How about I sit in with you?"

I nodded. "Yeah. Thank you."

Jack led us to the back sitting area and motioned for Winston to take the leather chair, and he and I sat on the couch facing him. I could hear the guys eating in the kitchen, but they were definitely keeping their voices low because they'd seen us walk past them into this room.

"What's up?" I asked, and for whatever reason, a sick feeling settled in my stomach.

"Karla is back in the picture and it's not good, Jace."

"What does that mean?" I leaned forward, resting my elbows on my knees as I clasped my hands together.

"Well, it means you've got a fight on your hands. She wants custody of the girls. They are requesting joint custody, but the mention of full custody was also mentioned." He rubbed his temples, and all the air left my lungs.

"What the fuck? Can she do that?"

"She's going to give it a try. She's got a lot of money behind her."

"Calvin? He's funding this?" I hissed.

"Calvin is her husband. She's been busy since she left here. Apparently, she went back to the city with him, and they had a courthouse wedding. He's got a ton of money to put toward this, so we've got to strategize if you want to win this."

My mouth dropped open. How the fuck was I the one fighting for my girls when I'd been the one taking care of them? "If I want to win this? They've been with me since the day they were born. How is this even open for discussion? She hardly saw them when she was here. She walked away and has never looked back until now. Two visits for less than an hour, and now she wants to be a mom again?"

"I'm not saying it's right or it's fair, but I've been doing this a long time, Jace. She's angry and she's coming with both guns blazing, so my best advice is to fight like hell. I've seen kids get lost in the shuffle and end up with a parent who doesn't even want them, but doesn't like the idea of being told they can't have them."

"I did what you fucking said. I let her see them. The kids were shaken after those visits, you know that. They don't *want* to be with her. Why is she coming back now?"

"I stand by that decision because sometimes that's enough. I hoped she'd go away after that, but unfortunately, she's ready for a fight and she's now got the money to do it."

"Fuck," I shouted as I moved to my feet and paced the room. I couldn't lose Paisley and Hadley. They were my heart, my world, and they needed me. I'd die before I'd let her take my babies away from me. There was not a doubt in my mind, this was spite. Karla wasn't doing this because she wanted the girls, she was doing this because she wanted to hurt me. I think that'd been her motive from day one.

"What's his best plan of action, Winston?" Jack asked, keeping his tone calm, but I could tell by the way his jaw ticced when he spoke that he was holding back his anger.

"Karla's attorney, Carl Hubbard, is a well-known divorce attorney from San Francisco who specializes in custody cases. He rarely loses, Jace. So, you are going to have to make some changes, and you're not going to like it."

"I'll do whatever it takes." I moved to sit down beside Jack and faced my attorney.

"All right." Winston looked between Jack and me, and I didn't miss his discomfort. "Listen, this is not something I enjoy, but I've got to guide you the best I can if you want to win this."

"Understood," I said, shaking my head as if nothing he

could tell me would be a hurdle, because I'd run through fire for those girls.

"In the grievance, it mentions your 'much younger nanny who you are also sleeping with.'"

"Jesus," Jack growled. "She's going to pull all the punches, isn't she?"

"What? I'm not sleeping with my nanny. We're dating. She lives with me. Ashlan is my girlfriend."

Winston nodded. "I know that, and I adore Ashlan, so this is not personal. But it does not look good for you to be shacking up with a woman who is a decade younger than you, who you hired to care for your girls. It just doesn't, Jace."

My mouth gaped open.

Winston added, "You're paying her for nannying, right? So, even though you're dating, the fact is you're sleeping with your employee."

I didn't answer his question, he was right. And I was fucking angry. "You've got to be shitting me. We're in love. Hell, I'd marry her today if she was willing to."

"I don't recommend that either. It'll look suspicious if you run out and marry her right after they filed for custody. She beat you to the punch. She got married a month ago, and I think all of this was part of her plan to come back and wreak havoc."

"So what the fuck do I do?" I was back on my feet again, running my hands through my hair in frustration.

Winston shared a look with Jack and they both remained silent before Jack turned to me. "I'm guessing your best plan would be to end things with Ashlan. At least for now."

"No fucking way. Are you serious?" I looked between them, and my hands fisted at my side. "How long will this take?"

Winston let out a breath. "Weeks. Months. Sometimes years. I can't tell you that, Jace."

"No way. I'm not doing that to Ashlan. I love her. It's not an option."

"I understand that. And I can tell you that you've been raising those girls on your own, and the judge will look favorably at you for that. But I have a hunch Karla is going to paint you as the villain. Were you ever unfaithful to her? You need to be honest here because this is going to get dirty. I've seen Carl Hubbard in action. And with Calvin funding this, they aren't going to stop until they get what they want."

"I never cheated on her. We didn't have sex for the last year of our marriage, and I never strayed. I'm fairly certain she did. Hell, I know she did. She ran off with that dipshit Zee and never called to check on our kids."

"Okay, this is good. But dating a younger woman, when you're going to be scrutinized—it's my job to tell you that it's a bad idea." He shrugged. "Understand, not legally, nothing to do with legalities, but it's all about how the courts view things."

Fuck me.

My girls were everything to me, but so was Ashlan.

"I'm not going to destroy what I have with the only woman I've ever loved because Karla suddenly wants to be a mom. I can't do that. I need to keep my family together."

Winston glanced at Jack again, and it was as if they were speaking their own language without words.

"Jace, I know you're a loyal dude. The most loyal I've ever met. And you're an incredible father. But Winston has a point. You're going to need to fight like hell if you want to keep your girls." His voice cracked as if the emotion was just too much.

Hell, I felt it too.

My legs were shaking, and I was sick to my stomach.

I had to choose between my girls and the woman I loved?

How the fuck was that fair?

"I'll do whatever it takes, but I'm not walking away from

Ashlan. What would that say to her? That she wasn't worth it? That I wasn't willing to fight for her? That I didn't love her enough?"

Jack nodded and shrugged because it was a lose, lose situation.

"No. I'm going to fight Karla with everything I have. But I'm not turning my back on Ashlan. This could go on for years. I can't do that to her." I pushed to my feet. I needed air. I needed to punch a fucking wall. "There's so much wrong with Karla and this shit. I can prove she's not a fit mother no matter what the fuck Calvin says, he doesn't know the half of it." And he didn't. I wasn't going to lose my girls. Nor was I going to lose Ashlan.

"All right. Let's meet tomorrow morning and start strategizing. This is going to get costly, Jace."

"I've got money in savings, and I can mortgage the house if I need to." I leaned my head against the wall beside the couch and took a few breaths. I was in for the fight of my life, for something that I already had—that someone wanted to take from me.

Karla wanted to gut me. She wanted to cut out my heart and leave me with nothing. I'd given her everything she wanted. She hadn't paid a dime of child support. She hadn't called to check on them when Paisley lost her first tooth, or when Hadley started peeing in the potty. I'd been there. And now it meant nothing? This woman was mental, completely unstable—I think I had enough to prove that too.

"I'm sorry about this. I don't know if she even wants the kids or if she's just a spiteful person who is doing this to hurt you. Which, if we can prove that to be true, it'll help your case."

"Unfortunately, I think it's the latter." I pushed away from the wall and turned to face them. "Eight tomorrow morning at your office?"

"Yep. We've got a lot of work to do. She's going to assassinate your character, so we're going to have to do the same."

I nodded. "That should be easy."

I walked out of there and didn't say a word to any of the guys. I was still processing everything that he'd said. I couldn't fucking wrap my head around it.

Before I started the car, I sent Ashlan a text.

Me ~ Hey. I need to talk to you. Can we skip the barn and meet at home?

Sunshine ~ Of course. I'm on my way.

Just like that. No questions asked. This girl was my ride or die.

How could I not be hers?

When I pulled into the driveway, Ashlan had just pulled up.

"Hey, are you okay?" she asked as she jumped out of her car, concern filling her pretty, dark gaze.

"Yeah. I'll explain once we get inside."

"Hadley fell asleep. We can just carry her upstairs and get her coat and boots off." She smiled, touching my hand as I reached for the car door.

She knew something wasn't right.

Because she knew me.

And if I lost these girls, I'd never be okay.

I could survive a lot of shit, but not that.

No fucking way was some other dude going to raise my daughters.

Not fucking happening.

I carried Hadley upstairs, and Ashlan followed close behind and pulled off her boots and coat before kissing her forehead.

Hell, this was going to gut her too. She loved the girls fiercely. She'd been there for them through everything.

My hand found the small of her back as we made our way

back downstairs to the kitchen. She pulled off her white winter coat and dropped it on the chair. "What's going on?"

I sat down to face her and buried my face in my hands because now that I was here, sitting with the woman I loved, I felt everything.

Vulnerable.

Scared shitless.

Terrified.

"Jace, what's going on? You're scaring me."

"Karla has hired a lawyer and she's filed for custody. Joint custody, but seeing as she lives in another state, sole fucking custody was also mentioned. She wants the girls."

She jolted back as if I'd slapped her. "What? She can't do that. No judge is going to give them to her after what she's done."

"She married Calvin, so she's got the money behind her. They've hired some fancy-ass lawyer, and Winston said it's not good."

"How is that possible? She hasn't even been in their lives for over a year and a half. That's half of Hadley's time on this earth. She didn't care about their first day of school or the first time they started speaking. No." She jumped to her feet. "She can't do this."

Tears were streaming down her face, and she moved toward me, falling into my arms as I settled her on my lap.

"It sure as fuck doesn't seem right, does it?"

"No," she croaked. "I don't think any judge is going to think she deserves custody when she left them so easily. She didn't even spend time with them when she was here. And you were fair about letting her see them, and still—she didn't care. She doesn't ache for them, Jace." Her body quaked against mine and she clutched her chest.

"I know she doesn't. Maybe this is just a tactic to scare me? I don't fucking know. But she's not getting those babies."

"No. They'd be terrified to go with her. We can't let this happen. What did Winston say to do?"

I was an honest guy to the core, but there were times when withholding the truth was for the best, and this was one of them.

I wasn't leaving her, so there was no point even bringing that up.

It would devastate her.

"He said we're going to be in for the fight of our lives."

Ashlan pulled back and put her hands on each side of my face. "So we'll fight like hell. I'll be with you every step of the way."

I nodded. Things were going to get ugly, but I was ready for it. As long as I had my three girls—I could do anything.

twenty-one

. . .

Ashlan

WE'D SPENT the night watching Christmas movies with the girls. With Paisley being on winter break, it meant they could stay up a little later as we didn't need to get up and get her to school. Jace and I did not discuss what was happening with them, as Paisley would not handle it well and the stress would be a lot for a little girl to handle. Charlotte was coming over to babysit the girls for us tomorrow morning since I wanted to go with Jace to Winston Hastings' office for the meeting. This was going to be a fight, but we wouldn't back down for anything. I'd spent a few hours online googling everything I could find about custody battles, and there was no doubt this was going to get ugly. But Jace had the truth on his side. He'd been there for his girls from the start. She'd walked away. I had to believe that good came to good, and everyone would see the truth and make the right decision. After we tucked the girls in and read a few extra stories because I think we were both feeling a whole lot of emotion, which made it tough because they had no idea what was going on.

We made our way to our bedroom, and he closed the door

after I stepped in. He pushed me up against the door and kissed me hard.

My fingers tangled in his hair as my lips parted for him. I could feel the turmoil pouring from his body.

I pulled back, my hands on each of his cheeks, searching his gaze. "It's going to be okay, I promise."

"I don't want to think about it, Sunshine. I just want to feel good right now. I need you."

"I'm right here," I whispered, walking him back until his knees hit the edge of the mattress. I reached for the hem of his hoodie and pulled it over his head before tugging at the button of his jeans and shoving the denim down his legs, taking his boxer briefs at the same time. He sucked in a breath, and I held my arms up for him to pull my sweater over my head before shimmying out of my leggings. I pushed him back to sit on the edge of the bed and straddled him, as his hand came around my back and unsnapped my bra. His mouth covered one hard peak, and I moaned. I leaned forward, claiming his mouth as his fingers slipped beneath the lace of my panties.

He shifted them to the side and teased my most sensitive area as I gripped his erection and positioned myself above him.

I teased his tip as I nipped at his mouth.

"You teasing me tonight, baby?"

"Is this what you need?"

"You are what I need," he said, his voice gruff and full of need.

"I'm all yours. Always will be." I slid down slowly, taking him inch by inch as he claimed my mouth.

I gripped his shoulders and took control. Jace was always in control. But tonight, I knew what he needed. I rocked my hips slowly, as we both found our rhythm. Nothing had ever felt better. Our breaths were coming hard and fast, our lips fused together. Joining us in every way. I pulled back to look at him. Steely blue eyes locked with mine as I moved faster. Our gaze never losing contact. His hands found my hips, moving me up and down his erection in the most delicious way. This man made me feel everything. And I only wanted more.

"Jace," I groaned, and his hand came between us, knowing exactly what I needed.

Our bodies slapped against one another as the last bit of moonlight peeped through the curtains, allowing me to take him in.

Muscled shoulders, tanned skin, and chiseled abs.

He was tall and lean and strong.

The building need grew, and I couldn't hold on any longer. My nails dug into his shoulders as my teeth found my bottom lip.

"Let go, Sunshine."

That's exactly what I did. My head fell back, and sensation moved through me with a force. Lights burst behind my eyes, and pleasure racked my body. Jace continued to pump into me—once.

Twice.

And he followed me right over the edge the way I hoped he always would.

His hands moved up my back as we waited for our breaths to slow.

"I love you," he whispered against my ear.

"I love you."

And we just sat like that, holding one another and not saying a word. The heaviness of the day was there, but we wrapped ourselves around each other and I knew that we could get through anything together.

"Thanks for coming with me," Jace said as we took the elevator up to Winston Hastings' office.

"Of course. There's nowhere else I'd rather be." I looked up at him, our fingers intertwined.

"I'm hoping he's got a plan because I don't know what the fuck to even do. She's not in Honey Mountain, she's in San Francisco. Is she planning to have them spend time there? I just can't fathom them being away from me."

I nodded. My stomach had been upset all morning. The girls had no idea what was going on. Charlotte had come over this morning to stay with them, and she brought a whole bag of Christmas crafts to do with them. The entire town was festive with decorations, and wreaths hung from every light post that we passed on our way here. Everyone was cheerful and in the holiday spirit, but this heaviness hung like a dark cloud above us, and I knew Jace was struggling.

"You don't have to put on a brave face for me. I know you need to do it for the girls, but you don't need to do it for me."

"This is the kind of shit I never wanted to drag you into. We should be celebrating your book deal and getting excited for our trip to New York coming up." He scrubbed a hand down the back of his neck.

I took a minute to take him in. The man was rarely standing still, but he was impossible not to stare at. His defined jaw peppered in just a bit of scruff, full lips that knew how to please me any time I needed, and blue eyes that could see into my soul. Yet, he carried the weight of the world on his shoulders.

"We have celebrated my book deal. And we'll celebrate with the girls in New York. But right now—this is real life. And you don't have to do it alone. I'm here with you. I'm not going anywhere."

Something passed across his face. I couldn't read it.

Was he nervous?

But he nodded just as the doors opened. "Thank you, baby."

He led me to the front desk, and the woman there smiled and greeted us before moving to her feet. We followed her down the hallway, and Winston was waiting for us with the door open.

He moved around his desk and shook Jace's hand before shaking mine. He was older and had kind eyes. He looked a bit tired, but I imagined this job kept him plenty busy.

He motioned for us to take our seats, and the woman who'd brought us here disappeared behind the closed door.

"I need you to tell me what her chances are, Winston. Be straight with me. I need to know exactly what I'm up against," Jace said, leaning forward so his elbows rested on his knees.

Winston cleared his throat. "It's not going to be easy. As I told you yesterday, she's hired a guy who's known for winning these cases. She clearly did her homework and planned for this because she got married a few weeks ago, which shows that she's more stable now. In a solid relationship. She quit her job so she isn't working for him any longer, and she claims that she's a stay-at-home mom to Calvin's son."

"She's not capable of being in a solid relationship nor taking care of a child full-time. The woman has the attention span of a small flea, and she always looks out for number one, which is herself," Jace hissed.

"I understand that, but on paper, in a court of law, she looks like a woman who has gotten her life together. Married a solid man in the community, with a lot of money to fund this custody battle."

"She wants them full-time? Does she actually plan to take them away from their home and move them to San Francisco?" Jace did not hide the anger in his tone, and I reached for his hand.

"I don't believe she has a chance at sole custody. You've been the consistent parent in their life. You've financially and emotionally provided for them since the day they were born. No judge is going to take that away from you, I don't care how much money her husband has. But she's got a shot at shared custody with the way she's presenting herself."

"So what does that mean? They'd live half the time with me and half the time with her? We don't even live in the same fucking city. Paisley's in school. Hadley's starting preschool in a few weeks." Jace pulled his hand away from mine and ran it through his hair. I glanced over to see the veins on his neck bulging, and his shoulders stiffened as he spoke. "How the fuck is that best for them?"

"Carl Hubbard sent over some paperwork today, notifying me that they purchased a home here, and they're closing on it in a week. I don't know exactly what that means, because her husband's job is not here. Maybe it's a summer home, maybe it's just a ploy to make them look committed to showing they want to keep some roots here for the girls. I really don't know. But again, they are getting their ducks in a row. Presenting the best picture possible. You need to do the same." Winston's gaze moved the slightest bit from Jace to me, and I saw something there. Maybe it was doubt or worry, I wasn't quite sure. But I didn't like it. Jace's hand found mine on instinct, but his attention stayed focused on his lawyer.

"What can we do right now? I need to fucking do something."

Winston nodded, and I saw the empathy in his gaze. "I know, Jace. Let's start with everything you can tell me about Karla from the first encounter you had with her. We're going to need to call character witnesses for you, as well as finding people to back what you tell me about your ex-wife if this goes to trial. Employers. Friends. I'm going to need lists, and we're going to have to dig up a lot of dirt, and they're going to do the same. So if you've got skeletons in your closet, you need to tell me. Do not hide anything from me, because I promise you, she's going to bring it up. And that's the only way she'd have a chance of taking them from you. We need to get ahead of anything that might be coming our way."

"Where do I start?" Jace said, glancing over at me and forcing a smile. The sadness that I saw there nearly broke me. There wasn't anything I wouldn't do to help him through this. He was an amazing father. His girls adored him. He couldn't lose them. I was ready to fight like hell right alongside him.

"At the beginning."

The next two hours were heavy, and I had a sick feeling in my stomach from all he'd shared. This brave man with a huge heart had dealt with a lot more than I'd realized.

He shared how Karla's best friend, Rayne, told Jace that Karla had put holes in the condom they'd used on their first night together when she'd conceived Paisley. She and Karla were no longer friends due to what Karla felt was a betrayal. He said Karla had admitted it was true, but this news had come a few days after Paisley had entered the world, and they'd had a fight over it—but ultimately, he'd looked past it because they shared a child.

"Man, the minute Paisley was put in my arms, something changed in me, you know?" Jace said as he leaned back in the high-back leather chair and stretched his long legs, crossing them at the ankles. "So, when Rayne came by the house and told me that, sure, I was pissed. I mean, who the fuck does that? But we had this beautiful baby, and I knew I needed to try to get past it for her. And that's what I did."

"So, the relationship was rocky from the beginning, correct?"

"Yes. She'd always been around and shown me interest years before we got together, and there'd just never been anything there for me." He winced and looked over at me to gauge my reaction, and I nodded. I knew they hadn't been in love, but I hadn't realized just how bad it was. "So, one night I had a lot to drink, and she was there. We'd been playing pool, and I went home with her. I'm not proud of it. But it brought me Paisley, and I will never regret that. But it doesn't mean I don't get angry with myself for putting my girls in this situation."

"And she admitted to putting holes in the condom that night at her house?"

"She did. She told me she'd had a crush on me for a long time. In her own twisted way, I think she wanted to tie me down, even though she was not ready for a child at all."

"How was she as a mother after Paisley was born?"

Jace let out a long breath. "It didn't come naturally. My mother moved in with us for a while. Karla had a postpartum disorder and was very detached at first. Between my mom and me, we got by. She did stop drinking during her pregnancy and for a few months after, and she really seemed to try for a little bit. That's how it was with her, she'd pull it together for a few months and then go off the rails."

"What does that mean? What would happen during the off times?"

"She'd drink pretty heavily. I could never leave her alone with Paisley, nor with Hadley after she was born, when she would go on these binges. I'd have to hire someone when I was at the firehouse. She was hardly ever alone with our girls. I lived on very little sleep for several years."

"Was the marriage ever good?"

"Not the way a marriage should be, but we had times that weren't awful. I wouldn't classify it as ever being good. She tried to turn things around after Paisley turned a year old because I'd talked to her about a divorce. She started making a bit of an effort with Paisley and with me, and in hindsight, I think it was just her way of holding on. And when Karla wants to put on a show, she is fairly convincing. I've just seen the reality of it too many times. But back then, I agreed not to file because she was really trying, or at least she pretended to be. I agreed to give it a try. I thought maybe this is just how marriage is? You've got your ups and downs. I've never been one to quit at things. And then she got pregnant with Hadley. Things went south quickly after she was born. Karla was done trying. She'd kept herself in check during her pregnancy, and then she'd started drinking and going out all the time. We'd moved into separate bedrooms. She didn't show interest in either of our girls, and I'd told her I was done shortly before she ran off with Zee." He clasped his hands together as Winston fired off a ton of questions.

But at the core of it was a woman who hadn't shown an interest in being their mother before now. She'd been a woman who'd wanted to hold on to Jace.

To trap him.

To keep him.

And that made me wonder if that's what this was all about.

"What if this doesn't have anything to do with the girls?" I said suddenly, unable to keep my thoughts to myself any longer.

"What do you mean?" Winston asked.

"Well, she's never shown any true desire to be a mother, but she's been consistent about keeping a hold on you," I said, looking at my boyfriend. "What if this is about controlling you?"

Winston raised a brow. "Yeah. A lot of times these cases are about a lot more than the kids. This could be fueled by anger and revenge, or even a ploy to get you back. I honestly don't know. When was the last time you spoke to her or saw her? How did she behave?"

Jace looked over at me, and I nodded.

"Ashlan and I ran into her on our way to dinner a few weeks ago. It wasn't pretty. She was drunk and she lashed out, which is typical for her." Jace told him everything about the encounter.

"So, she didn't like seeing you two together, obviously. But is that enough to make someone run off and get married and file for custody after walking away so easily before?" Winston asked as he shook his head.

"I wouldn't put anything past her," Jace said.

Winston looked between us, and I knew he wasn't saying all that he wanted to. But again, a look passed between him and Jace, and I wondered what I was being shielded from.

We couldn't fight this if I didn't know everything that was going on.

But I was determined to find out.

twenty-two

• • •

Jace

I HATED that I had to be at work right now with all that was going on. Ashlan had grilled me after the meeting. Wanting to know if she was missing something. But she wasn't.

We were going to fight this together.

I couldn't fathom a world where a judge would take my girls away from me. No. I had the truth on my side. I didn't need to break the heart of the woman I loved to prove that I was a good dad.

I wouldn't do it.

The alarm went off, and I was dressed and on the truck in no time. I sent Ashlan a text letting her know because she always worried.

"You all right, brother?" Niko asked as he took the seat beside me. "You've been quiet today."

"Yeah. Just that custody shit that I told you about." I shrugged as we hauled ass down the street to a house fire.

"She doesn't have a leg to stand on. She's just as selfish as she always was," Niko hissed.

"Ain't that the truth. But it's going to be a fight. She's got a husband who can bankroll her every whim, and today she is choosing to fuck with me."

"Well, you've got a famous hockey player that will bankroll this as far as she wants to take it if he needs to," Niko said, running a hand through his hair.

Yes, Hawk had called me immediately and offered any financial assistance that I needed. He offered to bring in more attorneys or do whatever it took to make sure the girls stayed with me. I appreciated it and told him I was fine right now financially, but it was nice to know I had a backup plan if this went on for years.

Because I'd never stop fighting for them.

"Yeah." I nodded. "I'm good right now. Hopefully, it doesn't come down to that."

"What does Ash say?"

"She's been fucking amazing. Ready to fight like hell right alongside me."

"Typical Thomas girl. They sure are fierce when they need to be," Niko said.

"Man, I need to get me a Thomas girl," Rusty piped in from behind me and Niko flicked him in the face.

"Get your ass back in your seat, and stop talking about my girls," Cap said as he yanked Rusty back down in his seat. "All right, boys. Get your heads on straight. Apparently, this is a doozy and with the wind shifting, it's threatening the Madelines' home next door." The truck came to a stop, and we jumped into action.

I was drowning in stress over losing my girls one minute and then charging into a burning building the next.

I just had to keep fighting, no matter where I was.

Jack had updated us that everyone was out of the house, but the family dog was trapped inside. Little Sarah Hopkins, whose house was currently up in flames, was sobbing to her parents about her dog named Champ, and my chest squeezed thinking about Hadley with Buddy.

"What's the plan?" I asked after we stepped away, and Rusty and Tallboy got the hoses ready for attack.

"Let's try to get this out, and if there's a safe way in, we get the dog. But we're not running into a death trap to save the dog." Cap gave both me and Niko a hard look.

"I agree. Remember that German shepherd last year that you guys brought out and then he bit me in the ass afterward?" Rusty shouted. "Not risking my life to get bit in the ass."

I tried not to laugh, but it had been funny as hell. The dude had to get a rabies shot and whined like a little bitch.

"Stop messing around, Rusty. Let's do this," Cap shouted.

I nodded and Niko looked over at me. We both had kids and we'd do anything for them. So, if there was even the slightest chance to safely get that dog out, we were going to take it.

The ladders were up, and I tried to assess the situation through the smoke and haze. All the neighbors had come out to gather around from the other side of the street to see what was going on. That was typical for Honey Mountain, where your neighbor would bring you a casserole if something bad happened, but gossip about it to anyone who'd listen on their way over.

"Let's see what we can do from inside," Cap called out, as Niko and I led Rusty and Tallboy toward the back entrance that was still standing and hadn't been touched yet by the growing fire. Our team was attacking the west side of the house with the hose, as our first goal was to keep this fire from spreading to the neighbor's house.

We made our way inside. The heat was strong but not the worst I'd ever experienced.

"Champ," I shouted, listening for a bark or a cry or anything that showed he was still alive.

Niko motioned for us to move forward, and we allowed Rusty and Tallboy to aim at the flames a few feet ahead as we continued to shout and they did their best to get things under control from the inside. The outside of the home was being hit hard by the rest of our team, and if we could contain this from both the interior and the exterior, it would get things under control much faster.

"Did you hear that?" Niko shouted, and I came to a stop. A sound that was something between a bark and a whimper came from a few feet away. Niko pointed for the hose and the guys cleared a path for us, holding the flames back long enough for us to continue on. I searched the area, and there in the corner under an end table that had yet to be engulfed in flames, was a small brown and orange pup. I hurried over and scooped the little dude up before we made our way out of there.

Once outside, I heard the shriek of a little girl just as Sarah came running toward me, screaming out Champ's name with her parents on each side of her.

I set the little guy in her arms and turned back to see the fire was almost contained from the outside. Hell, our guys were the best. Our team was strong, and I was proud to be a part of this house.

"Good work," Cap said as he clapped me on the shoulder.

We watched as our guys continued to get things under control, and Rusty and Tallboy came out to meet us by the truck.

"I'm not going near that little fucker. They always look nice, and then you lean down to allow them the opportunity to thank you, and they bite you in the fucking ass," Rusty said.

Niko barked out a laugh as I pulled my helmet off.

"That's probably the most action you've gotten in a while," Tallboy said as he clapped Rusty on the shoulder.

"Don't you worry your pretty little head, Tallboy. I do just fine." Rusty climbed into the truck.

And just like that. We were heading back to the firehouse, and it was business as usual.

When I arrived home the following morning, my girls were all in their jammies drinking hot cocoa at the table. Buddy was sound asleep beneath Hadley's chair. The fire was roaring in the family room, and the tree had more presents beneath it every time I checked. Ashlan was a sucker for the holidays and wanted this to be a special one for our girls.

Our girls.

They were ours, weren't they? My girls depended on her. They missed her when she wasn't there. They ran to her in the middle of the night now when they had a bad dream. They wanted her when they skinned their knees because apparently they thought she was gentler with the boo-boos than I was. We'd become a family over the past few months, and it was something I'd always wanted to give them but never thought I could.

And the thought of losing it—I couldn't fathom it.

This little slice of happiness was more than I deserved, but I was holding on for dear life.

"Daddy," Hadley shouted and jumped up. I scooped her into my arms and rubbed my scruff against her neck as her head fell back. I set her back down and kissed the top of Paisley's head before Ashlan pushed to her feet and wrapped her arms around my middle.

"Happy to be home. Missed my girls."

"I was just about to make waffles." Ashlan pressed up on her tiptoes and kissed me before moving toward the bowl she'd set out on the counter.

"With holiday sprinkles, right?" Paisley asked.

"Of course."

We spent the morning eating waffles, drinking cocoa, and making snowflakes out of paper that the girls wanted to hang like garland across the windows. The snow had started to fall and there was no sign of it letting up.

"How about we get dressed, take the sleds out, and go hit the hill by Honey Mountain Park?" I asked.

"Yes," Paisley shouted and pumped her fist at the ceiling.

"Can Buddy come?" Hadley asked, and I smiled because my daughter was starting to talk in complete sentences, which was a total win. Hell, I didn't even know if Paisley was talking this detailed at this age. My baby girl had come a long way.

"I think Buddy would love it," Ashlan said as we made our way upstairs.

What felt like nineteen hours later, but was actually about forty-five minutes of getting the girls in more snow gear than I knew possible, we were loaded up in the car.

I carried Hadley up the hill with two toboggans in hand, and Ashlan held Buddy in her arms. Of course, the dog had a ski sweater on, which I hoped none of the guys at the firehouse ever saw, because I'd never live it down. Paisley led the way to the top of the hill and the falling snow made it hard to see. I helped Ashlan and Paisley into the first toboggan, and Hadley, Buddy, and I took off in the second one. We raced down the hill, hooting and hollering as a few passersby stood there laughing as they watched us fly by.

Ashlan and Paisley's sled flipped over, causing them both to get covered in snow, and I couldn't remember a time I'd had so much fun. Just being together. Not doing anything special in particular, and yet it would go down as one of the best days I'd ever had.

We raced back up the hill, laughing our asses off. We had a full-blown snowball fight, with Buddy chasing all of us around as we took turns throwing them at one another.

After about three hours of running and sledding and laughing—we were completely exhausted. The girls fell asleep on the ride home, and Buddy was dozing off on Ashlan's lap in the passenger seat.

Her hand found mine, and she smiled up at me. "I loved today."

"I love you," I said when I came to a stop at the light, and my phone dinged. Ashlan picked it up to look at the screen.

"It's Winston. He said you need to call him." I didn't miss the panic in her voice.

It had been nice to turn off all the noise for a few hours. But reality was waiting for me.

And it threatened to ruin everything good in my life.

twenty-three

. . .

Ashlan

TO SAY that things had gotten stressful after Karla and Calvin returned to town was an understatement. They'd closed on a large home on the lake, and according to Winston, they were really painting the picture of the perfect family. Winston was hoping to settle things civilly via a mediator, but Karla didn't seem to care how this affected her children. She was ready to take this the whole way. My father had called Jace this morning when Winston had unexpectedly shown up at the firehouse because he thought Jace was on duty. I'd had a Zoom call with my publisher which he insisted I keep. He'd dropped the girls off with his mom and ran over to meet with his attorney. He called afterward and said that Karla was painting him as a terrible father, but he'd spared me most of the gory details and said he'd fill me in later tonight. The whole thing just seemed unfair and unbelievable. She was twisting the truth in the worst of ways, and I'd had a sick feeling in my stomach all day.

He was going to do some Christmas shopping on his own for a bit as the Christmas countdown was on. We were leaving for New York shortly after, so I was desperately trying to stay positive. We did our best to hide the stress from

Paisley and Hadley, and due to all the holiday excitement, they didn't seem to be aware of it at all.

I pulled up to my dad's house after my Zoom call, as I was meeting Dylan and Charlotte to go do some last-minute shopping myself this afternoon, but my dad had asked me to stop by.

"Hello," I called out as I walked in. The large tree was up in the family room, and I'd brought Paisley and Hadley over to help decorate it a few weeks ago. My sisters and I loved to do it together every year, and adding little ones to the mix made it all the more fun.

"Hey, sweetheart. I'm in the kitchen."

I walked in to find my father sitting at the kitchen table with a cup of coffee and a donut from Honey Bee's Bakery sitting untouched.

"Are you feeling okay? I've never seen you leave a pastry untouched," I said, giving him a kiss on the cheek before pulling out the chair beside him.

"Such a smart-ass."

I smiled. "What's up? Do you need Christmas gift ideas for the girls?"

He cleared his throat. "You know I'm not big on getting involved in your business. I know you're a grown woman and I trust your judgment, but sometimes I need to make exceptions."

My stomach dipped. My father was rarely serious, and he was most definitely not joking around right now. "Okay. What's going on?"

"Has Jace been straight with you about this custody case?"

"Yeah. Of course. I went with him to talk to Winston a few days ago. Why?"

"What has Winston told you regarding the relationship between you and Jace?" he asked, folding his hands together as his gaze locked with mine.

My heart raced at his words. "What would my relationship with Jace have to do with a custody case?"

"Shit." He covered his mouth with his hand as he took a minute to think about what he was going to say. "Winston has come to the firehouse twice now. The first time he warned Jace that Karla was going to use you against him to get what she wanted. And then they met again this morning, and Winston told him that they'd filed a motion with the court deeming him an unfit parent due to his relationship with you."

All the air left my lungs. "Me? Why would they use me against him?"

"You're almost a decade younger than he is. You're employed by him. Karla's claiming he's sleeping with his young nanny." He reached for my hand as the tears started to roll down my cheeks. "Listen to me, Ashlan May. We know that's not how it is. But she's got a very powerful lawyer, and Winston thinks she's got a chance of taking the girls back to California with her."

"No. A judge would never do that. Jace is such an amazing father. He's given everything to his girls." I shook my head in disbelief.

"I know. It's not right. But her attorney is playing dirty. I think Karla's new husband is pulling out all the punches to get her what she wants. They purchased a home, they got married. I don't think this is going away. I think maybe you should go speak to Winston on your own. I have a hunch Jace asked him not to talk to you about the way they're using you against him in this case. But I can't in good conscience keep this to myself. I know you. I know your heart. And you'd do whatever you needed to do to protect the people you love."

I nodded and swiped at my cheeks. "I can't believe he wouldn't tell me this."

"He loves you. He wants to protect you and the girls. But this might not be the way to do it, because by protecting you,

I think he may be putting himself in a position that will cost him—a lot." He didn't want to say the words. Being with me might cost Jace his girls.

Our girls.

Where did I fit into this equation?

I had no rights to Paisley and Hadley, yet they felt like mine. I would never survive losing them, and neither would Jace. I pushed to my feet.

"Where are you going?" Dad asked.

"I'm going to talk to Winston Hastings and find out exactly what's going on." I thanked him for telling me the truth and hugged him goodbye before hurrying out the door.

I couldn't call my sisters just yet, or I knew I'd lose it. I needed all the facts first, and then I'd figure out what to do. Jace called twice on my drive to see Winston and I sent him to voice mail. He hadn't been straight with me, but I hoped his attorney would be.

When I arrived at the law office, I made my way to the front desk. "Is Winston Hastings in?"

"Yes. Do you have an appointment?"

"I don't. Could you please let him know that Ashlan Thomas is here and it's important that I speak to him?"

Her eyes softened. "Of course. Take a seat right over there, and I'll let him know."

Not two minutes later, she led me back to his office where I'd been just days earlier, feeling like I was in this fight beside my boyfriend, but I hadn't had all the facts.

I hadn't realized that I was the weapon that Karla was using against Jace.

"Ashlan, come in." Winston came around his desk and shook my hand, ushering me to the chair across from him as he sat back down. His assistant closed the door and left the office. "Does Jace know you're here?"

"He does not." I folded my hands in my lap. "I just spoke to my father and learned that Karla is using my relationship with Jace against him. He hadn't shared that with me, and I'm hoping you can tell me exactly what all of this means."

He let out a long breath. "He's my client, Ashlan."

"And he's the man that I love. And I love those girls more than life itself," I said as my hand grasped my chest, and the tears started to fall. "I cannot be the reason that he loses them. Please, Winston. Just tell me what this means and what I need to do."

He nodded and shook his head. "She's pulling out all the punches. She filed a motion with the court today for unsupervised visitation at her new home. She claims the holidays just won't be the same without her girls, and frankly, it's a bit over the top for a woman who didn't even call them last Christmas. But it is what it is. She's got a lot of money behind her, and they aren't going away. And unfortunately, their biggest argument is that Jace is dating a young girl. She even requested that your birth certificate be checked as she's claiming you may be underage."

I gasped. "I'm twenty-three years old. I've graduated from college. Can she get away with this?"

"Well, I vouched for your age when I said you've grown up here, and I've known you most of your life. But Ashlan, it doesn't fare well for him. You were his nanny, and she's claiming that you two are living together out of wedlock. You're young and wild according to Karla, and it's not a good situation for her girls." He shrugged and put his hands up. "I'm not saying it's right. She's reaching here. But a judge that doesn't know you two could buy into it."

"Oh my gosh. This is crazy." I rubbed my temples. "We've been together for months. This isn't a fling. We didn't take this lightly. I've known Jace for years."

"Listen to me… you don't need to convince me. If this were up to me, I'd have agreed to a few supervised visits a year and closed the book on her. She hasn't shown that she's really changed other than marrying a man with money. I did file a request for her to be drug tested every three days as we proceed with supervised or unsupervised visitation, so at least we can find out if she's actually clean."

I reached for some tissue on his desk and wiped my face. "Just tell me what I need to do, and I'll do it. Am I going to cost him his girls?"

He closed his eyes and leaned back in his chair, letting out a breath. "I think your relationship right now is going to complicate things for him. And I hate saying it because I've known Jace a long time, and I've never seen him happier. But she's not going away, and this could drag out for a while. The only real thing that I see that they have on him is his relationship with you. She's painting it as inappropriate and she's using it to win this case, making it look like you two have the girls living in this bad situation. It's completely irrational, but right now, she's presenting herself as a reformed addict who's turned her life around. She's married. She claims to be sober. She sent proof of a program that she attended back in California. Calvin and Karla live in a large estate in California where they have fabulous schools nearby. They just bought a summer home here, so she's offering to bring the girls back and forth to see their father, but she wants to take them to California with her full-time, and I can't say that she doesn't have a shot at it. And that worries the hell out of me."

"Oh my gosh," I whispered. My head was pounding, and the falling tears blurred my vision. "I can't believe this. And you told all of this to Jace?" My voice cracked as his name left my lips.

"I did." He shrugged. "He's a stubborn man in a lot of ways, but I understand him too. He loves his girls, and he loves you. He's waited a long time to be happy, and what she's doing isn't right, and it isn't fair. He knows that. We know that. But the reality is—it doesn't matter if it's right or wrong right now. She's hired an attorney who's ruthless, and she doesn't care that Jace is a good father. She can't see past herself right now, and that's an equation for disaster."

"What did you tell Jace to do?" I asked. I needed to hear him say it.

"I told him that he should end things with you for now. Present himself as a single father focused solely on his girls. He can say that you two dated briefly and it ended with a friendship. Keep it simple, and get through this battle. Because it is a battle, Ashlan. And it's one that he is not winning at the moment."

"How long do you think this will go on?"

"It's hard to say. I mean, she's pushing to have the girls stay with her at their new home over the holidays. The judge may want to see how things play out for several months, see how the girls adjust, make sure Karla stays sober. I'll most definitely be making that a stipulation in any visitation agreement. But this could go on for some time—months, years. I wish I could give you an answer."

I nodded. I knew what I needed to do, but every inch of me was fighting the thought. I was desperate for any other option. "What if we got married?"

He smiled. "You know, he offered that immediately too. He said he'd marry you today if you were willing. But unfortunately, that would look highly suspicious at this point, seeing as she pointed you out as the problem. It would look like you two did this for the wrong reasons, which would make him look more unstable."

I covered my face with both hands and sobbed right there in Winston Hastings' office. Because sometimes life just wasn't fair. And I knew that better than anyone, didn't I? I'd lost my mom when I was only ten years old, and now I'd lose the man I loved because some crazy woman didn't want us to be together.

Winston came around his desk and put his hand on my shoulder, and when I pulled my hands away from my face, he handed me some fresh tissue. "I know it doesn't seem fair right now. Maybe this will all be over in a few months, or a year, and you two can pick up where you left off."

I blew my nose and did the best I could to clean up my face before pushing to my feet. "My priority is keeping those girls with their daddy first and foremost. Thank you for being honest with me."

"I'm sorry, Ashlan. I wish I could tell you that we'd beat her either way."

I reached for the door handle. "Me too. Take care, Winston."

I made my way to the elevator and immediately got on the group text with my sisters.

Me ~ I need you. It's bad.

Charlie ~ Come to my house. Dilly's here. We'll wait for you.

Vivi ~ On my way. I'll leave Bee with Niko.

Ever ~ Getting in my car now.

I tried my best to keep it together until I got in my car, and I sobbed all the way to my sister's house. Charlotte lived in Vivi's old lake house, and it wasn't too far from Winston's office. Everly and Vivian's cars were already in the driveway when I pulled in, so they must have left the minute I texted.

That's the way we always were when one of us was in trouble.

When I stepped out of the car, Everly was there in the doorway, rushing to help me inside. My sisters huddled around me on the couch as I told them everything. I sobbed and cried, and they hugged me even tighter.

"I will snap that little tartlet in half next time I see her," Dylan hissed.

"And that would be a great help," Charlotte groaned. "She's awful, but she's sure painting herself to be something she's not."

"What are you going to do?" Vivian asked as she stroked my hair away from my face.

"I have to leave, right? I mean, there's no other choice. Maybe someday down the road, we can find our way back to one another. But I can't be the reason he loses Paisley and Hadley." My words broke on a sob again. "I just can't imagine my life without Jace and the girls now. I think I need to completely remove myself from the picture, and I don't know how to do that."

I couldn't fathom it. I'd honestly rather die right now than live without them. My heart ached. The lump in my throat was so severe it made it difficult to breathe.

"Listen to me. You are not alone. And I know it's going to hurt like hell because I know how much you love them." Everly wrapped me up in her arms and sobbed right alongside me, which was very out of character for her to break down this way. "But you've got to be strong, Ash. Paisley and Hadley cannot go live with that woman. You've got to do whatever you can to make sure Jace doesn't lose them."

I nodded and buried my face in her chest. "Why is life so unfair to me? Why can't I have this?"

A glass shattered, startling us all, and I looked up to see Dylan standing there with her hands on her hips as we all stared at the vase of flowers she'd just shattered against the wall. Always the hothead. "I agree. I mean, you lost Mama when you were so young, and now you found your place with Jace and the girls. This just isn't fair," she shouted.

"You're going to get through this, Ash. We're going to help you. And we'll make sure Niko and Hawk are there to help Jace through all of this too. Maybe it'll all blow over in a few months and you two can get back together, and this will barely be a memory. You just need to do whatever you can to make sure he keeps those babies right now."

"He knew all of this, and he didn't tell me," I said. "He's

going to think I gave up on him when he didn't give up on me."

Charlotte bent down in front of me and put her hand on my cheek. "He's going to know how much you love him and the girls, sacrificing your own happiness to make sure they're okay. That's love. No question about it."

"Love sucks," Dylan hissed as she dropped to sit back on the couch.

"Not sure why you needed to smash my vase to prove your point, but I hear you." Charlotte shot a look at Dilly.

I couldn't help but laugh, which quickly turned into sobs once again.

I knew what I needed to do.

Now I just had to find the strength to do it.

twenty-four

. . .

Jace

I CALLED my mom on my way to pick up the girls and she said that Ashlan had called and asked her to keep the girls for a few more hours, so I made my way back home.

Ashlan hadn't been taking my calls all day, and I didn't know what the hell was going on. I'd had a shitty meeting with Winston, and I could feel the wheels coming off the cart, but I didn't know how to stop it.

Karla was twisting everything, and I felt like I was losing this fight. The truth was on my side, but no one seemed interested in that.

I sat in the kitchen when the back door opened, and Ashlan stepped in with her sisters behind her. All four of them. I jumped to my feet because Ash's face was swollen and red.

"What happened? Are you okay?" I rushed her, my hands on each side of her face assessing her pretty dark eyes as all four Thomas sisters moved past me and up the stairs.

What the fuck was going on?

"I need to talk to you, Jace. I need you to listen to me, okay?" She put her hands on my chest, backing me up to sit down in the chair as she took the one beside me.

"What is this?"

She reached for my hands. "You weren't honest with me."

"About what?" I couldn't look at her because I knew in that moment that she knew. "Who told you?"

"I went to see Winston today after I spoke to my father." She put her hands up to stop me from cussing them out. "Don't get mad at them. They both love you. You're going to lose your girls, Jace. I can't let that happen."

Tears welled in my eyes, and I shook my head. "We'll figure it out, baby. The girls have never been happier. Any judge will see that."

"That's not how this works. Right now, you need to fight like hell to make sure Karla does not get them. You don't need to worry about me. I'll be okay. And maybe someday—" Her words broke on a sob, and she leaned her forehead against mine. "Maybe someday we can find our way back to one another."

"Sunshine," I whispered. "I can't live without you."

"You can and you will." She pulled back to look at me, and tears streamed down my face just the way they did hers. "They need you."

"I need you," I said. "They need you."

She shook her head and her lip quivered something fierce. "I need all of you. But right now, I can't be a part of this. It might cost you everything and cost them their happiness. I won't do that, no matter how much it hurts."

"Fuck, Ash. This isn't fucking fair."

"Who said life was fair?" She shrugged.

"Please don't do this. We'll find another way."

"There is no other way, Jace. Winston is terrified for you and for the girls. This is not looking good."

"So, that's it?" I threw my hands in the air. I wasn't angry at her. I was angry at the situation. "You're giving up on us?"

"Don't do that. Don't make this harder for me than it

already is." She pushed to her feet abruptly as Dylan hustled past us with two garbage bags in her hands as she made her way to the back door. She looked back at me and forced a smile. I didn't miss her tear-streaked face or the sadness in her eyes.

Charlotte was next, and she set down the suitcase and lunged at me. Hugging me tight before pulling away and hurrying out the door. Vivian had a box filled with more of Ashlan's belongings and she set it on the table and reached for my hands. Tears streamed down her face.

"Love is doing what's best for the person who matters most, no matter how much it hurts," Vivian said. "Don't you forget that."

She grabbed her box and left just as Everly walked toward me. Her belly protruding out and making her waddle in my direction as she held Ashlan's laptop in her hands.

"Would you sacrifice everything to make her happy?" Her blue gaze hardened as it locked with mine.

"Of course."

"Then don't fault her for doing the same thing." She kissed my cheek and left.

I ran my hands through my hair and turned to face Ashlan as I wiped away the moisture running down my face. "What do I tell the girls? We're supposed to be a family."

"We are," she said as she pushed up on her tiptoes and gave me a chaste kiss on the lips. "Tell them that I love them enough to do the right thing. And remember that I love you, no matter how much this hurts. But life's not always fair, right? I think we can both attest to that."

And just like that, she was gone.

I'd never known a hurt like the one I felt in that moment.

But I loved her even more for it.

Because she was right.

She loved us enough to do the right thing.

And that's what love was all about.

Real love.

Caring that deeply.

The back door flew open, and Niko walked in. I swear the girls hadn't even pulled out of the driveway yet, and he was here.

"You all right?" he asked as he gave me a quick hug and slapped me on the shoulder.

I pulled out the chair and sat down, covering my mouth with my hands as I processed everything. "Not fucking all right, brother."

He grabbed me a beer and himself a bottle water out of the fridge just as Hawk burst through the door.

"I thought you were still in the city?" Niko asked. Hawk was in season, and they were still traveling quite a bit.

"Nope. We don't have a game for another week. I got back an hour ago, and I'll train here. Ever wants to be here as much as possible until the baby comes. She just told me what happened, so I came straight over. What can we do to help you?"

Niko took a long pull from his bottle of water. "It's a fucked up situation. We may not be able to help, but at least we can be here. We've got you, brother."

"I can't even fucking believe Karla can pull this shit. I swear to you, she doesn't want the girls. This is about revenge. She's pissed that I'm happy with Ashlan. This is how she is. She's always been spiteful, but this is next fucking level. Dragging our girls through this, and now Ashlan fucking jumped ship." My fist came down hard on the table and they didn't even flinch.

"Dude. She didn't jump ship. She's doing what's best for you and the girls right now. You'd do the same thing for her." Hawk walked to the refrigerator and grabbed a bottle of water.

"Give it time. Maybe this will all blow over, and you can get back to normal." Niko shrugged.

"And if she decides to drag this out for years? I just jump through hoops trying to convince everyone that I'm a good fucking dad when I'm the only one who's been here for them? She gets to come in and out of their lives and wreak mother-fucking havoc? How is this okay?"

"No one said it's okay, brother. But the reality is—she wants to hurt you, and she knows exactly how to do it."

"It's fucked up, right?" Hawk asked. "You let her go. She agreed to give you sole custody. You didn't go after her or make her feel bad about her choice, yet she gets to come back and fuck things up for you?"

"Not helping, dude," Niko said, shooting him a look. "No one said it isn't fucked up, but it's happening, and he has to do whatever it takes to keep those girls safe."

"Fuck. I need to call my mom. The girls are over there," I said, picking up the phone and dialing.

"How are you doing, sweetheart?"

Did she know that Ashlan had left?

"I've been better. How are the girls?"

"They're okay. Ashlan just came by to talk to them and explain things the best she could. There were a lot of tears from all three of them, but I commend her for putting the girls first. It's something their mama has never done," she said, keeping her voice low as she obviously wanted to make sure Paisley and Hadley didn't hear her. Even with all that had happened, I'd made it clear that no one was to speak poorly about Karla in front of them. She was still their mother, and I didn't want to be the one to taint the way they felt about her. They'd be able to do that all on their own if they chose to when they got older. As of now, Paisley had little fondness for her.

"She came by to talk to them?"

"Yes. And to me. She made sure I had you covered with

the girls until all of this is over. She reminded me that Hadley starts school after the holidays, so I'll come sleep at the house when you're on duty. Don't you worry about anything, son. We are going to get through this."

Of course, Ashlan was one step ahead of everyone, making sure we were all okay. That's who she was. The lump in my throat was growing, and I didn't know how to fucking process all of this.

I nodded. "You can bring the girls home. I'm here."

"We're decorating cookies, so how about I bring them over in an hour? They are welcome to spend the night too. You know we love having them," she said, and I knew she was just trying to give me time to deal with what was going on.

"I'd like to have them home with me tonight, but thank you. Can I speak to them really quick?" I needed to know how they were doing.

"Of course." She called out for them.

"Hi, Daddy," Paisley croaked, and I heard the sadness there. "Ashlan isn't going to live with us right now."

I scrubbed a hand over my face. "Not right now, baby. But we're going to be okay."

"That's what she said. I hope she comes back."

"Me too."

"Can we sleep with you tonight, Daddy?" she asked, and I heard Hadley saying my name in the background.

"Of course. I'll see you soon. Let me talk to Hadley." She said her goodbyes and handed the phone to her sister.

"Hi, Daddy. Wuvie go bye-bye."

I let out a long breath, and my eyes burned with the tears that threatened to fall again. "Yep. But we're okay. You want to sleep with Daddy tonight?"

"Yes," she said, but it was lacking excitement.

Damn, these two had been through more than any kids should ever go through at this age. It pissed me off. The fact that Karla felt no guilt over what she'd done to them and that she'd come back to do it again.

So fucking selfish.

"All right. I'll see you soon."

"Wuv you, Daddy."

"Love you, baby girl." I ended the call, and before I could stop myself, I reached for the bottle and threw it hard against the kitchen wall, as the glass shattered into a million pieces.

Neither Hawk nor Niko seemed fazed, but Niko raised a brow and pushed to his feet. "That's one way to deal with the anger. But the girls are coming home, so you best get it out of your system quickly, brother. You're going to need to show how stable you are moving forward, so this is it. Let it out, and then put it the hell away."

"He's right," Hawk said, standing up and making his way to the closet and coming back with a broom and a dustpan. "It's game time, brother. You need to fight like hell if you want to get your life back."

I buried my face in my hands. I had one hour to let all this shit go and put on a brave face for my girls.

"Give me that," I said, reaching for the broom. "It's my mess. I'll clean it up."

"I got it. You're not alone in this, Jace. It just feels like it at the moment." Hawk bent down and proceeded to pick it all up before going for the vacuum to make sure there weren't any little pieces left.

Niko handed me another beer and sat down to face me. "Let's do this again. Have a beer. Take the edge off. And then tomorrow—the fight starts. She wanted you single. Now she can deal with how fucking bad that plays out for her. You're here raising those babies and being a rock star dad. She has nothing more on you than dating your nanny. Her case will go away just as quickly as it started."

"I hope you're right," I said, holding up my bottle. "Because I can't lose them."

I'd already lost Ashlan. My heart felt like it was barely beating. But I knew the sacrifice she'd made, and I wouldn't let it be in vain.

Karla was going to have the fight of her life on her hands.

She'd already cost me the woman I loved—she wasn't getting anything more from me.

twenty-five

. . .

Ashlan

I DECIDED to stay at Charlotte's house after she'd pushed hard for me to come home with her. Dylan was spending the night with us as well, and I'd hugged Vivian and Everly a couple dozen times before I finally insisted they go home to their husbands.

I didn't want dinner. I didn't want to talk about it anymore. I just wanted to climb into Charlotte's bed and drift away. Of course, there was no privacy when it came to the Thomas girls, and Charlotte and Dylan had climbed into the cozy king bed on each side of me. Dylan wrapped her arms around me and hugged me tight.

"You did the right thing. I'm so proud of you," she whispered.

The tears started falling again, even after I thought I was all cried out. I'd put on a brave face when I went to see the girls. I'd insisted my sisters stay in the car as I didn't want to overwhelm Paisley and Hadley. I tried to make them feel like this wasn't a horrible thing. I'd hurried into the King house where I knew the girls were, as I'd been talking to Jace's mom about what was going on over the past few hours. And I owed them a goodbye at the very least. Some sort of lame excuse for why I wouldn't be there when they came home today.

"We're not going to New York anymore?" Paisley asked as I stroked her face.

"No. I think my work wants me to come alone after all. I guess there are a lot of meetings now that I have to attend, so it wouldn't be much fun for you guys." The lump in my throat made it difficult to keep my voice even, but I was determined. I didn't want to alarm them about what was happening with their mother. About the fact they could be forced to move and live with a woman and a man they barely knew at this point.

"And you have to leave now for the trip?"

"Pretty soon. I took all my things because I think I'm going to be super busy for the next few months, and so I might not be able to see you as much for a while." I needed to find a way not to scare them but still make it clear that I wasn't living there just in case Karla's legal team inquired.

"So you aren't living with us anymore?"

"Not right now, baby girl. But you know I'm still here, right? I love you so much." The tears were welling in my eyes, and I looked away and blinked a few times, doing my best not to cry in front of her. My gaze locked with Jace's mom's, and I saw her fighting back the tears too.

"Wuvie going bye-bye?" Hadley asked as she came up and rested her head on my shoulder as I sat on the floor in front of the pretty Christmas tree.

"For a little bit, yes. But you two need to take good care of your daddy." I pulled Hadley onto my lap and wrapped my arms around her as Paisley watched me carefully like she was trying to figure out what was happening.

My heart had already shattered when I'd left Jace's house, and the splintered pieces were cutting me deeply now.

"What about Christmas?" Paisley asked, and I tugged her close, pulling her onto my lap beside her sister.

"All of your gifts are under the tree, and I'll come by and see

you just as soon as I can, okay? I think I may need to stay in New York a little longer than I'd planned."

"No skating?" Hadley asked as her little hand reached up to pat my cheek. We'd had grand plans to ice skate at Rockefeller Center.

"Not this time, but we'll go back someday, okay?"

"I know we will, Ash. Because not all mamas leave, right?" Paisley pushed to her feet. "I think you'll come back for us."

The air whooshed from my lungs, and my lip started quivering out of control. I'd do anything to show them how much I loved them. To show them that not everyone leaves. That I'd be by their sides forever if they'd have me.

But the cost was too high this time.

"I hope so," I whispered as I pushed to my feet and set Hadley down in front of me. I needed to get out of here.

I needed air.

As if their grandmother had read my mind, she hurried over. "Okay, we need to let Ashlan get packed up for her trip, and the gingerbread cookies are all ready to be frosted."

Hadley jumped up and down and clapped. "Wuvie back soon?"

I nodded and sniffed a few times. The floodgates were threatening to open as I struggled to hold in the emotions any longer.

"I don't want you to leave," Paisley said as she rushed me and wrapped her arms around my legs. "I love you forever, Ashlan."

And that was about all I could take. I quickly leaned down and kissed the top of her head before squeezing Hadley's little hand. She watched me with complete confusion, because she didn't understand what was happening. I hurried for the door as Jace's dad followed me outside.

He reached for my arm and pulled me into a hug. "I know it's hard, sweetheart. But this is what real love looks like. Thank you for loving them enough to do the right thing for now. Remember, life has a way of working out. This doesn't mean it's forever."

I hugged him back before pulling away and pushing up on my tiptoes and kissing his cheek. I wanted to tell him that I agreed with him. But I didn't know if he was right. Everyone thought my mom would overcome her cancer, but she never did. She lost her battle, and she never came back. So, I wasn't naïve to know that things didn't always work out.

Oftentimes they didn't.

When I'd climbed in the back seat of the car, I'd sobbed all the way home, and my sisters had cried right alongside me because they couldn't stand to see me hurting. We'd always been that way. We felt one another's pain.

I'd cried myself to sleep, and when I woke up this morning, I was alone in Charlotte's bed, and I took a minute to remember all that had happened yesterday. My fingers found my lips that were chapped, my eyes heavy and swollen from crying late into the night, and my stomach wrenched.

I was physically ill.

I ached for Jace and the girls. They'd become my constant. And now I would wake up without them. There would be no morning snuggles with Paisley and Hadley, no stolen kisses from Jace.

I was completely on my own.

Obviously, I had my sisters and my dad, and I loved them dearly.

But the ache that I felt. The loneliness. The gaping hole in the middle of my chest—no one could fill that but Jace, Paisley, and Hadley.

When I'd lost my mom as a little girl, I'd felt this same gaping hole. But I hadn't understood it at the time. I'd been too young to grasp what it meant to mourn and to grieve for someone that had meant so much to you and was no longer there.

This was hard to wrap my head around. No one had died. But I couldn't hug them. I couldn't ask about their day. Winston had suggested I cut off all contact as Jace's phone could be used as evidence in the case. I couldn't bandage up boo-boos or read good night stories to them. I couldn't fall asleep beside Jace, who always woke before me and would smile at me the minute my eyes opened first thing in the morning. I remembered the way his light blue eyes would twinkle when I found them. The way he looked at me like I was the only girl in the room no matter where we were. The way we could communicate without words, with just a look or a touch.

I'd never felt more loved in my life.

I'd never felt more complete in my life.

Home.

Jace, Paisley, and Hadley were my home—and now it was gone.

My chest throbbed, and I pulled my knees up and wrapped my arms around them, trying to comfort myself any way that I could. A loud sob escaped my throat as the reality of what had happened set in. I wished I could go back to sleep. Wished I could forget.

Charlotte came hurrying into the room as she moved to sit beside me on the bed and stroked my hair. "You're okay, Ash. It's going to get a little better every day."

I shook my head as the tears streamed down my face. "I don't want to hurt like this."

Dylan walked through the door and came around the other side of the bed, climbing in beside me and reaching for my hand.

"One day at a time, Ash," she whispered.

I lay there crying as both of my sisters stayed with me until I dozed off again.

Sleep was the only place that I felt at peace.

"Okay, that's it. You slept for an entire day again. It's time to get up, Ash," Charlotte said as she handed me a glass of water.

Everly walked in, her belly leading the way. "Ashlan, let's go."

She paused at the bed and reached for my hand. I did what she asked and sat up before pushing to my feet. She led me into Charlotte's bathroom and turned on the shower.

I stared at her for a long moment. I wasn't ready for a shower. Hell, I wasn't ready for anything. My stomach felt queasy, and being awake just reminded me of what I was missing.

"It's snowing out. It's Christmas Eve tomorrow, and you leave for New York next week. It's time to pull up your big girl panties and push forward."

I leaned against the wall and tears welled in my eyes. No sound left my mouth this time as the tears streamed down my face because I had nothing left in me. "I don't want to go to New York. I'm going to see if I can reschedule it."

Dylan barreled into the bathroom wearing a black turtleneck sweater, her long blonde hair falling all around her shoulders, and she handed me a coffee mug. "No, ma'am. That's not happening. Do you know how rare it is to get not only an agent but a publisher who wants your story? I'm going with you. We'll make it a girls' trip. New Year's in the city. Holla," she sang out.

"I'm coming too," Charlotte said as she appeared in the doorway, brown hair pulled up in a high ponytail and an empathetic smile. "Come on, Ash. We'll do New Year's together in New York. It'll cheer you up, and you'll be meeting your publisher. There are still things to look forward to, even if it doesn't feel like it right now."

"Well, damn. I feel like I'm missing out, but there's no way I can travel when the baby's due in a few weeks."

I swiped at my cheeks and forced a smile. I stopped to glance in the mirror, and the dark circles under my puffy eyes told the story.

"Hello?" Vivian called out, and Charlotte shouted that we

were in the bathroom. She appeared with little Bee in her arms and walked into the small space, assessing the situation. "What's happening here?"

"We're making Ash take a shower and insisting she go to New York."

"You're going to New York. I know you're sad, but you can do this, Ash. I know you're hurting, but you can't stop living. Niko's been over with Jace, and he's feeling about the same way you are. But guess what? You two are doing what's best for those little girls. Now get yourself in that shower, and make them proud."

"Yes. You're a tomato, Rock," Dylan shouted out the Rocky Balboa speech, and I held my hand up.

"I'll take a shower if you stop with the speech. I can't handle it right now. Give me a minute alone to get cleaned up, okay?"

Everly studied me and then nodded. "We're coming back in fifteen minutes, so get a move on."

"You're going to be such a bossy mother," Dylan whined as they walked out of the bathroom, and I shut the door behind them.

The space was filling with steam as the water had been running, and I pulled off my T-shirt and leggings and climbed into the shower. The hot water stung my swollen face, but I let it beat down on me. The last time I'd showered had been almost a week ago. The girls had slept in, and Jace and I had snuck in a shower together. I leaned against the wall remembering the way he'd dropped to his knees and buried his face between my legs. The way he'd made me cry out his name because it felt so good. The way he'd gently washed my hair before wrapping me up in a towel and carrying me to the bedroom.

To our bedroom.

I stood under the water and I wasn't sure if there were

tears streaming down my face or just the sensation of the water, but I let myself feel all that sadness.

All that loss.

And then I thought of Paisley and Hadley and the way they jumped on their daddy when he got home from the firehouse. The way he carried them upstairs every night and tucked them in.

I turned off the water and swiped at my face.

No more being selfish and feeling sorry for myself.

My girls were going to be safe. Jace wasn't going to lose them.

And that was what mattered most.

twenty-six

. . .

Jace

TO SAY that the past few days had been a living hell would be an understatement. My babies were sad because they missed Ashlan terribly. Even after Karla had left a year and a half ago, they'd never had any sort of sadness over it. They'd appeared more settled with her being gone than they had with her being there. But Ashlan's absence had taken a toll on all of us.

They didn't like the food I cooked. They didn't like the way I did their hair. They didn't like the way the house looked. They didn't like the way I made the bed. They didn't like the clothes that I picked out. They didn't like the TV shows that we watched, even though they were the exact same shows we'd watched when Ashlan was here.

And I fucking got it.

Because I was miserable too.

Lost.

Broken.

The only reason I was even getting out of bed and moving forward was because Paisley and Hadley needed me. I'd taken a leave from work until after the holidays, so I could sort things out. Winston was on his way over to discuss the latest movement with our case, and I wasn't happy with him for what he'd shared with Ashlan, but I still had to deal with the man. This shit was still happening whether I was pissed or not. And it was the day before Christmas fucking Eve.

"Do you think Santa is still going to come even if Ashlan isn't here?" Paisley asked, and she crossed her arms over her chest like this whole thing was my fault. Did they not understand that I was fucking hurting too?

Of course they didn't. They were little girls who didn't have a clue the length Ashlan and I would go to in order to protect them.

"Santa's coming. But you best stop talking rude to your dad because Santa definitely doesn't like that." I raised a brow when the doorbell rang, and I pushed to my feet.

"No mean to Daddy," Hadley said, wrapping her arms around my knees and kissing my leg over the denim.

"Thank you, Sweet Pea. Daddy could use a little love right now, too. We're in this together, okay?" I stared at my eldest daughter, who rolled her eyes at me.

Well, I wouldn't win every battle. At least Hadley wasn't hating on me right now. I told them both to head up to the playroom so I could speak with Winston.

I made my way to the door, inviting him inside. "Hey. Thanks for coming here. The girls are having a tough time, so I didn't want to take them to my parents' house right now."

"I get it. It's no problem," he said as he followed me into the kitchen and sat down in the chair across from mine.

"I assumed something happened, seeing as you're here two days before Christmas."

"Well, yeah. And I know you're upset with me, Jace, but she asked for the truth, and since you'd brought her along to the other meeting, I figured she should have all the facts."

I let out a long breath. I wanted to hate him, but he wasn't the one I was mad at. "Just help me keep my girls, Winston. Can you do that?" I kept my voice down, checking the stairs to make sure no little ears were listening.

"I'm going to try like hell. I spoke to Carl Hubbard this morning. Karla was forced to take her first drug test today, and she complied. So, that's a start," he said, pulling out a notebook from his briefcase. "But he has made a request that you're not going to like."

"Well, let's see. She's come back and turned our lives upside down. Ashlan no longer lives here. The girls are devastated. I'm a fucking mess. What else could she possibly want now?"

"They're requesting a sleepover with the girls, unchaperoned. They're asking for good faith."

"Good fucking faith?" I hissed as I pushed to my feet. "No fucking way. She wouldn't even know what to do with them."

"Jace, listen to me. They can file a motion with the court, and they'll probably win. But it's Christmas Eve tomorrow, and they're asking for some time with the girls. Carl Hubbard and I are going to do what we can to mediate this between you two for now. They agreed to the drug testing. They know that Ashlan is not living here any longer, nor is she around the girls. That seems to have appeased them for now. You've got to give me something to take back to the table."

"What do you want, Winston? A limb? What's left of my heart? How much more do I have to give to a woman who has never put her children first? The only woman I've ever loved has left because of this shit—my girls are hurting, I can't expect them to stay the night with strangers. They won't *want* to go. Paisley doesn't like her. How about someone brings something to the table for us?"

He scrubbed a hand over his face and groaned. "I know you're right, and nothing about this is easy. What about a few hours on Christmas Eve? We agree that they can come pick up the girls. Calvin will be with Karla, as will his son. They can go get a burger or some ice cream. It'll show that you're trying to work with her."

"But I'm not," I said dryly.

"Big picture, Jace. She might just end up going away in the end. Let's try to find some peace for you and for the girls."

"Lunch. Two hours. And I will take them to a public place. And I'm going to be there, Winston. I'll sit at my own table. No way would I risk anything happening to them. I don't believe after her outburst at my house, that she wouldn't try to take them away from me. And I don't want her driving them when we don't even know if she's sober."

"I can make that work," he said as he pushed to his feet. "Let me make a call."

Winston left the kitchen, and I assumed he was calling Karla's attorney. I sat there sipping my coffee as I glanced over at the Christmas tree filled with packages. Just a week ago, I'd been the happiest I'd ever been in my life.

We'd been looking forward to Christmas.

To New Year's in New York.

We'd been a family.

And now I was sitting here negotiating where my babies would eat lunch on Christmas Eve.

"Okay. He thought that was kind of you to agree, and he was fine with you driving the girls there. He said that he would personally set up the restaurant location and he would be present this first time to make the transition smoother. He has to leave to head back to the city tomorrow as it's Christmas Eve, so he'll make sure that lunch is no longer than the two hours you requested."

"How big of him," I grumped.

"He's actually not a bad guy, Jace. He seems to be wanting to help mediate this situation and do what's best for the girls."

"He's getting a fat paycheck, Winston. If he wanted what was best for my girls, he wouldn't be defending a woman who didn't give two shits about them," I whisper-hissed. I was going to have to sell this meeting to the girls, and Paisley would not be happy about it.

"They seem to be backing off, so I think we count this as a win. They aren't talking about sole custody anymore, so let's just give them this visit and maybe they'll be heading back to the city after Christmas."

"One can hope. So, what does this mean if they don't push for custody? Can we go on with our lives? Or we're just on hold, waiting to see what Karla feels like doing from one day to the next?"

"I don't have an answer for you right now, Jace. All I know is that today they asked for a visit. That's a lot tamer than what they'd said just a few days ago. But it could change tomorrow."

"So, I just live like this, constantly worrying that she'll take my kids from me?"

"It's not forever. We're going to have a resolution with this. They want that as much as we do," he said, pushing to his feet. "Merry Christmas, Jace."

"Yeah. Merry Christmas, Winston. Give Veronica and the kids my best."

I tried to be genuine. Just because my life had imploded didn't mean I had to ruin everyone else's holiday. The girls and I were going to be at my parents' house on Christmas morning. They were supposed to come here as Ashlan had planned to make brunch, but everything had changed, and my mother said she would host since I sure as shit wasn't up for it now.

I walked Winston to the door just as my brother walked up the driveway. The snow was coming down, and Travis had nothing more than a sweater and a pair of jeans on.

"Mom would kick your ass if she knew you were out

without a coat," I shouted as he and Winston said their hellos before he made his way inside.

"Damn, it's fucking cold out there," he said, rubbing his hands together.

"The blizzard wasn't a solid clue that it would be cold?" I asked.

"I see someone is in the holiday spirit." He followed me into the kitchen. "I know it's a shitty time for you, so I thought I'd come over and hang with you and the girls."

"Hayden was here yesterday. I'm guessing Mom's having everyone take shifts?"

"Something like that. So, what was that about?" he asked, flicking his thumb at the door where Winston had just left.

"Karla wants to see the girls tomorrow. She isn't talking about sole custody at the moment, so he thinks we should appease her. I said no to them spending the night there, but I agreed to let them go to a public restaurant for lunch. Two hours. And I get to be present at a different table. She was also drug tested today, so she's at least complying with that."

"She's the devil," he whispered because he knew how I felt about him talking shit about her in front of the girls. We were standing over by the door, out of earshot. "She fucking put holes in a condom. The woman is twisted. The only good thing that she ever did was give you those two angels."

"Agreed."

"Any word from Ash?"

"Nope. I'd say that's done. She moved her shit out. She's made it clear that she'll be staying away." I heard Paisley call out for me, and I gave him a look that said we needed to drop the subject. "I need to let them know that they have to go to this lunch thing tomorrow, so help me out. Don't make it worse than it already is."

"I got you. I can sweet talk my nieces better than anyone." He shoved me out of the way and jogged up the stairs toward the playroom.

"Uncle Trav," Paisley said, and it was the most enthusiasm she had shown since Ashlan left. "What are you doing here?"

"I came to see my favorite girls."

"And Buddy?" Hadley asked as she continued petting her pup, who I swore was part narcoleptic because the dude loved to snooze.

"Yep. Of course." He scooped them each up in his arms and spun them around before putting them back down and dropping to sit on the floor.

"I just talked to Mr. Hastings, and he was telling me that your mama would like to take you two out for a special lunch and maybe some ice cream tomorrow."

"Karla? No. I don't want to go with her." Paisley huffed, just as I thought she would.

"Ice-scream? Mmmmmm," Hadley said as she rubbed her belly.

"Well, I think it would be nice, seeing as it's Christmas. I'll be there, and I'll just sit at another table. She and Calvin are married now, and he has a boy, and I think she'd like you all to go have a meal together. Do you think you can do that for me?"

"I don't get to see Ashlan, but I have to go eat lunch with Karla?" Paisley shouted before storming off and running to her room and slamming the door.

"Damn. That did not go well, brother. You are so in for it when that girl is a teenager," Travis said with a laugh.

"Shut the fu—heck up," I snarled and dropped to sit by Hadley on the floor and pet Buddy. I admired his life. He had no heartache. No angry kids. No crazy ex-wife. No stress. He just ate, shit, and slept.

It sounded like heaven.

"We'll give her some time to cool off. She'll be fine." The truth was, I understood her anger because I felt it too. She wanted Ashlan who had been consistently there for her. She'd shown up over and over again. Yet I was forcing her to go spend a few hours with a woman who hadn't been there. All because I was terrified of losing them. But sometimes you had to do whatever it took to get what you wanted.

And protecting them was most important.

Hell, that was the reason Ashlan left, right?

I closed my eyes as my brother and Hadley babbled back and forth to one another. I missed my girl something fierce, and I wondered if she was nervous to go to New York alone. I knew she was hurting too, and she deserved to be celebrated for all that she had accomplished. My fingers itched to text her, but Winston had told me my phone records could be easily requested by the court if this thing went to trial, so I needed to wait this out.

And hope the day would come that I could tell her how much being away from her sucked.

That there'd be a day when I'd get my heart back in one piece.

Christmas Eve was supposed to be magical. It was snowing outside, the tree was plugged in even though it was late in the morning because I was trying all that I could to get my girls through this day. Travis had spent the night in the guest room. I think he knew today would be tougher than I was letting on. Hadley was clueless, but she had made a few comments that she wanted to stay home with me today. Paisley had come out of her room yesterday but still insisted that she didn't want to go. And I had a pit in my stomach that had taken my appetite and had me on edge.

Winston had called to tell me that Carl Hubbard, Karla, Calvin, and Dawson would meet us at Honey Mountain Café at eleven thirty.

I got them dressed, but Paisley refused to wear what I'd

laid out for her, and she came out of her room wearing black leggings and a black sweater and her black boots.

"She looks like the Christmas angel of death today," Travis whispered in my ear as he chewed a handful of pistachios loudly, and it took all I had in me not to punch him in the face. "I think she's making a statement."

"I'm aware. But sometimes you've got to choose your battles," I said as Hadley pranced past us wearing a pink tutu, red and white tights, and an orange sweater.

"Jeez, it looks like you lost more than one battle today. That one looks like she's three sheets to the wind with that outfit and her waddle walk."

I pinched the bridge of my nose. "Can we not do this right now?"

"How about you let me handle the hand-off? You're far too emotional," Travis said, reaching for some more nuts out of the bowl on the coffee table and I smacked his hand, and the nuts went flying.

"Dude!" he shouted.

"Stop talking. Stop chewing. Stop"—I waved my hand around—"all of it."

"Yep. Definitely losing it," he whispered to nobody.

"All right, coats on, girls. It's time to go." I reached for Hadley's purple jacket, which only clashed with her outfit even more. I knew she'd be the easier one to winterize.

Someone knocked on the door, and Travis went to open it. Niko and Hawk strolled in.

"It's cold out there. Bundle up, girls." Niko was rubbing his hands together.

"This is nothing. I thrive in icy conditions," Hawk teased.

"What are you doing here?" I asked after I zipped Hadley's coat up and pulled her hat over her head and handed my brother the mittens to put on her hands.

"Thought you might need some backup." Hawk

shrugged. "Ever's wrapping last-minute gifts right now, so I thought I'd come check up on you."

"Vivi and Bee are over at her dad's house and I thought I'd stop by. Plus, we're hungry. We're going with you."

They knew what was happening today. They were here to make sure me and the girls were okay. I was grateful.

"Come on, Buttercup. Let's get your coat on."

Paisley stomped toward me, her baby blues welling with tears. "I don't want to go, Daddy."

"I know, baby. But we need to try. Can you do this for me?" I asked, and my voice cracked, startling me and Paisley because her eyes widened. I was at the end of my rope. I didn't want to force her to do this, but I didn't have a choice, did I?

She held up her arm and slipped her coat on. "Okay."

Travis gave me a look of empathy. She was such a good girl, and I was proud as hell of her in this moment. "Thank you." I kissed her cheek.

Hawk pulled her hat on her head and pulled it down to cover her face until she started hysterically laughing.

I was happy they'd shown up to help with this.

Because nothing about it was easy.

My girls got in my truck, and Travis climbed in the passenger side up front. Hawk and Niko followed behind us in Hawk's SUV.

I carried Hadley inside Honey Mountain Café, and Travis held Paisley's hand. Niko and Hawk stayed close behind us.

A man in a suit stood beside the hostess stand and he extended his hand. "I'm Carl Hubbard. Thanks for agreeing to this."

I glanced over to see Karla sitting in a booth, and I didn't see anyone else beside her.

"Where's Calvin and Dawson?"

"They aren't coming. It will just be Karla today." There was something he wasn't telling me.

"Don't you think she should come over here and greet these little girls? This is a lot for them, and they don't know you."

"Agreed." He walked back to the booth, and I couldn't make out what he was saying, but it sounded like they were arguing before she walked our way with a blatant case of resting bitch face when she looked at me.

"I hope you'll sit out of our sight, as we don't need a babysitter. I've already got Carl joining us, so I think it's safe to say we're fine," she said. "Are you girls hungry?"

"I'm not hungry," Paisley said quietly, looking up at her uncle to avoid Karla's gaze.

"Then you don't have to eat," Karla hissed.

There she is. Keep showing your true colors.

"Okay. Let's head over to our table," Carl said.

"See you in a little bit and we'll get ready for Santa, okay?" I kissed Hadley and set her down on the ground. She looked at Karla and then at Carl, and then back to me. She didn't say a word. Her eyes were wide, and she fidgeted with her hands, and I fucking hated this.

"Take care of your sister, okay?" I said to Paisley before bending down and pulling her into my arms. "It's just lunch, Buttercup. I love you."

She pulled back and a tear rolled down her cheek, and I swear the last piece of my heart that was hanging on by a thread cracked.

"I will, Daddy." She hugged me once more before she reached for her sister's hand and they followed Karla to the table.

And the four of us stood there watching them before Hawk cleared his throat and said he found us a table in the back. I'd be able to see the girls, but we were far enough away that they wouldn't be running over to me.

I nodded.

The lump in my throat made it tough to swallow.

"You all right?" Travis asked as I slipped into the booth beside him.

"Nope."

And I probably wouldn't be for a long time.

twenty-seven

. . .

Ashlan

"MERRY CHRISTMAS," Charlotte said as I stretched my arms and my eyes opened. I tried hard to find any bit of holiday spirit within me, but it was a struggle. I had a constant sick feeling in my stomach. My body physically ached for Jace and the girls. It felt like something was missing all the time.

The only peace I felt was when I slept. Those brief hours when I didn't have to think about all that I'd lost.

Dylan had talked to me about all the potential outcomes, as she was graduating from law school in a few months, and she knew how it all worked a whole lot more than I did. But she said custody battles were complicated, which is why they were called battles.

They weren't cut and dry. She was convinced my moving out and distancing myself from Jace, Paisley, and Hadley would be helpful for his case. Winston would probably write it off as some sort of fling or just say that I'd been working there, and we weren't actually together. I didn't know how they'd spin it, but it all stung. Diminishing what we'd shared, what they mean to me—it didn't seem right. But Dylan insisted I did the right thing, and I'd do it all over again if it meant the girls would be staying with Jace.

"Yeah. Merry Christmas." The lump in my throat was thick.

She reached for my hand and intertwined our fingers. "I know it's not how you thought you'd be spending the holidays. But getting out of the house and out of this bed..." she said, raising a brow because I hadn't wanted to do much more than sleep over the past few days. "It'll be good for you. You'll eat a good meal, open a few presents, maybe even eat a few of Vivi's cookies."

I'd always had a sweet tooth, but I hadn't had any appetite since I moved out of Jace's house.

"I know. I'll do it. No one will even know that I'm hurting, I promise," I said, sitting up and letting out a breath.

"I don't care about that, Ash. I know your heart is broken. The whole thing is just so sad, so I get it. But I'm worried about you. And according to Winston, this could go on for months or even years. So, you've got to move forward."

I nodded and swiped at my cheeks, irritated that there were still any tears left in me.

"And we've got Everly's baby shower in a few days. There are still things to look forward to."

"I just don't know where I fit now? That's what I've always struggled with. I never knew what I wanted to be or what I wanted to do after college, and then everything just felt so right, you know?"

"I get that. But your career has taken off, Ash. You're signing with a top-five publisher in New York. You're so freaking talented. You can do anything you want to do."

But none of that mattered now. The one thing I wanted, I couldn't have.

"Yep. I'll figure it out. I should probably move back in with Dad. I can't sleep in your bed forever." I chuckled, and it was the first time in days that I'd even smiled.

She pulled my head down to rest on her shoulder. "You know you can stay here as long as you want. I love having you here."

"Thanks. And I am looking forward to the baby shower."

"There she is. How about you jump in the shower, and I'll make coffee and heat up the croissants that Vivi brought over last night."

"Sounds like a plan."

I knew it was time to put on my happy face and try. It was Christmas after all. I wondered what the girls were doing this morning. I'd hidden the bag in our closet filled with all the stocking stuffers, and I hoped that Jace had figured it all out and that they'd had a magical morning.

I wondered if they were seeing Karla today. I got little tidbits from Vivian and Everly, as Hawk and Niko were doing what they could to support Jace through this. So, I knew they'd gone to lunch with their mama yesterday, but I didn't know anything else.

I was ashamed to say that I was more than just sad and heartbroken. I was jealous. Jealous that she got to see them open their gifts and see the smiles on their faces when they saw what Santa brought them.

She got to see them in their cute Christmas dresses that we'd gotten them.

She got to hug them. Kiss them. Tuck them in.

I leaned against the shower wall and allowed myself a few minutes to fall apart privately before I forced myself to be in a good mood for Christmas.

I dropped to sit on the floor as the water rained down on me, and I hugged my knees and cried.

Cried for what I missed.

Cried for what I'd lost.

Cried for what would never be.

And then, I pushed to my feet, washed my hair, and climbed out of the shower.

I was determined to pull myself together and not let my sadness drown everyone else on this special day.

It was little Bee's first Christmas.

Everly was about to give birth.

Hawk was in the middle of a winning season.

Niko and Jace had started working on the huge house they'd purchased, and everyone was excited about that. I'd gone with them to pick out all the finishes and knew it was going to be stunning. I wondered if I'd even get to go by and see it now. I knew I had to keep my distance, but how long would that last? Until this custody battle was over? I wouldn't be allowed to see any of them?

I wrapped a towel around myself and pulled a brush through my hair as I stared at the mirror, and I was overcome with a feeling of missing my mom in this moment. This happened to me often over the years. At my graduations, school dances, and apparently, my first heartbreak.

"I wish you were here, Mama," I whispered. "I'm so lost."

I covered my face with my hands and shook my head.

I'm not going to cry anymore.

It's time to pull yourself together.

And just like that, my mom's words flooded my head.

"It's okay to feel things, baby girl," Mama said after I'd cried when she told me she was sick and the chemotherapy wasn't working. "Don't push those feelings away. That's what happens when you love someone and you're afraid of losing them."

She pulled me onto her lap, and I buried my face in her neck. She smelled like fresh gardenias which were her favorite flower.

"But what's going to happen if you don't get better?" I croaked.

"You're going to keep living either way, my love. I'll always be with you. That's the way love works. When it's real... it never leaves. And I will love you until you take your last breath."

"I love you too, Mama."

"I know this is scary. Loss is hard, and it's a lot for you to handle right now. I'm so sorry that you have to go through this so

young. But remember this, Ashlan May… I'd do it all again if it meant I got even a few years with you. Because love is a gift. Don't be sad about what we're losing, be happy about what we've had. Because being your mama has been my greatest gift."

I gripped the bathroom counter and squeezed my eyes closed. Loving Jace and Paisley and Hadley had been my greatest gift.

I wasn't going to be sad about what we'd lost.

I was going to remember what we had.

I let out a long breath and towel-dried my hair before slipping into a pair of black leggings and the matching hoodie that Dylan had bought each of us to wear today. It had a photo of Santa wearing a pair of black shades in the center and it said: I do it for the HOs. I hadn't laughed when she gave it to me, but I laughed now as I slipped it over my head.

I dried my hair with the blow dryer and put on a little bit of moisturizer, lip gloss, and mascara.

I pulled the door open, and Dylan and Charlotte were sitting at the kitchen counter, most likely gossiping.

"Well, looky here. There's a *HO* in the house." Dylan jumped to her feet and hugged me. "And she's not looking like death this morning, so I'd call that a win."

I pulled away and rolled my eyes, but I could feel the smallest smile trying to come out. "Thanks for that."

"Of course. What are sisters for?"

"Ummm… well, emotional support. Starbucks runs. Doing your hair and makeup. Sharing clothes. Great Christmas and birthday gifts, just to name a few." Charlotte handed me a plate with a croissant and some jam on the side.

I made my way to the barstool beside Dylan and sipped my coffee. "Thank you."

Dylan looked down at her phone and then set it on the counter. "Vivi and Ev are on their way to Dad's house. Time to open presents."

"We can't keep little Bee waiting. It's her first Christmas,"

I said, taking a bite of my croissant and pushing to my feet. I chewed quickly and tried to force it down. I couldn't eat. My stomach was still twisting and turning, and the thought of food just wasn't appealing at the moment.

"Please. Little Bee is mesmerized by a Cheerio, she is hardly going to remember this Christmas." Dylan snorted as we slipped into our jackets and made our way out the door.

When we got to my father's house, Christmas music was playing through the surround sound speakers in our family home. Everly was in the kitchen putting two casseroles in the oven while Vivian set out a platter of pastries on the kitchen island.

Christmas morning was just for our family. My dad, Everly, Hawk, Vivian, Niko, Bee, Dylan, Charlotte, and me. My chest tightened as I thought about how Jace, Paisley, and Hadley were supposed to be here too. I pushed the thought away as Hawk pulled me in for a hug before passing me down the line to Niko, Vivi, and Everly. My dad set his coffee mug down and walked over to me.

"How are you doing, baby girl?" he asked. I hadn't seen him since the day he told me about what was going on with the custody battle. But we'd talked almost every day. My dad wasn't big on crying, so he gave us our space when we needed it. But he was always there when we were ready to talk.

"I'm fine. Merry Christmas," I said, hugging him extra tight.

We made our way to sit around the tree, and just like always, Dylan passed out the gifts. She'd never been patient on Christmas morning, so it had always been her job. We went around opening endless gifts, one at a time. Sharing, laughing, and being grateful. Niko stood and moved to the entryway before making his way over to me and handing me two packages.

"Jace asked me to bring these to you."

The room fell silent, and I cleared my throat. "You don't have to stop talking. I'm fine. I left him the presents for him and the girls, so of course he wanted to pass these on."

I turned over the first package which was small in size, and it was wrapped in red paper with little sleighs on it. I smiled at the memory when he and I ran to get some gift wrap and he took forever to choose one roll of wrapping paper, while I'd loaded the cart with five rolls. He said the little sleighs reminded him of our day out sledding.

I pulled out a gorgeous silver frame and turned it over to see a photo of Jace lying on his stomach on the floor with Buddy tucked beside him, me on top of Jace, my belly pressed to his back, Paisley lying on top of me and little Hadley on top of her sister. We were all laughing in the photo and my eyes welled with emotion as I stared down at it. Paisley had asked us to try a pyramid picture, and Jace had propped the phone on the floor and set the timer and it took more than a dozen tries to get Hadley on top before the timer ran out. It was the sweetest picture, because we looked—happy.

We looked like a family.

"Let me see it," Charlotte asked, and I passed the frame to her and tried to focus on the next package.

"It looks like little Hadley is about to topple over," Everly said as she looked at the photograph and chuckled.

"Yeah. She fell off so many times before we actually got a picture with everyone in it."

Everyone continued passing it around and smiling as they looked at it. I tore off the gift wrap on the next package and my mouth gaped open. It was a white Apple box, and I lifted the lid to see the rose gold laptop inside. I shook my head and tried everything I could to keep the tears away. Jace knew I was looking to purchase a new laptop now that I was writing full-time.

"That was very thoughtful," Vivian said as she leaned into me and wrapped an arm around my shoulder.

I swiped at the single tear running down my cheek and nodded.

"Okay, let's eat," I said, wanting to take the attention off of myself.

Niko helped me to my feet as I set the laptop over with the stack of presents I'd already opened.

"You okay?" he asked.

"Not really. But I will be, right? Time has a way of healing."

"He's miserable too, if that makes you feel any better." Niko bumped me with his shoulder and smiled.

"I can't text him right now, so would you mind thanking him for the laptop and the cute photo for me?"

"Of course, I will."

I wanted to ask Niko to tell Jace and the girls that I loved them. But they already knew it.

Loving them wasn't our problem.

It never had been.

twenty-eight

. . .

Jace

"I DON'T UNDERSTAND why the judge wants to see me. Doesn't he communicate with you normally?" I asked Winston as I pulled off my black trench coat. The weather was crazy cold, and the snow had been falling over the past week since Christmas morning.

"I don't know, Jace. I received a call from Judge Flores, and he asked to speak to both of us. I reached out to Carl Hubbard, and he said he would be meeting us here, but he didn't tell me anything further. There's been no communication with Karla, so I have no idea what we're walking into."

"Fuck. Who knows what she's going to ask for now? Paisley said Karla barely spoke to them at lunch last week, and I could see that she was on her phone the whole damn time. She said Carl talked to them more than their mother did. I just don't know what her end game is anymore."

"You aren't alone in that. I can't figure this woman out for the life of me," Winston said as we approached Judge Flores' office and checked in with his receptionist.

She led us down a hallway before knocking on the office door and pushing it open. Carl Hubbard was already there, and they appeared to be deep in conversation.

"Are we late?" Winston asked, and I didn't miss the irritation in his voice.

"Nope. We wanted to discuss a few things before you got here," Carl said, nodding at me as Winston sat beside him and I sat in the chair on the other side of my attorney. Judge Flores clapped his hands together once.

"So, our goal here is to look out for the best interest of your two little girls, Paisley and Hadley King."

You could have fooled me with the way they'd allowed Karla to come in and out of their lives, but I'd keep my mouth shut about that. My stomach wrenched with nerves, wondering if he was here to tell me he was granting Karla custody.

"I feel comfortable saying that's the goal for all of us," Winston said, glancing over at me as he cleared his throat a couple times.

He was fucking nervous, which had me sitting forward in my chair and resting my elbows on my knees as I waited for Judge Flores to proceed.

"I have a few questions for you, and all that I ask is that you're honest with me." His dark gaze locked with mine, and I nodded.

"Do you feel you've provided a safe home for your children in their mother's absence?"

"Absolutely." There was no question about it. My girls were happy, well cared for and loved beyond words.

"And is it true that you had an affair with your children's nanny?" he asked, catching me off guard. Winston started to respond, but I held up my hand.

"It wasn't an affair. I've known Ashlan Thomas for many years, which is why I'd hired her to nanny for the girls. Because she's an amazing woman and I knew that before I hired her."

"And she's young, according to these notes that I have." He rested his chin on his interlocked hands.

"She's twenty-three years old. She's graduated from college. She took care of my babies like no one ever had before. She's wise and kind and smart. She's a brilliant writer, and my girls love her."

"It sounds like they aren't the only ones?" he asked skeptically, and Winston shot me a look. But I was done with the lies. I had nothing to be ashamed of.

"I'll be straight with you, Judge Flores," I said, sitting forward and letting out a breath.

"Please." He nodded.

"Ashlan Thomas and I were family friends when I hired her. We fell in love somewhere along the way, and I love her fiercely. She stepped up for my girls in a way that their mother never did. We built a family together, and I'm not ashamed of that. It was a beautiful thing because she's an amazing human being and my girls are crazy about her, as am I."

His gaze narrowed, and he looked back through his notes. "I was under the understanding that she was no longer in contact with any of you."

"She's not. She moved out of our home, and we have had no contact with her whatsoever since she left. When Karla filed for sole custody, Ashlan was told that the two of us being together would be frowned upon by the court. She was terrified that she would cost me my girls and that they would be put in a home that was not in their best interest. She moved out immediately."

His head cocked to the side a bit, maybe surprised by my honesty, or moved by the story that I was sharing, I wasn't sure.

"That was a very mature decision on her part."

"It was." I agreed, and I saw Winston's hands gripping the chair, knuckles white, as if he were ready to have a full-blown panic attack.

"Well, I thank you for your honesty. I can't say that

happens very often these days, but I appreciate it. Unfortunately, in my line of work, I don't always get the truth. I don't always get the full picture either, because I get presented with things like *underage girl living in the home with the children* from the attorney on the opposing side," he said, glancing over at Carl Hubbard, who shrugged.

"It's my job."

"Well, a twenty-three-year-old woman, one who's already graduated from college and steps up for two little kids who were left by their mother, is hardly the picture that was painted. And I'm sorry, Mr. King, that you had to choose between the woman you love and your two little girls; however, I commend you and Miss Thomas for putting the children first. So few people do that anymore."

Winston glanced over at me, eyes wide and a slight smile on his face as his hands relaxed and moved to his lap.

"Thank you. I didn't turn my back on her as I couldn't find it in my heart to do so. She made the final decision." I shook my head and shrugged. "The truth is, your honor, I love my daughters more than life itself. I also love Ashlan Thomas, and that doesn't make me a bad father. I'm just a man out here working hard, doing the best I can to show up for my girls. And I don't think it's right that I have to prove that every time their mother strolls back into town and shows the slightest interest in them. I'm here every day, and I have been since the day they were born."

He sat back in his chair and glanced over at Karla's attorney. "Why don't you take this moment to fill them in on the current situation?"

"I met with Judge Flores this morning to let him know that we will not be proceeding with the petition for custody."

I studied him, processing the words that he'd just said. "She doesn't want custody anymore?"

"Listen, Mr. King, this is my job, but I do try my best to

represent my client when I can. I don't know what the actual motivation was behind this case, but I highly doubt it had much to do with your daughters." He reached for his bottle of water sitting on the desk and took a long pull before setting it back down. "Calvin has already started the paperwork to terminate the marriage. I believe there are a lot of factors that played a role in that, but at the end of the day, she failed her drug test last week and has not been honest with him. She'd signed a prenup when they married just a few months ago, so I don't foresee her having the resources to pursue anything further."

"Well, seeing as she failed the first drug test we gave her, she has other things she needs to focus on," Judge Flores said, his voice stern as he gave a hard look at Karla's attorney.

"So, it's over?" I asked.

"The motion has been dropped," Carl said, pushing to his feet. "I am sorry for putting you through so much over the holidays. If it's any consolation, Calvin actually wrote a letter to the judge about how he felt the girls were already with the parent who would best care for them, which I submitted to Judge Flores this morning."

"Wow. I'm just—relieved. A little surprised, but very pleased," I said, pushing to stand. "But what does this actually mean, as Karla has a habit of disappearing and reappearing with demands?"

"This has all been documented, along with the first time that she left. I think it's safe to say that she'd have a hard time showing up again and threatening you in the future. For the record, I wouldn't have granted her custody even if she had passed the drug test. I would have allowed her some visitation and insisted she prove that she was making a real change in her life over the next several months. She can't keep coming in and out of their lives making demands." Judge Flores looked between both attorneys and they nodded in agreement. "I'm sorry that you had to jump through hoops to prove that you were doing your job all along. The system is not always perfect, Mr. King, but our intent is to make sure your children are best cared for. And it sounds like they most definitely are," Judge Flores said.

"Thank you. I'm not sure how to ask this, but is me dating the woman I love going to cause a problem for me if Karla were to decide to show up again in a couple years?"

Judge Flores looked up from his paperwork, the corners of his mouth turning up the slightest bit. "Nope. The court does not frown upon healthy relationships which enrich the children's lives. In other words—you're allowed to be happy and be a good father at the same time."

I nodded and moved forward to shake his hand. "Thank you, sir."

"Keep doing what you're doing. We need more fathers to step up to the plate and fight for their kids."

I nodded. "Will do."

Carl, Winston, and I made our way out of the office before stepping on the elevator.

"So, Karla isn't going to be showing up at his door, is she?" Winston asked. "You can answer off the record. Just tell us what we're dealing with."

"She's gone. Ran off with some ex-boyfriend." Carl shrugged.

I snorted. "I'm guessing we're talking about Zee."

"Yep. You didn't hear that here though," Carl said.

"Poor Calvin. He seemed like a stand-up dude."

"He is. He asked me to send you his regards and to apologize for the part he played in this. Love can be blind sometimes." He chuckled as the elevator doors opened and he stepped off.

"It's been a pleasure, Carl. But I hope we don't meet again anytime soon," Winston said as we walked through the lobby.

Carl barked out a laugh and saluted him. "You can't

imagine how often I hear those words. I normally like to win, but this time—I'm pleased with the outcome. Judge Flores is correct. This has all been documented along with her failed drug test. Potentially, if she comes back to you in the future with intent to take custody of the girls again, the courts will frown upon her behavior. She's proved her instability too many times, but I'm sure you've already figured that out. Take care, gentlemen."

Winston and I came to a stop beside my car, and he extended his arm. "I'm happy for you, Jace. You deserve this. You're a great dad and a good man. Thanks for trusting me to help you with this."

"Thank you. I'm happy it's over."

"I'm guessing you're going to go find that girl of yours, huh?" He winked. "She's one-of-a-kind, the way she sacrificed her own happiness without a second thought to do what was right for you, Paisley, and Hadley."

"You're preaching to the choir, buddy." I laughed as I climbed into my car and drove straight to my mom's house to pick up the girls.

I greeted my parents and hurried over to see Paisley and Hadley.

I scooped them up and hugged them extra tight. I gave my parents the short version of what happened, and tears streamed down my mom's face and my dad looked like he was about to burst into tears himself.

"Come on," I said, holding Hadley and reaching for Paisley's hand.

"Where are you running off to?" my mom shouted.

"We need to book our flights to New York. Go find our girl," I shouted as I hurried to my car.

"Daddy, we're going to New York?" Paisley asked.

"Yep." I kissed Hadley's forehead after I buckled her in.

"We go get Wuvie?" she asked.

"Damn straight," I said, climbing into the driver's seat.

"Daddy," Paisley shrieked. "That's a timeout for you. Damn's a bad word."

"You can put me in timeout once we get on the plane." I chuckled.

And for the first time in several weeks, I felt like everything was going to be okay.

twenty-nine

• • •

Ashlan

"THAT WENT SO WELL," Willow said as we sipped our coffee at the cute café downstairs in the high-rise where we'd just had our meeting with the publisher.

"It did. They're so great. I can't believe they want me to write an entire series for them." I shook my head. "It doesn't even seem real."

The meeting had been amazing. I hadn't even written the other books, but they liked my outline for the series and liked it enough that they wanted to contract them all. The publisher said that she loved my voice and that should have meant the world to me. And I smiled, genuinely happy for the moment, for the first time in two weeks. But it didn't mean that my heart wasn't still in shambles. Dylan and Charlotte had come with me to New York because I truly thought they were worried I'd climb into bed in my hotel room and never come out.

But I knew Jace would be proud of me for seeing this through.

I thought that the day I signed the contract would be this euphoric moment in my life, and it was in a way. I'd accomplished something that I was proud of. But it was bittersweet because I couldn't share it with the man that I loved. I wished I could tell Paisley and Hadley all about the lady I'd met with, who was dressed like Cruella de Vil.

Now I had to write the books, and to write romance when my heart was in the shitter was going to be the biggest undertaking of my life. I'd have to dig down deep into the memories and find those stories, those moments, and it was going to hurt.

"So, it's New Year's Eve tomorrow, and you're in the best city in the world to celebrate. What are you going to do?" Willow asked. She had blonde curly hair and beautiful green eyes. She dressed extremely chic in her winter cream business suit, and she was someone I knew right away that I'd have a long friendship with.

I shrugged. "Dylan made reservations for the three of us to have dinner, and then I'll probably climb into bed and watch a movie. I know… I'm the lamest twenty-three-year-old out there. But I've just never been big on going out on New Year's Eve."

Jace and I had planned to watch fireworks with the girls from our hotel room and order room service. That was my perfect way to ring in the New Year.

"Oh girl, you don't need to tell me. I'll be curled up with Nate on the couch with Winston and Rowen, my two pups, cuddled up with us." She chuckled.

"You doing okay with everything?" she asked as she set her mug down. "I know it's been tough for you since you moved out. I know you're missing them something awful."

The compassion I saw in her gaze had my eyes watering. Willow and I had grown close, even though this was the first time we'd actually met in person. She'd been checking on me daily, and even sent a baby gift to Everly for her baby shower. It had been a beautiful day, but I'd just gone through the motions, just as I had for the past two weeks.

"I'm hanging in there. One day at a time, right?"

"You know, if you need a fresh start, I could totally see you living here in the city. This is the mecca for the publishing world after all." She smiled and broke off a piece of her sugar cookie and popped it in her mouth. "Plus, we could hang out all the time, which would be the best."

I smiled. It meant a lot to me that I'd found such a special friend in my agent. "Thank you. I'd love that. But Honey Mountain is my home. It's where I've always seen myself living. It's where the words come for me and where my heart is."

Jace. Paisley. Hadley.

She swiped at the tear rolling down her cheek. "And this is why you are going to find yourself at the top of the New York Times Bestseller list. Keep being you, Ashlan Thomas."

"I will."

"Excuse me, are you Ashlan Thomas, the famous romance author?" a familiar voice said from behind me, and Willow's eyes bulged as she took him in. I whipped around to see Jace standing there. Black sweater, dark jeans, boots, and a black trench coat. He looked like he'd just stepped off a *GQ* photo shoot.

I jumped to my feet. "What are you doing here?"

"I came to ring in the New Year with my girl." He tugged me against him.

"Um. I'm guessing you're Jace? Or this is just going to be the next romance book she writes?" Willow stood, her mouth gaping open as her gaze moved from me to him.

"I'm Jace. You must be the infamous Willow Cowles." He extended his hand, and she took it.

"I most certainly am. Okay, then. I'm going to give you two a moment." She giggled and then mouthed *oh my god* once she was standing behind him and only I could see her.

I laughed and waved. "I'll call you later."

"No rush, girl. Happy New Year. And congratulations.

Only good things for you moving forward, Ashlan. Nice to meet you, Jace."

He smiled and thanked her, but his eyes never left mine as he moved to sit in the chair I'd just vacated and pulled me onto his lap.

"What are you doing here? Are we allowed to be seen together?"

He chuckled. "It's over, Sunshine. She's gone. Failed her drug test. She ran off with Zee and Calvin filed for divorce." He snorted.

"Oh my gosh, you're serious?" I croaked as a tear ran down my cheek. "What does that mean for us? What if she comes back?"

"It's all been documented. Judge Flores, Winston, and Carl all agreed she wouldn't have a leg to stand on in a court of law. She can't hurt us anymore." He tucked my hair behind my ear and stroked my cheek.

He told me how he'd told the judge about us before he even knew that Karla was gone. He said he wanted the truth to be out there. Because he couldn't imagine his life without me in it, and he needed the judge to know that he loved all three of us.

"I can't believe it." I shook my head. "It's been really hard without you guys."

"I know, baby. We've been just existing. It's hard once you've had all that sunshine and then you take it away."

"Where are the girls?"

"They're with Charlotte and Dylan, taking a horse and carriage ride."

"They're here?" I jumped to my feet. "Let's go see them. I was so worried they'd think I left them."

"They never thought that. They must know you because Paisley told me she knew you'd never leave them. Not really. So she talked to you every night when I'd tuck her in. And Hadley would shout, 'We wuv you, Wuvie.'" He snorted.

"They never lost faith in you. In us. In our family. Because they're able to recognize when someone is all good. Pure sweetness."

"Oh, yeah? You think I'm pure sweetness?" I teased, my lips grazing his.

"I know that every inch of you is pure sweetness. And I've missed you so fucking much." His mouth covered mine, and I sank into him. His arms wrapped around me as we stood there kissing in the middle of a busy New York coffee shop.

When I pulled back, I could feel my cheeks heat as I glanced over to see two older women watching us with big smiles on their faces.

"Let's go find the girls."

He took my hand. "All right. And we'll have dinner with them, but tonight you're mine. I got a room at the same hotel as yours, and Charlotte and Dylan have agreed to babysit. I bribed them with room service and Disney movies."

"Ah, you know a way to a Thomas girl's heart, don't you?"

"The only heart I care about knowing is yours." He lifted my hand to his lips and kissed it. "I love you."

"I love you."

I texted my sisters and they were just pulling up in front of the hotel. When I saw the horse and carriage in the distance, Paisley stood up and shielded her eyes, and I waved at her. She started bouncing up and down, and before I could stop myself, I took off in a full sprint just as Charlotte lifted Paisley out of the carriage. She took off in my direction and lunged herself into my arms.

I hugged her tight because I'd missed them both so much.

"I missed you, Ash." She pulled back, and tears streamed down her face. I'd never seen Paisley cry before. She was stoic like her daddy, and seeing that emotion from her had my heart ready to explode.

"I missed you too, sweet girl."

"Are you here to stay?" she croaked, and my throat felt like it was closing.

"Forever."

"Wuvie." Hadley was holding Dylan's hand and her little legs were hurrying in my direction even if she wasn't making much progress. I set Paisley down and smiled at her before bending down as Hadley jumped into my arms.

"How's my girl?" I asked.

"Me and Buddy miss you."

"I missed you too." I kissed the tip of her nose and she giggled.

"Well, I'm just so happy we don't have to deal with this sad sack anymore. I mean, you want to talk about depressing —she has been a hot mess express," Dylan said.

"Thanks for pointing that out." I chuckled.

I pushed to stand, and Jace came up behind me and wrapped his arms around me, my back to his chest. Paisley found my hand, and Charlotte scooped up Hadley.

"No more sadness, baby." He leaned down and kissed my cheek.

"That sounds good to me."

"Okay. Let's go celebrate someone signing her book deal today. Dinner's on me," he said.

"There's a lot to celebrate tonight," I said, smiling up at him as he reached for my hand and led us into the hotel.

You deserve it all, my sweet girl, my mom's voice entered my mind.

Yeah, maybe I did.

The next few weeks were a whirlwind. Hadley had started preschool, and she was thriving. The girl was talking up a storm. In fact, her preschool teacher said she was the chattiest one in the class. I had started writing the second book in my series. It was a brother's best friend, enemies-to-lovers romance—so I was having a lot of fun with this one. The first book in the series was currently in editing. The whole process was exciting, and most days I had to pinch myself to believe it was real.

"I've always loved this old farmhouse. So, this is the next one you guys are going to renovate?" I looked ahead as we pulled up to the home Jace, Niko, and Hawk were working on next. When he wasn't at the firehouse, and I wasn't writing, and the girls were at school, we took that time to spend most days together.

"Yeah. I mean, we have a ways to go on the other house, but there was just something about this one." He reached for my hand and led me up the steps to the oversized front porch.

"Oh, wow. Look at all that natural light. These windows are amazing." I ran my fingers up the black panes on the windows.

"Yeah? It's got good bones, right? You think you can help me pick the finishes out for this one too? We just had a realtor visit the other project, and she commented on the finishes. I told her my girlfriend has an eye for this stuff."

"Maybe your girlfriend just has a great eye for a good-looking man," I said, pushing up and planting a chaste kiss on his lips.

"I can't argue with that," he teased. "So, what do you think?"

"It's the prettiest house I've ever seen. I'd love to help you pick the finishes. You are going to sell this one fast. I think it might be worth it to stage it with furniture, you know, make the buyer see themselves living here."

"Really? That's not a bad idea. Tell me what you'd put in here."

"I'd do a huge sectional over here, with light colors and a big throw rug. A farm table in this oversized dining room like the one we have now, and I'd do a built-in banquette, right here in the kitchen," I said as I moved through the space.

"Yep. That sounds like a plan. You really think it'll go fast?"

"Absolutely. Cool light fixtures, and some flowers, throw pillows, curtains. I can see it," I said as I turned slowly in the room and pointed out where I'd put things.

"I can see it too. But do you know what I see over here?" He walked toward the kitchen island.

"What?"

"I see you and me cooking in here. I see Hadley and Paisley sitting up here at the island eating breakfast. I see Buddy running around in that big yard," he said, pulling me close. "And I see a high chair or two next to that banquet you're talking about."

My eyes doubled in size. "Oh, really? Do you now?"

"Do you see it, Sunshine?"

I couldn't hide my smile if I wanted to. "I think I've always seen it with you."

"I want this for us. I put in an offer a few days ago and they accepted. Niko agreed to help me with all the renovations as long as I provide him with free food when he's working. Hawk said he'd work with us when his season ends. This is our fresh start, baby."

My breath caught in my throat. He turned me toward the family room and pointed at the front office. "I think that should be your writing room. We can put in bookshelves along the walls and French doors there so you can keep me and the kids out when you need to work."

"No doors. I like the distraction."

"Oh, yeah. I'm happy to distract you anytime."

"Tell me about those high chairs you saw next to the table," I teased as I tugged him close and tangled my hands in his hair.

"I'm not saying we need to do it all today. Right now, I

want to be with you and the girls and start living our lives together. But I see it all with you, Ashlan. A house full of babies and marriage and a long life together sitting on that front porch. Hell, I just ordered a shit-ton of wood to build a white picket fence. I'm all in."

"I'm all in too. What do you say we go home before we pick up Hadley and celebrate?" I asked, nipping at his bottom lip.

His hands moved down my hips and settled on my ass before he lifted me up and my legs wrapped around his waist. "You're speaking my language, baby."

His mouth found mine as we moved through the house, and he carried me out the front door to the car.

"You ready for forever, Sunshine?"

"As long as I'm with you, Jace King."

This man was my forever.

My own happily ever after.

My everything.

epilogue

. . .

Ashlan

I RAN down the long labor and delivery hallway of the hospital until I saw Dylan's head pop out of a room and she called my name. "Prepare yourself. You might want to stay up top by her head unless you're ready to see the only parts of Everly you've never seen before." She shuddered dramatically.

I snorted. "You're so crude."

"Why? I didn't even say vagina because Charlotte just lectured me that it's inappropriate to say vagina when someone is giving birth. I have news for all of you... the vag rules in here. This is labor and delivery. The vagina is their crowned jewel."

"And there she goes again. You somehow manage to keep saying it," Charlotte hissed.

"Stop being a prude. Babies come out of vaginas. It's no secret. Hawky player, are you offended by the word?" Dylan asked as she reached for the water sitting on the table beside Everly and took a long swig. Vivian rolled her eyes and yanked the glass out of Dylan's hand and refilled it, before setting it back on the table next to Everly.

"I love vaginas." Hawk shrugged. "Especially Ever's."

"I'm going to hurt you if you talk like that while I'm giving birth to our son." Everly shot a look at Hawk.

"Baby. She asked the question. And I have to say, you have a magical vagina."

Everly groaned. "Why did I invite all of you here? You're a bad influence on him."

"You didn't. You invited Vivian. I called you out for being shady because you clearly only invited her because she already has a baby. How do you think that makes the rest of us feel?" Dylan asked, taking the peanut M&M's from Hawk and pouring a bunch in her hand before popping a few in her mouth.

"I don't care. I did invite Vivian because she has a baby. I knew she'd be calm and help me relax because she's been through it."

"Everly. You do understand that, in a way, that is like maternity profiling your own sisters. So, Charlotte can't help you relax because she hasn't had a baby. I mean, listen to yourself." Dylan chomped down on the candy and handed Hawk the bag back.

"Charlotte is a relaxing person by nature, unlike you. So is Ashlan. But if I invited all three of them and not you, it would be mean, am I right?"

"Very mean. And here I am talking up your vagina with your baby daddy, and you're talking smack. I'll cut you a break since you have a giant human in there and he's threatening to come out of places that should never be on display for a room full of people the way I'm guessing this whole show is going to go down. Don't you worry, Sissy. I've got you."

Hawk and I broke out in a fit of laughter. Vivian rolled her eyes and made every attempt to hide her smile. Everly shook her head with irritation and then reached for Hawk's hand. And Charlotte was busy staring down at her phone in the corner of the room, completely entranced with whoever was texting her.

I made my way over to her.

"What are you doing over here?"

She startled and tucked her phone into her back pocket. "Nothing. Just filling Jilly in about the baby."

"How is she doing? She finally picked her venue for the wedding. Is she excited?"

"Yeah. She's excited for Ledger to get here and see everything that she's picked out. Apparently, Garrett asked him to be his best man in the wedding, so we'll be walking down the aisle together."

"Ahhh… and how do you feel about that?"

"Me? Why would I care? He's Jilly's brother. Haven't even thought about him coming home," she said in a huff, hands flailing and way more dramatic than Charlotte normally was.

"Okaaaaay. It's not a bad thing to admit you're a little nervous about it. I mean, every time he comes in town, it seems like you make sure that your run-ins are quick. But you're going to be seeing him a lot this time."

"Yeah. So? Why would that matter?" she asked defensively.

"I just meant that you might be a little nervous to be around him so much after all these years."

"I don't care, Ash. I don't care that he's home or what he does or if he brings a date to the wedding. I don't care that I'm walking down the aisle with him. I haven't given any of that a thought. I care about Jilly's wedding," she huffed.

Sure, she did. That's why she was acting like a complete lunatic.

Because Ledger Dane was coming home and she was on edge.

Whether she wanted to admit it or not.

"Okay. Got it."

"Oh my gosh, Hawk. Ohhhhhh," Everly screamed, and

we all jumped to attention. I hurried over to grab her hand. Dylan chugged some more water before moving to the other side and taking her free hand. Hawk stood at her legs, massaging her calves and telling her how much he loved her. Vivian ran to get the nurse, and Charlotte wrung out a washcloth and placed it on Everly's forehead.

"Dude. We're literally thirty seconds into this thing. She's hardly sweating," Dylan said to her twin.

"*Dude.* I'm going to kill you if you don't change your tone while I'm giving birth," Everly shouted as the nurse came through the door.

Everly wanted to have a natural birth so she'd foregone the epidural, much to Vivian's insistence that she should get it.

"How are you feeling, honey?" the nurse asked just as the doctor came through the door.

"Oh, Dr. Cabot, I'm so glad you're here. I think I'd like to get that epidural after all," Everly said before letting out a blood-curdling cry that had all of us on edge.

"Get her the goddamn epidural!" Hawk shouted. All of this excitement was heightening the anticipation of their new baby, and all I could think about was that I couldn't wait to have one of my own. I put my left hand over my stomach thinking about this moment.

Dr. Cabot's voice remained eerily calm, and he gently pushed her legs apart before taking a look and doing some sort of inspection down there while I tried not to look.

"Wow, you really just go right in there, huh?" Dylan asked, craning her neck to see what he was looking at.

"You're well past the point of an epidural, Everly. It's time," he said.

I watched as Everly squeezed her husband's hand, nodding she'd be okay. I could see Hawk was ready to fly off the handle.

Two more nurses walked into the room, and everyone

seemed to be busy moving around as they prepared for the big moment.

At least that's what I assumed was going on. I'd never been in the room while someone was having a baby before.

"Baby, you've got this," Hawk said, taking her hand from Dylan and moving closer before he kissed her forehead.

"I love you so much," Everly cried out before the manic screams started again.

Charlotte kept the cool washcloth on her head. Dylan had moved down to her feet with Dr. Cabot as if she were there to assist him.

"Tell me where you want me, Ever," Hawk said, his voice completely calm and full of love. "You want me up here or down there with the baby."

"Stay here," she said as she shouted out in pain and squeezed his hand. "I need you to get me through this."

"Please tell me that is not a head I'm seeing. Jesus. How is that thing going to fit out of her—" Dylan paused to look up at Everly and then smiled. "Her yoohoo. She's got something against the word vagina."

Dr. Cabot chuckled but didn't respond. "Everly, it's time to push. I'm going to count to three and then you're going to push as hard as you can, okay?"

"You can do it, baby. You've got this," Hawk said as he stroked her face and kept telling her how much he loved her.

"Do you need any help? His head looks rather gargantuan. He clearly gets that from his father. No offense, Hawk," Dylan said, moving closer to Dr. Cabot.

"I think I've got it." He glanced up and gave Dylan a confused look. "Here we go, Everly. One. Two. *Push*."

Everly let out a cry that sounded like something out of a horror film and I swore she broke my fingers, but I just stood there watching her in awe.

My sister was a rock star.

Brave and strong and fearless.

"You've got this, Ev," I cried. "You're going to be the best mom. Your little boy is ready to meet you."

"Oh. My. God. Hawk, you need to come down here. He's coming." Dylan looked up, tears streaming down her face.

"Go, baby. Dylan, come hold my hand," Ever shouted.

"One more push, Everly. You're doing amazing. Here we go. One. Two."

Everly shouted just as Dylan took her hand. Her scream felt like it lasted forever as she just kept going. Her face was bright red. Her hair soaking wet, and face covered in sweat.

Hawk was standing beside Dr. Cabot with tears running down his face. "You did it, baby."

Everly fell back, gasping for air, just as a little cry came from between her legs.

"Would you like to cut the cord?" the nurse asked, and Hawk nodded.

The sweetest little angel was set in my sister's arms as we all gaped and sobbed at the newest addition to the family.

Everly was crying and laughing as she took him in, and Hawk moved beside her and kissed her forehead. "He's perfect."

"Are you finally going to tell us his name?" Dylan asked.

Hawk and Ever shared a look before my brother-in-law looked down at his son. "Welcome to the world, Jackson Dune Madden."

They'd named him after both of their fathers, and we all swooned.

The nurses quickly hurried my nephew away to check his vitals and clean him up, while Hawk wrapped his arms around my sister and hugged her.

The next few minutes were madness. Hawk hurried out to let my dad and his parents know that everything went well.

The nurse brought little Jackson over to my sister for a few minutes and the five of us were there, crying and laughing and taking in the miracle that we'd just witnessed.

"I'm glad you guys were here for this. Even if Dilly was extra annoying with all her vagina talk," Everly said.

"Hey. I'm proud of my vajazzle. I can't even imagine how proud I'd be if I pushed a giant-headed human out of there. You're amazing, Sissy."

Everly laughed. "I love you guys. He's a lucky little boy to have all his aunties here to welcome him into the world."

"We're the lucky ones," I said. Because we were.

We'd all had our ups and downs, but in the end, we were all okay.

We had each other. And that's what life was all about.

Family.

They took Jackson to the nursery to clean him up, and Everly was being taken to a room.

I made my way out to the waiting room with Vivian, Charlotte, and Dylan.

Jace was standing next to Niko and my dad, and Paisley ran toward me with Hadley on her heels.

"We have a new cousin," Paisley said proudly.

"You sure do."

Jace made his way over to me and pulled me into his arms. The waiting room was loud and filled with family and friends.

"All right. I need food. Watching someone give birth is both exhausting and emotional. Who wants pizza?" Dylan asked.

"Perfect. I need to go nurse Bee first. How about you pick it up and come to my house?" Vivian said, taking her baby girl from Niko.

"I want to meet my grandson first, and then I'll stop by," my dad said.

"We'll be over in a little bit," I said as we all started hugging and saying our goodbyes.

Jace and I made our way to the car, Hadley in his arms and Paisley's hand in mine.

"Are you guys up for pizza? I know it's been a long day."

"Yes." Paisley pumped her fist toward the sky. "I love when we all get to be together."

"Me too," I said.

Because there was nothing better.

THE END

Do you want to see what happens when Charlotte Thomas comes face to face with her childhood crush, Ledger Dane!

DOWNLOAD SIMPLY MINE (BOOK 4)

HERE https://geni.us/SimplyMine

Would you like more of Ash and Jace? Click here to see them share a very special date night...

https://dl.bookfunnel.com/nk30cj63gz

Catch up with the series HERE:

Always Mine

Ever Mine

Make You Mine

Simply Mine

Only Mine

acknowledgments

Greg, Chase & Hannah…you are the reason that I continue to chase my dreams every day. I love you more than I could ever put into words. Thank you for always supporting me and believing in me. I love you forever!

Willow, I could not begin to thank you for being such a bright light in my life! Thank you for reading my words, for sprinting with me, for making me laugh and for always being there. I am so grateful to be on this journey with you. Love you!

Catherine, I am so thankful for YOU! Thank you for talking me through all the things, for making me laugh and for being there during the "spiraling moments." Love you so!!

Nina, I'm not sure how I functioned before you—and I am forever grateful to be on this journey with you! Thank you for your guidance, your encouragement and your friendship!! It means the world to me!

Christine Miller, I cannot thank you enough for all that you do for me. I am so thankful for YOU!

Kim Cermak, Thank you for keeping everything organized when I'm certain that I don't make that easy for you!! Thank you for keeping all the dates straight and staying on me when needed!! I am so grateful for YOU!!

Sarah Norris, Thank you for the gorgeous graphics and for all that you do to make my releases extra special! It means the world to me!

Megan Corbett, Thank you so much for helping to get my

books out there on TikTok and being so supportive and patient! I am so grateful!

Kelley Beckham, Thank you so much for all that you do to help me get my books out there! I am truly so thankful!

Valentine Grinstead, I absolutely adore you!! I am so happy to be on this journey with you! Cheers to many years of working together!

Doo, Annette, Abi, Pathi, Natalie, Caroline, Jennifer and Lara, thank you for being the BEST beta readers EVER! Your feedback means the world to me. I am so thankful for you!!

Emily, Thank you for creating this gorgeous special edition cover for Jace and Ashlan! I love working with you so much! Xo

Sue Grimshaw (Edits by Sue), I love being on this journey with you. I would be completely lost without you. I love your feedback and talking through all the things with you!! I am so grateful for your support and encouragement.

Ellie (My Brothers Editor), I am so thankful for you!! I love being on this journey with you, and I am so grateful for all that you do for me. Love you!

Christine Estevez, thank you for all that you do to support me! It truly means the world to me! Love you!

Mom, thank you for your love and support and for reading all of my words! Ride or die!! Love you!

Dad, you really are the reason that I keep chasing my dreams!! Thank you for teaching me to never give up. Love you!

Sandy, thank you for reading and supporting me throughout this journey! Love you!

Pathi, I am so thankful for you! You are the reason I even started this journey. Thank you for believing in me!! I love and appreciate you more than I can say!! Thank you for your friendship!! Love you!

Natalie (Head in the Clouds, Nose in a Book), Thank you for supporting me through it all! I appreciate all that you do for me from beta reading to the newsletter to just absolutely being the most supportive friend!! I am so thankful for you!! Love you!

Sammi, I am so thankful for your support and your friendship!! Love you!

Marni, I love you forever and I am endlessly thankful for your friendship!! Xo

Jenn, I cannot put into words how much I appreciate you! Thank you for the gorgeous book bibles that help me keep it all straight!! Thank you for talking through issues and always being there when I need you!! It truly means the world to me!! Love you! Xo

To the JKL WILLOWS… I am forever grateful to you for your support and encouragement! I treasure your friendship and love you all so much!! Xo

To all the bloggers and bookstagrammers who have posted, shared, and supported me—I can't begin to tell you how much it means to me. I love seeing the graphics that you make and the gorgeous posts that you share. I am forever grateful for your support!

To all the readers who take the time to pick up my books and take a chance on my words…THANK YOU for helping to make my dreams come true!!

keep up on new releases

Linktree Laurapavlovauthor
Newsletter laurapavlov.com

other books by laura pavlov

Find all books by Laura Pavlov HERE

Cottonwood Cove Series

Into the Tide

Under the Stars

On the Shore

Before the Sunset

After the Storm

Honey Mountain Series

Always Mine

Ever Mine

Make You Mine

Simply Mine

Only Mine

The Willow Springs Series

Frayed

Tangled

Charmed

Sealed

Claimed

Montgomery Brothers Series

Legacy

Peacekeeper

Rebel

A Love You More Rock Star Romance

More Jade

More of You

More of Us

The Shine Design Series

Beautifully Damaged

Beautifully Flawed

The G.D. Taylors Series with Willow Aster

Wanted Wed or Alive

The Bold and the Bullheaded

Another Motherfaker

Don't Cry Spilled MILF

Friends with Benefactors

follow me...

Website laurapavlov.com

Goodreads @laurapavlov

Instagram @laurapavlovauthor

Facebook @laurapavlovauthor

Pav-Love's Readers @pav-love's readers

Amazon @laurapavlov

BookBub @laurapavlov

TikTok @laurapavlovauthor

Printed in the USA
CPSIA informati
at www.ICGtes
LVHW011927
794499LV

9 781088 27557